(Originally published under the title of III: A Christmas Story)

Walter D. Harvey

Wilde Rabbit Media
Ennis, Texas
USA

Wilde Rabbit Media LLC
Publishers Since 2012
Ennis, Texas

This is an original work of fiction loosely based upon ancient writings, historical facts, the traditional Christ-child story and early Christian church writings. The events and characters described herein are created by the author and are products of his imagination. This is neither intended, nor offered, as a theological treatise, exegesis, or commentary on the story of the biblically referenced Magi, the Christ-child's Bethlehem birth nor related scriptures from the Holy Bible about The Christ, of which the author is a practicing believer.

Copyright © 2016 Wilde Rabbit Media LLC. All Rights Reserved. Worldwide Copyrights secured, in association, but not limited to, the Berne Copyright Convention, Universal Copyright Convention, and The Pan-American Copyright Convention. This work, or parts thereof, may not be reproduced, stored in a retrieval system, nor transmitted in any form, nor by any means, electronic, mechanical, photocopying, recording or otherwise in any known form or to be known in the future throughout the universe without the prior written permission from the author, Walter D. Harvey & the publisher, Wilde Rabbit Media LLC.

Library of Congress Cataloging-in-Publication Data

Harvey, Walter - August, 2016
Magi Manuscripts: Vol. 1 / by Walter D. Harvey

ISBN-13: 978-0692775301
ISBN-10: 0692775307

Dedication

This book is dedicated to my mother and father. Mom, I hope you have been reading it over my shoulder from your heavenly home and approving. Thanks for buying all those books throughout the years and encouraging me to read good writing. Dad, you continue to be an inspiration to so many people and you are my hero.

Walter D. Harvey

Acknowledgements

Once a fire is burning, no one typically remembers who started it. In this case, I want to tip my hat to the fire starter, Sam Taylor. Were it not for his coaching, cajoling and confidence in me, the fire would have never begun. Thanks for being the spark, Sam.

It is rare in life to find a Hampton Keathley. Thank you for your technical expertise; without it this book would not have gone very far. Your cybertronic, extraterrestrial brain which understands all things e-book and electronic was a true Godsend.

I have to thank my official reader, Richard Bennett. He read and recorded each chapter aloud and then sent it to me so I could hear the voices of the characters. This reading kept me going and encouraged me at two in the morning sometimes.

A special thank you goes to my son Matthew and my wife Susan. Matthew was my first audience. He would sit at night and listen to Daddy read the next chapter. He laughed at Jandak and loved the sword fights. I couldn't ask for more. Susan, your support has been unwavering and your work on this book has taken it to a new level. You have helped turn all of this into something better than it ever would have been without your touch. I love you and would do it all over again.

And finally to all my friends and extended family members who have supported me as I talked and talked about this book for so long. Thank you. Thank you. It is finally here.

Ever so grateful to my Creator who makes all things possible.

-Walter

Chapter 1
The Race

Speed. It was the reason Balthazar raced. That and the fact he loved winning. Looking back at the other riders after a dash across the desert always lifted his spirits. Dirty, disheveled and deranged from the heat, his competitors vanquished.

The starting gong echoing through Balthazar made him focus on the task at hand. Jandak, his camel, didn't wait to break into a full run. He leaped into the lead, and it was a lead Jandak rarely relinquished.

At times Jandak and Balthazar would tease the other riders, letting them catch up just long enough to harbor a twinge of hope. And then, magically, mystically they would pull away leaving the other racers with a bitter mouth of dust and a lasting aroma that stopped camels and riders cold. No one could explain the mysterious cloud Jandak left everywhere he went but everyone bowed to the camel that never lost a race. Somehow, the smell was Jandak's way of saying, "If you don't want to smell me, then beat me."

With the fastest camel in the realm firmly in the lead, first place was almost a formality. The other riders could fight and feud with each other for second and third place. Second and third also meant an automatic bid to enter the Desert 100, a madcap race of mayhem and disaster that challenged man and beast. It was the pinnacle of the camel racing world and it guaranteed the winner a year of bragging rights. Balthazar and Jandak had won it five years in a row; no other camel and rider had claimed first prize more than three consecutive years.

Balthazar knew he and Jandak were achieving a status few others would ever match. He tried not to rub it in, but sometimes he just couldn't help himself. This was especially true with his friend and racing nemesis, Gaspar.

Gaspar from Persia. He and Balthazar had known each other forever. Deep down they had an unheralded friendship and grudging respect for each other's intellect, but it galled Gaspar to the core that he had never beaten Balthazar and Jandak in any camel race.

At first glance, Gaspar actually looked much more the part of a racer than Balthazar. Short and dumpy, Balthazar waddled more than he walked. Gaspar, however, was fit and trim, light as a feather. He had the appearance of a camel racer whereas Balthazar resembled an overfed cow sitting on top of a camel. However, it never bothered Balthazar that he didn't look the part. Looks never mattered to him; results were the only thing that counted.

Balthazar kneed Jandak hard to avoid a standing palm tree and a scattering of hidden boulders. They cut through a small abandoned oasis and headed into the sun, the overbearing and unrelenting sun. This was the part of the race that cut into the heart of camel and rider, and it was the only part of the course Balthazar dreaded.

He blinked his eyes rapidly trying to keep his salty sweat from rolling into them. He pulled a piece of his turban over his eyes and mouth, relying on Jandak to avoid any trouble spots and hazards until they could put the sun behind them.

Balthazar knew the sun and its position in the sky better than anyone in the kingdom. He was the Royal Astronomer for the King of Babylon, and he understood the sky and its secrets, at least as much as was possible from his rooftop observatory. He had mapped the sun, the stars and anything else in the sky that moved. He had discovered more stars and named more heavenly bodies than anyone in a hundred years, and it had paid off handsomely for him. The King was fascinated by the night sky and he looked forward to the weekly reports from Balthazar.

"What have you seen in my sky this week, Balthazar?" The King always claimed the sky was his. (Kings tend to do that sort of thing).

"Oh, my King, I have seen a new star and named it after your third son, Kildesh."

Balthazar always carried his star maps with him when he went to visit the king. He would unroll his map for the King pointing out his latest find in the sky. It pleased the King that so many stars and celestial beings were named after his family members.

Balthazar was no fool. He knew how to make the King happy and keep him happy. And who was he to question why the King was so infatuated with the night sky. Balthazar loved his job and he was good at it. He was the best astronomer in the known world.

Jandak had slowed considerably and Balthazar squinted into the sun. There was the reason Jandak had slowed, a faint cloud of dust directly in his path, his competition no doubt.

"How did they get past me?" Balthazar asked himself. It was impossible!

"Am I off course?" He glanced up and saw the unmistakable landmark—Quanan Tower, built before he had been born. "Well, that's correct."

He knew the route of the race. Balthazar had laid it out and gone over it in his mind a thousand times.

He stared into the cloud of desert dust as best he could. It was moving toward him. Why would the other racers be going the wrong way? They must have taken some strange shortcut and would be disqualified even if they did beat him.

Suddenly, three quick shimmering reflections of steel and bronze told him everything he needed to know. Bandits. Desert marauders. They must have overpowered the guards along the race route and now they were after him and Jandak. Capturing Jandak would bring a hefty ransom. It might fetch a province or two and even one of the King's daughters as a bride.

Jandak was fast. He could run for a long time, but he couldn't run forever. Even he had his limits. Balthazar knew he could not outrun the marauders and had to think of a plan. He sifted through every scenario in his head and pointed Jandak in the only direction he could think of where they might be safe, the mirages. It was the perfect time of day for them to be at their peak and, with a little bit of acting and luck, he just might be able to fool the thieves.

The sound of swords clanging and the deep throaty yell of men in pursuit washed over Balthazar and for a moment he feared they might actually overtake him. He begged Jandak to give him every ounce of speed he could muster and the straining dromedary did.

He dashed into the area of the desert where the mirages appeared regularly and quickly dismounted. The marauders paused and Balthazar could see they were gazing into the mirages looking for him and Jandak.

He had just enough time to prepare himself and Jandak for their great charade. He pulled the saddle from Jandak and scattered everything Jandak was carrying on the ground. Then he waited.

The bandits eventually found them and surrounded the two of them. The leader dismounted and pulled out an oversized silver sword flashing it at Balthazar.

Balthazar wailed as loudly as he could, "Nooo. Not Jandak."

There was one other trick Balthazar had taught Jandak, besides the mystical winds he released. Balthazar had trained his camel to play dead. He quietly gave the command. Jandak transformed from a perfectly normal camel into a whirling dervish. He spun in a circle three times, coughed up a ball of foul residue, kicked each leg out separately, then threw all four legs straight out simultaneously and fell flat on the ground. He heaved and huffed until his stomach swelled up to three times its normal size.

Balthazar cried again, "No. He just can't be dead." Balthazar grabbed Jandaks neck and squeezed hard.

Jandak released what every bandit knew was a death wheeze. Then he rolled over onto his back, stiffened his neck and pointed his legs straight into the air.

The bandit leader put his face over Jandaks nose to see if he was still breathing. He wasn't.

Balthazar stood up screaming at the bandit. "Do you know what the king will do to you for chasing his prized camel to death? You won't be able to find a hole deep enough or big enough to hide from him!"

The bandit grabbed one of Jandaks legs and pulled the leg towards him. Jandaks leg stayed stiff and straight as the bandit rocked him back and forth in the sand. Balthazar knelt back down beside Jandak, sobbing.

"I might as well kill myself because the King will when he finds out I let this happen."

Balthazar pulled his own sword from his tunic and plunged himself onto the blade until it protruded from his back. His blood oozed around the blade, soaking into the sand.

The bandits scattered like black desert cockroaches and never looked back.

Knowing the coast was finally clear, Balthazar pulled the trick sword from his back. "My trusty trick sword and a little spilled wine." Balthazar stared at his scene-stealing camel and thought Jandak enjoyed fooling the bandits even more than he did. He was still playing dead.

"Alright, Jandak. They're gone you can get up now."

The more pressing matter was the race. Balthazar had to decide if he still had a chance to win.

It didn't take him long to spot what he knew had to be the remaining racers. Gauging the distance to the finish line and the amount of ground he had to cover, he believed Jandak could make up the difference and build upon his legend as the fastest camel in any province.

Balthazar pointed Jandak toward home and spurred him into a hard trot. The next few hours passed quietly. Balthazar listened to Jandak's breathing as he bobbled along perched on top of his camel streaking over the sand toward the gates of town. Every few minutes, Balthazar would recalculate the distance between him, the other racers and the finish line. He knew it would be close but they were closing the gap.

Balthazar overtook the first three laggards just outside of town. He flew past the Well of Ithgar where several riders had stopped for a quick fill of their water skins.

Ill prepared, thought Balthazar. No wonder they never win. And he flew on.

Balthazar was feeling comfortable about his position. As he fumbled with the number of riders in his head, he realized there was still one rider and camel missing. Surely, they weren't so slow that they had never passed him during his ordeal with the bandits.

Balthazar and Jandak wildly careened around the corner at the Crypt of Kashir and just ahead saw his answer.

It was the missing camel and rider. Coming in from behind, he did not recognize who it might be. He only knew he had indeed miscounted and miscalculated the speed of this one camel and rider. They must have been significantly ahead of the others and he had just overlooked them. He seethed. He had been so smug.

"Yaaah, yaaah." He yelled urging Jandak harder than he had all day.

Little by little they inched closer to victory. The ba-da-dump, ba-da-dump of Jandak's hooves pounding past the gate entrance near the center of town was all Balthazar could hear.

Balthazar was beginning to worry that Jandak would fall just short of victory but there was one advantage Balthazar had over the unknown rider. The Slide. His only chance of catching this camel and winning the race lay at the Slide of Sadir.

Balthazar knew it well but kept the secret of the slide to himself. If this unknown rider did not know to lock his camels' legs and drift through the slippery cobblestone corner, then the Slide of Sadir would claim another victim.

Balthazar didn't see it, but the groans from the crowd told him everything he needed to know. The Slide had claimed another victim. Slipping through the Slide of Sadir, he saw the face of the other rider for just a moment.

Was it Gaspar?

Balthazar looked back at the fallen rider and could not believe it. It was Gaspar! After all these years and all the chances for him to finally win against Balthazar, he had fallen short, just a palm tree's length from the finish line.

After crossing the finish line Balthazar stood up and cheered for himself. Even if it was just by a camel's whisker, he and Jandak had done it! Their unbroken string of victories would remain unblemished.

That afternoon Balthazar basked in the glow of the crowded amphitheater. The servants lay down palm fronds before him as he walked the victors' trail to the dais. Gaspar stood hunched over, just a few feet beneath him on the second place pedestal. The third place finisher was so deflated he didn't even show up for the ceremony. He sent a lowly palace guard to stand in his place.

After the winner's ceremony there was a grand royal party. All the racers and invited dignitaries were there, except for Gaspar. Balthazar relayed the escape from the bandits to the King. The King listened intently, but he was only waiting so he could ask his Royal Astronomer the weekly question.

"What have you seen in the King's sky this week? Besides another victory." The King laughed but Balthazar knew the King cared about one thing even more than racing; he loved the sky and the stars in it.

"Well, oh King, I…"

A bronze royal gong was struck. (It took two people to lift the mallet). The sound rang out across the royal hall. The guests all quieted down looking toward the King.

"Before you show me what you have found I have had a special sculpture made in honor of your having been the Royal Astronomer for me."

The King clapped his hands and two servants rolled into the royal hall a mysterious moving shape. It was taller than most camels and it barely fit through the archway leading into the hall. The shape was covered by a purple cloth but Balthazar could tell this thing had moving parts, as the purple cloth billowed up and down.

The servants paused in front of the King and removed the covering. Beneath the cloth was a large moving sculpture of stone and metal. In the center was a tall pole of granite. Extending out from this granite pole were several bars of bronze. On the end of each bronze bar, granite spheres were attached and these spheres spun around the center granite pole. It was fascinating to watch and even Balthazar marveled at the ingenuity of this moving sculpture, but there was one piece of it which held him mesmerized.

For some reason all the bars and bronze spheres moved at the same pace and direction except for one. It moved gracefully in and around the others swooping and diving in the opposite direction.

"I have built you the sky you are always telling me about," said the King proudly walking over to the sculpture. "Now what can you tell me about my sky?"

Balthazar was flabbergasted. Had the King been spying on him? Was the King toying with him? Balthazar was the only one who had seen his latest map. He had carefully locked it up every night. Yet, here was the King's sculpture with this one granite sphere moving counter to all the others.

"Oh, yes my King. I do indeed have something to tell you, but it is intended only for you to hear. So, with my apologies, let's celebrate Jandak's latest victory!"

Balthazar was not prepared to reveal his latest map to the King but he knew after the party he must. If the King thought he was keeping something from him, Balthazar might lose more than just his job as the Royal Astronomer. But first, Balthazar had to get back to his observatory, then recheck and rethink his calculations one more time.

Chapter 2
One Star

It had been several months since the victory party and Balthazar was still taking measurements. He scribbled a few notes on the well-worn parchment resting on the table and then went back to the sky, gazing intently and muttering under his breath,

"Well, that can't be, it just can't be."

He was the King's mentor and Royal Astronomer. After all these months, how could he go back to the King with no answers? It wasn't a shooting star; they careen across the sky in the blink of an eye. And it wasn't that stars don't move, they do, but this one small star was moving backwards, like the only rebellious star child in the sky.

At first he thought there must be other stars moving against the flow in this nightly ballet of light, but Balthazar had scoured the sky watching and waiting for months. Nothing.

Every other star he could find was obeying the heavenly conductor and moving in the same direction. Balthazar had checked his old maps and there was no denying it. Further and further, this one star moved against the grain, against the universe. He wanted to know more. He needed a closer look. Balthazar roamed around his little rooftop observatory, then glanced out at the city in the direction of the star.

"My answer lies out there somewhere," he said into the night, watching his breath hit the cold night air and gently rise up to form a frosty mist encircling the moon.

He turned back to his table of parchments and tools and began putting them away when a glint of light caught his eye. It was quick and short but he had seen it. The lightest, faintest shaft of light reflected from a glass lens lying on the table. He stared back out into the night. Was it brighter? No. It... Yes.

Yes. It was brighter, almost imperceptibly brighter. Only an eye trained in the night arts of astronomy would even notice. Balthazar grabbed a magnifying glass from the table, held it up to his eye and looked back out into the sky.

"My land map, I must find my land map."

He dropped the lens into one of the many pockets on his coat and scampered across the length of the roof to a tall standing wooden cabinet. It creaked when opened and almost immediately things began to pour out of it. A crystal ball fell on Balthazar's head without him even noticing. It bounced off, skittered across the roof and finally came to rest against the ledge with a hodge-podge of other astronomers' tools and trinkets, a small treasure trove of forgotten and broken things.

In a flurry of activity, Balthazar fumbled through the contents of the cabinet tossing every instrument out onto the rooftop: rulers, rods, compasses. Then just as suddenly he stopped and pulled a folded parchment from the bottom shelf. It was cracked and pieces flaked off and drifted down around his feet.

Balthazar gently picked up the few pieces that had fallen, cradled them with the map in his arms and walked over to the ladder that led downstairs into the building from the rooftop.

Balthazar was a very intelligent man. In fact, the King referred to him as a 'wise man', although he didn't necessarily look the part. His short, round, arms couldn't quite hang straight by his side. Some people thought if you poked him with a knife he would just deflate until all the air was gone and only a pile of clothes would remain.

However, no one made fun of Balthazar, because he was so wise. When he was a child his father thought he was just a daydreamer and would never amount to anything. But Balthazar was doing more than staring up into the night sky. He was learning about the heavens and it had served him well. Here he was in the palace of the King of Babylon who, by the way, might have somehow heard about his latest discovery.

It was a sturdy ladder but the noises generated from the weight of Balthazar made it complain loud and long every time

Balthazar climbed up or down. As gingerly as he could, Balthazar stepped down from the last rung of the ladder and walked along a torch-lit hall into a small side room largely filled with a single table. The flickering light in the room gave him a better view of the parchment as he unfolded it onto the table top. His excitement increased as more and more of the parchment came into view.

"Ahh," said Balthazar "It has been a long time since I have seen the map of Babylon and Persia. Now I will find out where my little star is headed."

Balthazar pulled the star map from his robe and spread it out onto the table next to his land map. Quickly glancing back and forth and scribbling a few notes, he put a dot on the land map; then he placed another, and another. Soon he could see the arc of the star in relation to his old dusty land map. The stars trajectory was taking it closer and closer to the edge of it.

"My map. My map!" he exclaimed.

The star was clearly moving somewhere off his map and above an unknown part of the world. "I must know where you are going little star." Balthazar scratched his head and sat numb with his eyes straining and his mind wishing his map extended to the west. But there it was, his star dangling at the edge of his parchment at the end of his world.

He just couldn't stand it. His curiosity and fascination about the star was too much for him. He knew where he had to go, and who he had to see. Gaspar!

Balthazar's mind wandered back to the last race just months before. He could still clearly see his gold victory plate and Gaspar looking down at his silver, second place bowl.

"Ahh, victory," Balthazar whispered to himself.

He would have to swallow some of his pride if he expected Gaspar's help. Gaspar was the only person who would have reliable maps of the Mediterranean Sea and the surrounding area. Balthazar's calculations showed the star was headed in that direction. Like it or not, Gaspar was the only option if Balthazar was going to solve this riddle in the sky.

He gingerly rolled up both maps and put them into a leather tube. He capped the tube with a large cork, extinguished the torch and quickly stepped into the hall; the only observer was a wisp of smoke which followed him from the room.

It was morning. Balthazar had hardly slept at all. He knew he had to act quickly and travel lightly.

"Just enough food and water for two weeks," he said. "That should be enough time to reach Persia."

Normally, the trip would take three weeks but if he traveled alone, and without his usual entourage, Balthazar thought he could make it to Persia in two weeks.

"Boaz!" he yelled.

"Yes Master."

"Get my best camel Jandak, and load these bags. I must leave immediately." said Balthazar, without even looking at Boaz.

"And where is my master going?" inquired Boaz. He generally didn't ask, but Balthazar was so agitated and excited it made Boaz curious.

"To see Gaspar," said Balthazar, blindly throwing another robe into a knapsack.

"Gaspar?" asked Boaz, with just the slightest bit of hesitation.

"You think I shouldn't?"

Balthazar stopped for a moment gazing at Boaz.

"I can hear the hesitation in your voice. Speak freely."

"Well, after you defeated him during the latest camel races I didn't think he was very happy with you."

"Oh surely he's over that by now. That was pure luck and good fortune."

"Well, word around the tents was you had fed Jandak a mixture of unknown contents before the race and this mixture, Ummm... let's just say it made Jandak's stomach unstable, which in turn, created a very odiferous race. People alongside the race course complained. As I recall, it stopped Gaspar and his camel in their tracks at the start of the race. If it hadn't been for that incident, he might have won."

"Gaspar will just have to get past that. This is too important." said Balthazar as he threw one last goat skin bag onto the pile in the middle of the room. "I'm leaving as soon as you can get all of these things and Jandak to the front gate. In the meantime, I must tell the King."

After explaining to the King that he didn't know where he was going, nor how long he would be gone, nor exactly what he was chasing, Balthazar realized maybe it was all nonsense. He was beginning to think the King would say no; but in the end, the King's love of the stars and the temptation of his name being remembered forever won the argument.

As Balthazar was leaving the city he turned in his saddle and could see the King and all his entourage standing in the king's private alcove at the top of the wall. The King had even gotten out the royal banner of blessings. Several servants waved the huge scarlet and gold banner above the King's head.

Balthazar knew he had the King's full support now. Making a king believe they are important and will be remembered forever is a very good thing when you need permission to do something a little strange like tracking a star in an unknown part of the world.

As Balthazar sat around his first campfire that night, he remembered saying, 'You O King of Babylon will be remembered forever.' It made him smile. After all, Balthazar was a very wise man. He doused his small fire, got out one of his magnifying lenses and focused his eyes on the wandering star. He had no reference point out here in the midst of the dunes, but he knew it was still moving, still taunting him.

"As soon as I arrive at Gaspar's city I will see where you've gone, my little firefly in the sky. You will not be a secret much longer. Then, I shall return home and receive a handsome reward."

With a few animal skins for warmth and a sand dune for a pillow, Balthazar curled up in the cleft of a rock and fell asleep dreaming of fireflies and stars.

Over the next few days the dullness and sameness of each day weighed on Balthazar. Sometimes the nights were so cloudy he couldn't see the star and he wondered what he might do if the next night the star disappeared completely. The searing heat of each day combined with the frosty cold nights made him delusional. These delusions played tricks on his mind and created doubts, like a procrastinating friend who might or might not be there when you needed them the most. Was he losing his mind? What if he got to Gaspar's city and there was no longer any star? Or worse yet, what if all his calculations were completely wrong and there was no movement at all? Not only would he have to live with the derision of Gaspar rolling over him like a sudden and unforgiving sandstorm, but he would have to return to his own country and declare, "I guess it was just my imagination." He would find himself back in the abandoned part of the kingdom.

His curiosity always got the better of him. That was Balthazar's problem. At times it was his greatest strength and at other times the bane of his existence. Through the haze of the heat Balthazar looked into the horizon.

"Why do I even care about this star? My curiosity is going to be the end of me," he said aloud. But the only answer was the consistent soft swishing of the sand with each step Jandak took.

Balthazar had become so disoriented he couldn't remember how many days he had been traveling. He hoped somehow his astronomy skills were at least keeping him on track and headed in the right direction. The terrain had changed since leaving Babylon. Now, rather than one rolling sand dune after another there were walls of rock and wisps of vegetation. He had even spotted a few farmers and herders, but if he didn't see the city soon he knew he would be in trouble. Traveling alone wasn't the smartest thing he could have done, and in this land if he wandered even just the slightest bit off the trade route there would be some robbers or ruffians who would gladly take what little he had, leaving him for the desert to claim as another trophy. He had seen more than one windswept whitewashed skeleton standing eerily at attention, moving at the slightest breeze.

Jandak would save him. Jandak might be the smelliest camel in any kingdom but he was also the fastest. He had saved Balthazar on more than one occasion; he could do it again, if necessary. Balthazar smiled as he fondly thought of his camel. Jandak was also pretty smart for a camel and either through trickery or physical speed, Jandak had never let him down.

"I wonder if those bandits are still spreading the rumor of our demise." Balthazar patted Jandak and laughed quietly.

The humor was a small distraction but it didn't entirely remove the anxiousness Balthazar was feeling about how long this trip to Gaspar's City was taking. Balthazar had begun sleeping in the saddle, and his backside was letting him know it wanted some rest. Jandak could use a good night's sleep too, but where were they? How close was the city? If Balthazar only had some sort of assurance that he was…not seeing a mirage.

It couldn't be a mirage. Balthazar slapped his face to snap out of his dreary stupor. He fumbled for a magnifying lens, almost dropping it off the edge of the cliff where Jandak had stopped. He held the glass in front of his eye.

"The golden minarets of Persia!" he exclaimed. And guessing at the distance they couldn't be more than a day's travel. "Gaspar, I bring a gift of peace," Balthazar said to himself. He was building up his courage in order to face the man he had beaten in the camel races six years in a row. He patted a silk purse tied to the hilt of his saddle and it jingled lightly. "This purse of gold will make him forget all about the camel races." And with that, Balthazar turned Jandak around and began the descent into the Valley of Flowers, which would lead him to Gaspar's castle.

The Horn of Mithra could be seen for miles. The giant, golden, scythe shaped horn glistened from any angle whenever the sun was up. Balthazar needed no directional help the last five miles to Gaspar's castle. The Horn of Mithra sparkled and flashed the sun's rays in every direction. Gaspar's city was a marvelous sight from afar, but up close it was breathtaking. The massive minarets and white city walls reflected the sun brightly for miles in every direction, creating an unbroken pool of mirages. It was said one of the mirages was real, and when found, it would offer the lost traveler eternal life here on earth. More than one poor soul from the city had gone mad looking for it. Countless others had left the city in search of this *'Oasis of Life'* and never returned. Balthazar knew the legend and after seeing the beauty of the city, understood how someone could succumb to its' allure after all these years. Jandak sensed they were near the city and he quickened the pace.

Jandak and Balthazar finally stood before the massive city gates. The doors were twenty feet tall and at least that wide. The metal hinges alone took six men to lift them into place when the gate was built. A small wooden window cut into the city wall opened as Balthazar dismounted and walked toward it.

"Who goes there?" said the sentry, no more interested than necessary.

"I am Balthazar, Wise Council and Royal Astronomer to the King of Babylon. I wish to speak to Gaspar the Magi. I mean, Gaspar the Mighty Magi and Maker of the Maps of Kings," said Balthazar, correcting himself and giving Gaspar his due title. After all, he had some bridges to build if he was going to have any chance of attaining Gaspar's much needed help.

Outside the city gate, jutting out from the wall was a sun dial. After watching the sun dial slowly make its way from one hour to the next the sentry finally returned and opened the small wooden window in the wall. He cleared his throat to read from a scroll. "May all men know by this decree that Gaspar the Mightiest Magi and Maker of Maps beyond Balthazar's puny attempt to make a map the least bit comparable..."

"Excuse me," inquired Balthazar, "is this going to take long? Can you just get to the part where he says, No."

"Alright; let me see here, cheater of camel races, hmmm, Ahh, yes here it is at the very bottom. No." The sentry slammed the window shut.

Balthazar shook his robes clearing them of the final remains of desert sand. He stood as straight as he possibly could and politely knocked on the window again. It remained shut tight. Balthazar knocked harder. Still nothing. He took a coin from a pocket and passed it through a slit in the window. It dropped onto the sandy floor with a soft thud inside the city walls.

From inside the walls Balthazar heard the muffled voice of the sentry. "I think there must be someone outside. No. I don't hear anything. They have probably gone away."

Balthazar dropped another coin through the slot, a gold coin this time. The window slid open and the sentry stuck his head outside, inches from Balthazar's face. "Oh, it's you again. Did you have something you wanted to tell Gaspar? Gaspar thought it was a little early for you to come by. The camel races aren't for another few months, but if you were considering withdrawing..."

"I'll wipe the desert floor with..." Balthazar stopped in mid-sentence realizing he would have to make nice no matter how much it galled him. "... a broom and pave the way for Gaspar and his superior camel if he will but grant me an audience. I believe he will be intrigued by what I have to show him."

The gate window closed. Balthazar heard the soft shuffling of sandals on the sandy floor moving away from the wall.

"Ohhh, this desert sun is making it hard to swallow such a statement," he said to himself. But it wouldn't matter if he could get Gaspar to see and confirm his findings. This waiting and bowing and bending backwards would be worth it then. And who knows, Gaspar wasn't without his own ambition and curiosity. He would want his name attached to this discovery if it proved financially worthwhile and elevated them into a permanent place in history.

"Yes, Gaspar. Your name will be just below mine in the annals of great discoveries," Balthazar whispered to himself as he shuffled his feet stirring up a small dust cloud.

The thick wooden gate began to shudder and open. The opening of the gate created a swirl of dust and silt which engulfed Balthazar, temporarily hiding him and his plans of riches and fame from view.

Chapter 3
Gaspar

"Balthazar must want something very badly," said Enoch, Gaspar's bald and lanky attendant. "I mean to travel such a great distance alone."

"Alone?" said Gaspar quite surprised. No one traveled that distance by themselves unless it was a very pressing matter. Gaspar knew it couldn't be about the camel races; even Balthazar wasn't that obsessed with winning.

"Maybe there is some kind of emergency in Babylon that requires my expertise," said Gaspar.

"Perhaps," agreed Enoch, "shall I bring him in to see you?"

"Yes, I think so."

Balthazar waited for the dust to settle, and as soon as it did there were two splendidly attired attendants with gold encrusted feathers protruding from silver head bands sitting on their shaved heads. Their sandals were emblazoned with precious stones and their tunics were woven out of purple velvet with some type of exotic fur for trim. They carried no swords.

"Well, that's a good sign," mumbled Balthazar.

In the courtyard he was greeted by six female servants. Balthazar couldn't help but notice the attendants Gaspar had sent to usher him into the palace and up to his private living quarters. All of them were strikingly beautiful women and they all looked identical. Jet black shoulder length hair kept in place by intricately designed golden serpents woven into their hair. Flowing translucent tops with the smallest green emeralds sparkled around the neck and waist. They wore gold sandals and puffed purple silk pants. Balthazar walked with them down several marble halls lined with gold and silver framed tapestries hanging on the walls.

"Impressive," said Balthazar as he shuffled down the hall behind the wall of women.

Balthazar didn't have the heart to tell him, but it was this very fallible character trait of showing off which allowed Jandak to win the camel races year after year. Gaspar's camels were always weighed down with unnecessary jewels and precious metals, so by the end of the race the poor camel was completely worn out. While it was true Jandak had the look of a vagabond, he didn't carry an ounce more than necessary. Besides, with Balthazar riding him, Jandak already had quite a handicap.

Balthazar kept trying to find some sort of difference in any of the six women escorting him but he couldn't. In fact, he became so distracted and determined to find some flaw he failed to notice they had walked right into Gaspar's private chambers.

"Ahem." Gaspar standing behind Balthazar cleared his throat.

Balthazar turned and snapped to attention giving an appropriate bow.

"Arise," said Gaspar, with enough emphasis Balthazar knew who was in charge for the moment.

Gaspar raised his hands and waved the attendants from the room. There was an awkward pause as Gaspar walked around Balthazar gazing at him, probing him with his eyes as if he could will the request from Balthazar without having to ask why he had traveled alone.

"Please sit down. You must be tired from such a long journey." Gaspar pointed toward a group of zebra skin pillows with gold tassels lying on the floor.

Balthazar took off his sandals and wondered how long it would take before Gaspar would ask him why he was there. Gaspar clapped his hands together twice and two well-dressed male attendants entered the room offering drinks. For just a moment Balthazar realized how tired he really was, and how far he had traveled. A little nap would be nice. Besides, in the middle of the day they couldn't see anything in the sky, so Balthazar resigned himself to being as pleasant and amiable as possible.

"How are things in Babylon?" Gaspar asked nonchalantly.

Balthazar, wobbling and woozy from his trip gave the best answer he could.

"Well, you know the King always has an agenda..."

Balthazar paused and blinked his eyes quickly trying to keep awake, but his eyes and his head were winning the battle for sleep. He snapped his head back up off his chest and finished his thought, "...and I am his dutiful servant."

"Oh, those kings. Always with their own agenda."

Gaspar laughed and turned to pick up his golden goblet for a drink. When he turned back around there was Balthazar, a dusty, dirty curled up chameleon asleep in the pillows.

"Well, I suppose whatever it is can wait."

Gaspar got up, pulled a pillow from beneath Balthazar, allowing his head to hit the floor.

"That should give him a nice sore neck or at least a bump on the head." Gaspar looked down at Balthazar, "That's for the Desert 100. Sleep well."

"Owww! My neck!" Balthazar awoke in a complete panic. He was so tired he couldn't remember where he was or how he had gotten there. He could tell it was night as he looked through the high columned windows, and saw torchlight glittering and shimmering on the wall just across the courtyard from where he was sitting. Bolting toward the nearest window, he looked outside and knew it was close to midnight.

He needed his maps and a table. There was a large marble table in the room just down the wall from where he was standing and the maps were on Jandak. He hurried out of his room and down the giant marble staircase into the courtyard. Jandak would be in the holding pen near the front gate.

After retrieving the leather tube and returning to his room Balthazar laid out both maps on the marble table. He double checked his math and the maps one more time. It was absolutely undeniable. His star had moved again during the two weeks he had been unable to follow it.

"I hope Gaspar will be willing to help me double-check my math and trajectories." Balthazar's finger landed outside the boundaries of his old, outdated map. Mumbling, he realized he was thinking out loud and for some reason he had begun pacing back and forth across the room.

"I must awaken Gaspar." This could not wait. Balthazar clapped his hands twice and an attendant stepped into his room immediately.

"Yes Master Balthazar. I am your willing servant, Demetrius. How may I be of service?"

"I need you to take me to Gaspar's room."

"He will be none too pleased to be awakened at this hour."

"It cannot be helped. I must speak to him, now." Balthazar stepped in front of Demetrius and waited for him to lead him to Gaspar's chambers.

"Wake up." Balthazar gently rocked Gaspar back and forth. "Wake up." He said again just a little louder.

"No, I don't want to go to school." Gaspar whispered then rolled over.

"Oh bother. He's dreaming. Well, this should wake him up." Balthazar pulled a camel horn from inside his tunic. It wasn't the loudness of the camel horn or its physical size that made it so noticeable. The horn made such a disturbing noise it was said spirits long asleep would awaken if it was blown just right. Balthazar blew it just right. Gaspar was thin; almost a waif compared to Balthazar, and it was impressive how high he jumped out of bed.

"Balthazar!" screamed a now fully awakened Gaspar. "Is that why you came all this way? To scare me to death? I will call the guards and have you dragged through town behind that stinky camel of yours."

"Drag me through town?" Balthazar grinned. "Don't you think a royal guided tour would be more appropriate?"

"I'll give you a guided tour right out the front gate." Gaspar stared at the small ornate horn Balthazar was holding. "What is that thing?"

"It's my camel horn," said Balthazar. "I'm sorry to have scared you so badly but I have something far more intriguing to show you than this silly camel horn. Follow me."

Demetrius lit a torch and the three of them walked back to Balthazar's room.

"This better be worth it," said Gaspar as he gathered himself.

"Oh, it is. It is," said Balthazar as he took the torch from Demetrius motioning for him to stay in the main hall.

The torches in Balthazar's room had been extinguished hours before, but he re-ignited the one by his work table and waved for Gaspar to come over to him.

"Now listen to me," declared Balthazar. "What I have come to your kingdom to discuss would mean nothing to most people, but I believe before the night is done you will be very intrigued indeed."

"Middle of the night," grumbled Gaspar. "This had better be more than intriguing or I'll drag you back to Babylon myself."

"Alright Gaspar, let me start with the stars." Balthazar turned to look directly at Gaspar and waited for a little curiosity or interest; but none was forthcoming. "You are no astronomer, but I know you understand enough about the earth and the heavens to realize all the stars move…"

"In the same direction," Gaspar blurted out rudely. "Oh please don't tell me this is why you've gotten me out of bed tonight. Children know that much."

"Yes it's true," said Balthazar ignoring the sarcastic response, "that is why what I am about to show you is so remarkable. I want you to take a look at this."

Balthazar pointed at the two parchments laid out side by side; Balthazar's star map, and Gaspar's old cracked parchment with the outlines of the countries still barely visible.

Gaspar stared at both parchments for a long time. He ran his fingers over the creases of Balthazar's old worn map. "How long have you had this? It's ancient. It must be... It is. It's the first map I ever completed of the area between Babylon and Persia. Where in the world did you get it?"

"Well," said Balthazar sensing the pride in Gaspar's voice over seeing the old map, "you gave it to me, and it is a key piece of the puzzle you are about to see for yourself."

Balthazar sat down on the marble bench in front of the table and started telling Gaspar what he knew about the star. He told his story with his hands, drawing an arc in the air and pointing to the path on his map. He carefully showed Gaspar the calculations and trajectories determining the path of the star.

"Look for yourself. Use this." Balthazar pulled a magnifying glass from his robe. "Check the coordinates against your map." And so, the night was spent looking and plotting and staring out into the heavens; one star inexorably pulling two men closer together and putting them under its spell.

"Amazing. Undeniably amazing." Gaspar stopped his accolades, turned toward Balthazar and stammered, "I see. I believe what I see, but why would you share your greatest discovery with me? What do you need me for?"

"You see the old map of yours sitting here on the table?"

"Yes. What about it? What's wrong with it?"

"What's wrong with it? It stops right here." Balthazar pushed his round pudgy finger onto the edge of the map knocking one more piece off onto the floor. "I need to know what is out here beyond this edge of the map so I may continue tracking this star." He paused and swallowed hard to keep his pride from showing. "I have no one else who can help me."

Gaspar pushed himself back from the table and walked over to the balcony still staring at the star. It was now teasing him, pulling him in and drawing him toward it just as it had Balthazar.

"Oh you need another map alright. No doubt about it, and I have the map, but you need something more, and you don't even realize it." Gaspar left the room.

Balthazar stood still, his mind reeling. What did Gaspar mean he needed something else? What could it be? Did he have this something else in his possession, too? Could this trip still be a complete waste of time? Yet there was the star, still twinkling and twisting its way into Balthazar's mind. He only hoped Gaspar and his maps would help him discover something more about it.

Balthazar didn't have long to wait. Gaspar returned to the room followed by three servants with armloads of maps, parchments and scrolls. Gaspar began sorting the scrolls and parchments until they were piled so high the large marble table was obscured from sight.

"What is all this?" asked Balthazar.

"I hope the answers we seek will be found somewhere in the midst of all this." Gaspar said from inside the wall of parchments.

Gaspar walked out of the maze of manuscripts and over to Balthazar.

"You go back to bed Balthazar. I just want to go through a few things before I try to sleep. You have had a long trip. We will talk in the morning."

"A few things?" Balthazar stammered. "This much material will take you weeks to read."

"Oh, I will glance at these manuscripts and know in short order if the information I seek is here. Now, go on to bed. I won't be long."

"I don't understand what all these things have to do with my map of the stars."

"All in good time my wise friend. Some things cannot be rushed."

"But, you have the land map we need. What is all of this for?

"Bed. Now. Something about your star has changed and you don't realize it. Let me check your calculations one more time and overlay them on my map. Then we shall see if I am correct or not," said Gaspar turning abruptly and marching back to his table and his work.

Balthazar could think of nothing to say, so he walked over to his bed and fitfully fell asleep while Gaspar worked away in the soft torchlight that filled the room.

Yawning and stretching, Balthazar noticed the pile of manuscripts had been moved across the room and the sun was striking the opposite wall from when Balthazar had gone to bed so he knew a new day had arrived. Gaspar was still hunkered over the table full of maps.

"You've been up all night?" asked Balthazar.

"Yes. Yes, I have and it's your fault you know." quipped Gaspar. "I was quite happy here in Persia with my work and position as King Arsaces' advisor but no, this is how you want to see me end my time here, driven insane by a single misbehaving, miscreant moon."

"Technically, it's a star."

"Alright, it's a star. It doesn't matter to me what it is but there is something very pressing which I cannot answer. I've been scouring through all of this material." Gaspar waved his arm at the tall pile of scrolls and manuscripts.

"Oh, now I remember." said Balthazar. "You mentioned there was some other information I would need. Then you told me to think about it." Balthazar paused, afraid to say what was really on his mind. Gaspar sensed this and finished the unspoken thought.

"You want to know if I have the maps you need in order to give a full report back to your king and make a name for yourself and this star."

"Very much so," said Balthazar in a whisper, "I just need a larger land map so I can continue tracking the star from Babylon."

"You are welcome to the maps I have here but I think I have some information which will keep you chasing this star. Something you've missed."

"What? Oh, you're just trying to get back at me for all those losses in the Desert 100," said Balthazar.

Gaspar ignored the slight. He had found something the brilliant Balthazar had missed. Deep inside, Gaspar was beaming and couldn't wait to drop his discovery on his guest.

"Your star is slowing down, Balthazar," blurted Gaspar.

"What did you say?" Balthazar tried to feign only slight interest but this news took him completely by surprise and Gaspar could sense it.

"The star is slowing down and I believe it will be stopping very soon," said Gaspar louder than necessary just to make certain Balthazar had heard him.

"The star is stopping?" asked Balthazar. This was unexpected information indeed and Gaspar knew Balthazar's curiosity would not allow him to go back to Babylon now.

"I, I, I," stammered Balthazar, "I had come here expecting to map the star as far as I could. Name it. Have you verify I discovered it, and return to Babylon. But now I..."

"Now you want to know where I think it is going to stop."

"Yes, of course."

"I can't be certain yet, but I believe it will eventually stop somewhere in this area," Gaspar pointed at an area on the map where he had drawn a circle, "near the Mediterranean Sea."

Balthazar stared hard at the map. "I guess I won't be going back to Babylon quite yet."

Balthazar paused. "A star stopping in the middle of the sky? It is undocumented in the history of astronomy... This is no ordinary heavenly light."

"What is this area called where the star may be stopping?" asked Balthazar. "And why is it stopping?"

"To answer your first question I believe the star will stop somewhere over the area called Judea. Concerning the second part of your question as to why it is stopping," said Gaspar. "I do not know. But, if there are answers to that question, I know who has them." And with a confident look Gaspar went back to his maps.

"Wait just a minute," Balthazar tapped Gaspar on the shoulder. "You don't get to just go back to work on this. Who has these answers?"

"Well," said Gaspar with a deliberate smile crossing his face, "concerning that, I have a good decree and a bad decree."

"Oh, will the sands of time fill your turban to the brim," seethed Balthazar, "a good decree and a bad decree?"

"Yes. The bad decree is I don't have any information about why this star has appeared or why it is stopping. The good decree is I can help you track it with my maps and get you an audience with the man who will likely have the answers you seek."

Balthazar walked around the table and stared at the new trajectory of the star on Gaspar's map. Gaspar pointed at the recalculated arc on both maps and plotted a point in the middle of Judea: Jerusalem. He then took out a compass and drew a circle with Jerusalem in the center. The edge of it went through Beth Hanina, Elzaria, Anata and a tiny town called Bethlehem.

"Considering the stars current speed and trajectory, my best guess is it will stop somewhere in this area. If we can get closer to Judea, I can probably pinpoint it on the land map more precisely." Gaspar pulled the map from the table and held it up in the air shaking any loose debris from it.

Gaspar walked away from the map table and made his way to a pile of pillows on the floor. A servant offered him a drink and he took it; then he sat down. Balthazar took a drink from a tray and sat on a separate set of pillows directly in front of Gaspar.

Gaspar took a quick sip and eased back into the pillows. "Balthazar," he began, "have you ever heard of this happening before? Do you know of a prophecy or event that is foretold by such a thing as this star?"

"No. I do not."

Balthazar leaned further back into the comfort of the pillows to reconsider things. No, he had never heard of such a celestial disturbance as this being foretold, not in Babylonian history for certain. Perhaps this was a Persian sign of some sort. He wasn't as confident of his Persian history and prophecies.

"I have never heard of a sign like this before either." Gaspar drew a deep breath and continued. "That is what to me is most puzzling. During the night I scoured through all of the material I had concerning Persia, and I did not find any historical reference or foretelling of such an event."

"We are missing the historical documents and written prophecies of the region where the star is headed—Judea. I believe we will find the answers when we find those ancient writings. We need to find Melchior."

Gaspar paused, waiting for any reaction from Balthazar. "You've heard of him haven't you?"

"Oh, yes. Of course. Who hasn't?" Balthazar had been bested by Gaspar once already and once was enough. But to be truthful, he had no idea who Melchior was.

"Isn't he from Meohg Efe," Balthazar deliberately muffled his voice to hide the fact he had no idea where Melchior lived.

"What did you say? Mesopotamia?"

Balthazar nodded his head as he took a sip from his golden goblet.

"That's right. We are going to the kingdom of Mesopotamia." Gaspar got up, flipped his long trailing robe higher than normal and walked over to the map table. He wanted Balthazar to see the map one more time. He placed his finger on a city just south of Babylon—Najaf.

"Najaf is where we must go to find Melchior the Magnificent. He is the greatest living historian and oracle in the world. He will know the history of Judea, and if the foretelling of this star has ever been recorded on a manuscript or scroll, he will know about it."

Balthazar rolled off his pile of pillows and made his way over to Gaspar. With a sense of hope in his eyes he said. "So you think Melchior can help us answer why this star has appeared?"

"Yes. Yes I do," said Gaspar as he reached for his drink. "If I didn't, I wouldn't go on this crazy journey. Knowing why this star has appeared will help us prepare for our quest and possibly tell us what lies beneath it."

"I feel somewhat better Gaspar, and I want to thank you for…"

"Don't thank me yet. It is a troubling journey we are about to embark upon. The last band of tradesmen I sent out all returned but they were missing…" Gaspar shook his head at the memory and could not continue.

"Missing what?"

"Their heads," said Gaspar. He got up from the comfort of the pillows and went to the map table. He rolled the maps up carefully and turned to face Balthazar who was still seated on the floor with his mouth wide open.

"And what about your king?" said Balthazar. "Will he just let you leave like this?"

"Oh, I will tell him that I have heard of a camel in Mesopotamia faster than the fabled Jandak. He will let me go if I have discovered a chance to finally win the Desert 100."

Balthazar grinned sheepishly and shrugged his shoulders. "What will he say when you mention you are traveling with me?"

"That wouldn't be very smart now would it Balthazar? I will tell him you are a travelling trader sent from Mesopotamia to open a new trade route with us."

Gaspar turned and walked toward the marble hallway. "If the king should see you, just keep your head down and keep quiet. And for goodness sake don't feed Jandak anything until we are well out of the city." He turned at the edge of the hallway. "I'm going to tell my king. We will leave tomorrow morning at sunrise. Meet me at the front gate. I shall have everything loaded and ready to go. We must travel lightly and quickly to attract as little attention as possible. It will be a dangerous journey." Gaspar took one last look at Balthazar and disappeared down the hallway his flowing robe whisking around the corner behind him.

"Balthazar." Demetrius entered his room. "I am here to help you prepare for your journey."

Balthazar began pointing and Demetrius started packing. With each passing moment the anticipation and anxiety stirred in Balthazar's mind.

"I hope Gaspar knows what he is talking about," he mused.

Balthazar spent the rest of the day checking his and Gaspar's calculations. It certainly appeared Gaspar was right. Najaf would be their next stop. One last time Balthazar double checked he had all his instruments and maps. He climbed into bed while Demetrius doused the torches in the room.

It seemed Balthazar had just closed his eyes when Demetrius woke him up. "Master Balthazar. It is time to be going."

Balthazar got up, dressed and hurried outside while Demetrius brought his things down to the courtyard. Gaspar was already there, mounted and at the front gate. The silhouettes of the guard towers and the Horn of Mithra cast a moving, wavering set of shadows against the gate of the city. Then, just like a mirage disappears in the desert, the gate opened and the shadows fell to the ground giving way to the sun just beginning to appear on the horizon. The opening of the gate froze Balthazar in his tracks. Suddenly, it wasn't the star that awaited him, it was all of the questions he had about the star in his mind.

"Balthazar. Balthazar." Gaspar turned just under the guard tower. "Are you walking to Najaf, or riding?"

Balthazar's stare was still transfixed on the opened gate and what lay beyond.

"Well," said Gaspar, "I'd recommend riding."

Balthazar still did not move. He stood with Jandak's bridle in his hand and Jandak on all four knees waited for his master.

"Oh come now Balthazar, you came to me and convinced me to go on this journey. Now you have questions? Melchior will help us. He will know what is beneath this star. Who knows, this star might even make us famous someday. Now let's go."

Gaspar turned and urged his camel through the gate and out into the desert. Balthazar was jolted out of his daze by Jandak who pulled on the reins and snorted loudly. Balthazar mounted Jandak mostly out of instinct and hurried him through the gate which had already begun to close. They rode out of the city squinting at the first peek of the sun as the gates slammed shut behind them.

Chapter 4
Sand Cobra

Balthazar and Gaspar initially chatted about family and friends, but not long into the day they ran into a wall of swirling heat and wind determined to pour sand into every conceivable crevice of man and beast. This was decidedly not the time to talk. The sand and the constant heat made talking too taxing. And so, the two men rode in silence, silhouetted against the dunes, bobbing up and down in the soft, shifting sand.

The first place they stopped that night was actually quite refreshing. Since it was only a day's ride from Gaspar's city, it was a place quite familiar to him. They were greeted by a family of herdsmen living nearby. The herdsmen loaned Balthazar and Gaspar a tent to sleep in for the night. In the morning they even gave the two travelers a sheepskin sack full of wine and some of the best bread and cheese Balthazar had tasted in a very long time. After eating and saying their goodbyes, it was back out into another day of dunes, dust and dreariness.

"Balthazar" asked Gaspar, "this star you found. Have you ever wondered if anyone else has noticed it?"

Balthazar looked back out toward the horizon hoping the star might still be visible in the early morning. The sun had not fully risen yet.

"No. I've never really thought about whether anyone else has seen it or tracked it." Balthazar rode on for a moment and then added. "I personally have told no one else except my king."

"And your king was he interested?"

"At first I didn't think he was overly curious or concerned, but my king is obsessed with the heavens and bade me go and discover what I could and then return. Why do you ask?"

"Well," said Gaspar, "I have a very strong feeling this kind of heavenly sign is reserved for immortals or gods and beings of the upper realms."

"Yes, I suppose it could be for something like that." Balthazar shifted in his saddle.

"I must admit at one point I thought this star might just lead me to some great city of gold, or it was calling me to be a king in some foreign land," said Balthazar.

But, the one thing he couldn't bring himself to reveal to Gaspar was what had initially led him to the star. But Balthazar knew the reason he had decided to begin this journey, three reasons to be exact.

"The crystal orbs have done nothing since I left Babylon," he muttered, "I'm not sure why I brought them."

The soft steady plodding of the camels lulled Balthazar into a semi-dream state and he remembered the orbs. Balthazar pulled on the strap around his neck and they jostled inside the leather pouch. When the orbs first revealed themselves he thought it must be a trick or a dream. The same thing happened every night.

Balthazar would go to bed as usual and the next day when he would make his way to the rooftop observatory, there would be the three globes sitting on the ledge in the same formation. One crystal would be positioned in front of the other two like the tip of an arrow. At first Balthazar thought he must have just forgotten to put the crystal orbs away, after all...

"I'm not known for my tidiness," Balthazar said. He glanced over at Gaspar's perfect impeccable taste in full display on his camel. Everything was in its proper place, shiny and new.

"I've been collecting things since before Gaspar was born," Balthazar said laughing to himself. And to be honest, he had no idea where the three globes had come from or how long they had been in his possession. One night Balthazar deliberately put each globe in a separate drawer inside the wooden cabinet.

"I remember locking the cabinet and going to bed."

Balthazar closed his eyes and went back over the experiment. In the morning the three globes were out of the cabinet, lined up in their arrow formation at the edge of the roof.

So, that night he took the three globes to bed with him. He set them on a table in his bedroom and locked the door to his room. In the morning they were gone. Sure enough, when he went upstairs onto the roof, there they were on the ledge again arranged in their familiar arrow formation.

After a few nights of this, Balthazar realized the globes were always pointing toward the same location in the sky. Aside from being a great astronomer he was a pretty good magician too. But these crystal globes were no magicians trick; or at least not one he could comprehend.

He began studying the night sky in the direction the globes were pointing and soon discovered the star he had been tracking ever since.

"I guess I won't need them anymore if the star has stopped," Balthazar said, staring at leather satchel hanging by his side.

Ever since the night he had decided to follow the star the globes had been dormant. No pointing, no disappearing, nothing. He had brought them with him purely out of curiosity. He opened the leather pouch and stared in at the clear crystal orbs.

"Is there another purpose for you?" he asked. Then he closed the pouch and guided Jandak back into position alongside Gaspar.

The sand cobra is not a good bed fellow. This was only the second night of their journey and now Balthazar thought it might be his last. The beady yellow eyes of the snake followed every move Balthazar made. The head swayed from side to side, the neck flared out and the tongue tested the air as it flicked in and out, in and out, keeping time like a bizarre, venomous metronome. How much longer would it wait before it struck? Balthazar tried being absolutely still and the snake might have thought he was dead were it not for the sweat trickling down Balthazar's nose. Perhaps the snake was waiting for the first drop of sweat to fall because just as it pooled on the end of Balthazar's nose and dropped toward his lap, the snake made its move. It uncoiled and hurtled itself swiftly and silently toward Balthazar. Balthazar fainted and fell backward making his peace with the few seconds of life he had left. Once bitten, he would quickly die out here in the desert.

He moaned knowing the venom would swiftly do its work. His whole body felt cold and he knew he was dying. It didn't feel like he had imagined. Balthazar slowly moved his right hand to the side of his body and touched the ground. 'The afterlife feels like sand. How odd,' he thought.

Balthazar's hands sifted through the sand of his tent floor and he felt something squirm and twist itself around his fingers. It was the sand cobra! Then the cobra twisted its body up out of the sand. It was just too much for Balthazar to endure.

Gaspar had heard men scream in battle. When someone was about to die it always had an indescribable, primal edge to their scream. Whatever was happening, this was one of those screams. In fact, it was so frightening Gaspar didn't even recognize the screamer as Balthazar. He only saw a ball of man flash by in front of his eyes and disappear behind the dune where they were camping for the night. Gaspar immediately got up and followed the screams. Luckily for Balthazar, Gaspar was quite the sprinter and quickly caught up to him. Gaspar grabbed Balthazar by the shoulders and spun him around. Then he stopped and stared at Balthazar.

There was the sand cobra dangling from Balthazar's neck. Writhing and twisting in the night it was hard to see what had happened. But on second glance...

"Oh Balthazar," Gaspar turned and sprinted for the camp, "you're going to be fine. Just wait right there and don't move."

Then, he was gone behind the dune.

"Don't move," said Balthazar gasping for air and sweating profusely.

It was the most difficult thing he had ever done, standing absolutely still with a snake hissing and spitting just inches from his face. Gaspar returned with a silver scimitar in his hands. He approached Balthazar slowly.

"Please take my life before the poison does," pleaded Balthazar. He stuck his chest out waiting for the blow. The scimitar whistled through the air slicing the sand cobras head from the rest of its twisting body. The cobra's body fell to the ground and spun in circles around Balthazar's feet. Gaspar began to laugh and cry at the same time.

Balthazar was shaking so badly it took him some time to gather his wits. He was still alive! Gaspar had not swung the blade to kill him but to kill the snake.

"What are you laughing about?" demanded Balthazar.

"You are destined for this journey is all I can say," said Gaspar followed by a very long exhaled breath. "Do be careful when you remove the remainder of your snake necklace."

Balthazar looked down and finally realized what had occurred. Somehow when the snake leaped toward him, its fangs had gone into the leather bag and become entangled in the webbing inside.

Balthazar carefully pulled the pouch over his head and laid it on the sand. Then he took Gaspar's sword and pried what was left of the snake's body from the pouch. The snake's head snapped futilely in the sand like it might somehow still find its body, join it again and finish the deed. In his relief, Balthazar plunged the sword into the snake's head, pushing it into the sand and out of sight. Then, he pulled the pouch off the sand and looked inside. There were his three orbs, still unbroken and apparently undisturbed by the snake's fangs.

"Maybe this was your purpose," he said.

Balthazar closed the pouch cover, thankful he had brought the leather pouch and the orbs with him.

The next morning Balthazar and Gaspar sat outside their tents eating a breakfast of honey, nuts, dried fruit and a small portion of goat meat. Neither said a word as both of them were lost in their own thoughts. In particular, Gaspar was curious if the sand cobra would be the worst of it or if something more frightening was over the next rise waiting for them. Balthazar sat still but he flinched every time the wind blew across the dunes and created an image of multiple snakes rippling across the sand.

"I shall not ever come so close to death again without actually dying," he blurted out without even realizing he had verbalized the thought. Gaspar nodded his head in agreement and continued eating his breakfast. A lack of conversation and words would mark the journey for the rest of the day.

As they stopped that night and prepared their campsite, Gaspar finally broke the silence, "Balthazar, do you know anything about this Judea? It's culture, rulers, history? Anything?"

Balthazar had to think for a moment as he sat down at the entrance of his tent. "I have heard about the Maccabees and some great battles at Beth Horon. I know there is the story of a great flood which destroyed almost all life on earth, but that is about it. I suppose you are going to tell me more?"

Gaspar drove the last tent stake into the sand and secured it with a small rock. "I know the land has been the center of great conflict for many years. At one time, I heard it was called the land of milk and honey. I am anxious to speak with Melchior the Magnificent. I hope he has the answers we seek."

"You hope?"

"I mean, I know he has the answers we seek. Good night Balthazar." Gaspar turned and stooped to enter his tent. Just as he closed the flap he stuck his head back outside. "No snakes. Alright?"

"No snakes." said Balthazar. Just the thought of it made him shudder. He entered his tent and checked the straps securing the opening, twice.

Over the next few days the journey settled into a sameness which was comforting to Balthazar. Unlike the first leg of his journey, he had company this time and it was making all the difference. Not a great deal of conversation was happening but it wasn't necessary. Just having someone with him lightened the burden he felt. Someone he knew and respected believed in him and the star. It was beginning to bolster his confidence.

Gaspar was worried but didn't want to overburden Balthazar so he kept it to himself. The heat had climbed significantly and the wind had dropped low, very low. He knew this could be a prime time for a dust devil, but so far the horizon had been clear and perhaps it was a little of his imagination that was making him unusually nervous. Typically dust devils weren't very deadly, but they could wreak some havoc on occasion. The real danger was they could appear unannounced and leave before any action could be taken. He would keep his eyes open and watch for any signs a dust devil might be forming.

"West. That's the direction we need to go." Gaspar said. "There should be an oasis a short distance from here."

Balthazar pulled the reins and guided a lumbering Jandak west toward the unseen shade and water.

After arriving at the oasis, Gaspar dismounted, tied up his camel and made his way over to a low wall built by some earlier travelers. It was not a large oasis and only a traveler with the most recent map would be able to find it. "Hmmm," Gaspar glanced up at the sun. "It's just after midday. We should be somewhere between the edge of the Syrian Desert and Phoenicia. Let's look at the maps." Balthazar joined Gaspar at the wall and pulled the maps from their protective case. They cleared some space on a flat outcropping jutting out from the wall and laid both maps on it. The wall separated them from the elements and neither one of them noticed the slight change in the direction of the wind.

Chapter 5
Dust Devil

Wind is a very tricky thing. It can change speed and direction on a whim. And, even though it may be traveling at a great rate of speed it can be more invisible and silent than a sand cobra. Gaspar and Balthazar's only clue something was amiss was a slight breeze which caused the corners of the map to furl and curl up. Balthazar picked up a few rocks and began placing them on the corners of the map to keep it in place.

"Get down. Dust devil!" yelled Gaspar. He wasn't sure Balthazar heard him.

The serenity of the oasis was split in two with the sound of a thousand camel horns being blown simultaneously. Neither one of them could hear or see anything in the midst of the sand swirling around them.

Gaspar could feel the unrelenting stinging sand and shards of palm leaves tearing at his exposed skin. He was lifted off the ground. Then, just as quickly as it had picked him up, the storm laid him gently back down. The deafening sound continued for a moment, then all was quiet, and the dust devil gone.

Gaspar's hand reached up onto the ledge where the maps were. His stomach tightened and his heart sank. All that time, all that effort.

"The maps. The maps are gone."

Gaspar got up and stared blankly at the shelf where they had been just moments before.

"Gaspar, are you OK?" Balthazar's voice came from the other side of the wall. He too, had been lifted up by the storm and survived.

"Yes, I'm fine," Gaspar said weakly. "But, the maps are missing."

Balthazar walked around the corner of the wall. "So are the camels! Gaspar, climb up here and see if there is any sign of them."

From the top of the wall Gaspar could see a great distance out into the desert. He shielded his eyes from the sun, squinting and scanning for the camels.

"There they are, just over on the next dune. You stay here. I'll fetch the camels. Keep looking for the maps. We must find them."

The dust devil had really complicated things. Just like a truculent toddler on its way to the bath it had strewn things everywhere. Tunics, towels, tools, everything was spread out haphazardly over the desert floor. Balthazar picked up a tunic and flask. He spotted a saddle in the sand and draped the flask on the saddle horn. In a daze he turned back around and momentarily was blinded by the sun reflecting off something buried in the sand. He parted the sand and there they were – the three orbs. Balthazar stared at them for a moment. Even though they were made of glass, the wind and sand hadn't broken them. They were unscathed and unscratched. As he continued cleaning up their camp he found the leather pouch too. He opened the pouch and placed the glass orbs inside. He closed the pouch, sat the orbs down and began assembling what few things he could find.

It took Balthazar quite a while to gather enough pieces of his tent to assemble it. He was really sweating now and he thought about how working for the king had its privileges. Balthazar hadn't set up his own tent since he had started working for the king. There were always servants and stewards to do those mundane and manual tasks. It took him a few fits and starts to get his tent right. And besides that, it was a daunting task to keep up with all of Gaspar's things. In spite of being in a hurry to leave, it seemed he had packed enough for ten people.

Balthazar knew they could not survive out in the desert without the maps. That fact alone would allow them both the opportunity to turn back with their dignity intact.

Balthazar sat down in front of his tent next to the pouch containing the orbs. The orbs were the only thing Balthazar could think of that might allow them to continue their journey. It was time to test them and Gaspar.

Jandak and Gaspar could be heard before they were seen. Gaspar was complaining loudly as he and the camels wandered back into camp. All Balthazar could tell from Gaspar's rambling was that he and Jandak, a kangaroo rat and some cactus had all met; and it was not a pleasant meeting.

"Your camel..." Gaspar said, "you can have him. You found the maps I hope? Please tell me some good news."

"No. I did not find the maps."

"Without them we must turn back. I can't guarantee our direction or safety. Ouch," said Gaspar as he pulled a cactus needle from his back side.

"I think we should make our decision in the morning." Balthazar paused and took a deep breath. "I have both tents ready. Let's just stay here for the night."

Balthazar stood up and pulled the leather pouch containing the orbs off the sand. He reached into the pouch and one by one handed the orbs to Gaspar.

"I want you to take these three orbs and hide them around camp but don't tell me where you put them. If I'm right, we will know in the morning whether to continue or not. Good night Gaspar."

Balthazar excused himself and entered his tent.

"Oh, and one more thing," came Balthazar's voice from inside his tent. "I want you to tie my tent opening up tight so you will know I did not watch you hide the orbs."

"The dust devil and the cobra have taken your mind haven't they." There was no answer from inside Balthazar's tent.

"I will play your little game and hide the orbs and tie you inside your tent, but I am afraid without our maps we will have to go back to Persia. The lost food, flasks and maps have forced our hand. The star search is over."

Gaspar tied the front flaps of Balthazar's tent closed. Then, he stepped away and walked through the camp staring at the glistening globes and wondering what he was doing burying them in the middle of the desert. He dug hiding places for the orbs without even making a mental note of where they were hidden.

"What difference does it make if we can find them in the morning or not? We're turning around anyway." Gaspar said quietly as he stood in front of his tent.

As an omen and right on cue, the light desert breeze shifted and began blowing gently in the direction of his city.

"Even the wind agrees," he said shaking his head. Then he stepped into his tent and drew the front flap closed.

Balthazar could not remember ever having such a wonderful night's sleep which was odd considering he had somehow managed to slip off his cot, fall onto the floor and continue sleeping. He could not explain the happiness he felt or the lightness in his step. He had this unwavering confidence the orbs had done something during the night. Even if they hadn't, he would be headed back to Gaspar's city and a gorgeous camel hair bed. Once there, if the star was still visible he would ask Gaspar to make him another map. Then he would decide what to do next.

Balthazar walked to the front of his tent forgetting it was tied securely from the outside. Instead of his tent flap opening, the entire front of his tent flopped forward taking Balthazar down with it. He landed face first on the front of his tent tearing the stakes from the corners. The rear of the tent stuck straight up into the air like a giant inflated flag. Everything inside the tent collapsed on top of him with a crash. The cot, the pillow, his clothes, everything fell on top of him as the tent came crashing down. When Balthazar was finally able to stand up, he took a few steps in the sand and from the outside the tent looked like a poorly dressed, sand-shuffling mummy.

Of course, Balthazar couldn't see where he was going and after a few more steps he stumbled across Jandak who was fast asleep. Jandak jumped up; saw a mummy staring him in the face and began to run. Inside the tent, Balthazar realized this was not a good thing. Before going to bed, Balthazar had secured Jandak to his tent just as he always did. Now that the tent was no longer secured this would allow Jandak to run amok unimpeded except for the tent which had become partially draped over his eyes completely blocking his sight. This spooked Jandak even more causing him to run faster and change directions more often.

Gaspar had not slept particularly well as the quandary of their predicament and his curiosity about the orbs kept him awake most of the night. But even if he had slept well the ruckus outside his tent would have woken him up.

Gaspar had encountered many surprises in his life but seeing a camel run by in front of him wearing a tent with a man screaming inside it... Well, he could honestly say he had never seen such a sight. This was something even Balthazar might enjoy watching.

"Balthazar you..." Gaspar turned, and where Balthazar's tent should have been there was nothing but sand. Four loose strands of rope and the stakes they were tied to was all that was left. He looked back in the direction of the camel and realized it was Balthazar and Jandak.

He wasn't sure how long he laughed but he could feel the tears streaming down his face leaving tracks of joy. A free show in the desert. This was worth every camel race he had ever lost. Jandak weaved to the right and Gaspar could hear Balthazar hollering, "Slooooowwwww doooowwwnnnnn, st, sto, sto, stooooopppppp!" Jandak darted to the left. The tent swung out wide and struck a cactus then a palm tree. Balthazar yelled even louder.

"I better put a stop to this before Balthazar gets really hurt," said Gaspar hesitantly to himself. It was hard ending something as entertaining as this. Gaspar stood up. "Jandak. Jandak!" he called but it didn't faze the blind panic gripping the camel. As a last resort he used a camel mating call. It had been passed down to him through the generations. Making this sound, which is like a cross between a male lion and a grunting pig, was the wrong thing to do. Immediately, Jandak did a hard turn straight for the sound. Gaspar realized he was standing right in front of his tent in the middle of the camp. He flailed his arms and screamed but the mating call had buried its way into Jandaks mind and there was no deterring him. He had heard the mating call and at a full tilt maintained his direction. Jandak hit Gaspar and his tent without ever slowing down.

There are a few moments in every life when you realize you have done a very silly thing. Sometimes these silly things can turn very serious and you only hope you survive; for Gaspar, this was one of those moments. Jandak's head caught Gaspar between the legs and lifted him high into the desert sky. His body became silhouetted against the sun and just for a moment his eyes locked onto Balthazar's. They both waved goodbye to each other as Balthazar was thrown under Jandak and Gaspar flew over.

The dust did finally settle but neither man could remember anything causing so much destruction in such a short period of time. And the camp, or what was left of it, looked worse than it did when the dust devil had turned everything inside out. They would be lucky to find half of what was now strewn across the desert. One sandal here, half a tunic there. The dust devil had been a hindrance, but this would be the straw that broke the camel's back as far as their journey was concerned.

"Jandak!" Balthazar bellowed from inside what was left of his tent. "You just wait until I get my hands on you."

Balthazar finally extricated himself from his canvas prison and the sight he beheld took his breath away. He crawled back inside his tent and closed his eyes.

"It's just a dream; it's all just a dream." He kept saying to himself over and over. Then he slapped and pinched himself.

"Oww!" He screamed, "I'm not dreaming."

A weak and warbled response from Gaspar echoed across the oasis. "Ohhh, you're not dreaming. Ohhh, my head."

Jandak had thrown Gaspar completely across the watering hole which was in the center of camp between two groves of palm trees. Balthazar and Gaspar sat up and stared at each other from opposite sides of the oasis.

"I'm sorry," was all Balthazar could muster, "I really am."

"Well if we are to end our journey, we certainly did it in a most unusual manner," mused Gaspar.

Balthazar realized they would probably never find the orbs now, but in the sand around him he saw a shiny sparkling shimmer of light. He quickly dug into the sand thinking at least one of the orbs had found him in all the chaos. But it wasn't an orb after all. It was just a jewel which had fallen off one of the camels during the ruckus. He would have traded all the jewels he had ever owned to see his globes sitting in the sand pointing the way out of this predicament, but he did not see them anywhere. Balthazar placed the jewel into a pocket of his tunic.

"Yes, our journey has ended." His voice trailed off and one dusty tear trekked down his face and disappeared into the sand. "Let's gather what we can and go back."

"I don't want to, Balthazar, but I truly do not see any alternative. We have no maps and no tools. Look at this place."

Balthazar glanced down at his lap full of sand. He got up and brushed himself off.

'Well,' he thought, I will wash myself, help gather our things and go home.

He walked to the edge of the watering hole, splashed his face with a hand full of water, then dried off with a partial tunic lying nearby, and sat down.

"Gasper, I must ask you where you hid the orbs."

"I don't remember. What difference does it make? They could be anywhere."

"Or," said Balthazar as a growing smile began to cross his face, "they could be right there."

He lifted his hand and pointed toward the center of the watering hole. There they were, all together with one orb in front and the other two behind, bobbing together on the surface of the water, untouched and unbroken. The water glistened around them as they floated together in their magnificent arrow shape.

"The orbs I buried," said Gaspar, "Will you look at that."

"They're back!" yelled Balthazar.

He stood staring at the hollow glass globes floating on the water. Perhaps they could find enough of their gear to trudge on to Najaf and the books of Judea. Balthazar could not stop smiling. The orbs had returned.

Balthazar hiked up his cloak and stepped into the water. He walked out toward the orbs, gently picked them up one at a time and placed them in the leather pouch. Then he carried them back to shore where Gaspar was sitting.

"So," said Gaspar, "you have not told me everything about our journey, now have you?"

"No, I suppose I have not," confessed Balthazar, "but I was afraid you would think I was crazy if I had told you about the orbs. Originally, they are what led me to the star but since leaving Babylon they have remained still and showed no signs of their power."

"What power?" asked Gaspar. "What are you talking about?"

"I'm not certain myself but that pattern they formed on the surface of the water just now. Well, they would do that every night back in Babylon."

Balthazar got up and walked along the edge of the water.

"I finally realized they were pointing to the same location every night. So, I began charting the stars in that quadrant of the sky and I found this one star going the opposite direction of all the others. It intrigued me."

"As it would any good astronomer, especially one of the world's most renowned astronomers," Gaspar said, giving Balthazar a nod.

"Well, last night I thought we had nothing to lose by testing them. That's why I had you bury them."

"But, Balthazar what are they aiming at now?"

"I don't know."

Balthazar sat back down on the sand next to Gaspar, opened the pouch and gently laid the orbs on the ground.

"What else have the orbs done?" ask Gaspar.

"Nothing, except they forced me to seek your help," said Balthazar. "I assume they are leading me in the direction of the star but I have no way of knowing what they are attempting to do. I don't even know if we can trust the orbs or not."

Gaspar picked up one of the orbs and examined it closely.

"We can trust the orbs? Who are you talking about? Have you got a kangaroo rat in your pocket? I should think you would understand if I chose to go no further. Leading me out here into the heart of the desert only to be blown about by a dust devil and attacked by a runaway camel with a tent over his head and my friend inside it screaming for his life."

Gaspar laughed until Balthazar couldn't help himself and he joined in chuckling at what a sight it must have been.

"I wouldn't miss the rest of this adventure for anything in the world," said Gaspar as he winked at Balthazar.

Balthazar gazed around the campsite at the recent wreckage, then rummaged through his tunic pockets until he found the jewel he had picked up earlier.

"This may be all that is left of your magnificent jewelry. I hope we can find the frankincense and myrrh."

"Keep the jewel Balthazar, as a souvenir."

Gaspar and Balthazar got up, and cleaned up the campsite, again. Eventually they did find everything they really needed, but they never did find Gaspar's jewelry or his gilded sandals. For now they had what was necessary to continue.

Separately, they were both changed that day. Gaspar had finally seen a side of Balthazar he had never experienced. Balthazar had always seemed so confident so above the need for others, so able to go it alone. Gaspar hoped he was proving himself a worthy companion and wise man.

Balthazar realized how much he had overlooked Gaspar in the past. Gaspar had recalculated the azimuth, zenith, speed and trajectory of the star and found something he had missed.

"Of course if I had been given access to the proper geographical maps in the first place, I wouldn't have made that mistake." Balthazar said out of earshot of Gaspar.

He was still trying to blame Gaspar's original map for his miscalculations even though that wasn't the real issue. He was having a hard time accepting Gaspar as an equal and an even harder time grasping the fact that as brilliant as he was, he had made such a beginner's mistake.

Chapter 6
The Leper Colony

It didn't seem possible the sun could get any hotter, but it had. Neither man spoke what they were thinking, afraid that somehow verbalizing how hot it was would only make it hotter. The camels were affected too. Their pace had slowed and their tongues were dry and hot. At the ascent of every dune their spirits would rise as they imagined seeing some sign of a city, only to be disappointed. Their spirits would then drop as they descended into the next trough toward the bottom of yet another dune of sand. This battle between their spirits and the sand raged on.

Over the top and into a trough, over and over again. It reminded both men of an old saying, 'In the desert, any water will do.' Neither one of them spoke it but it was written on their faces. They were running out of water.

Melchior the Magnificent lived in the city of Najaf near the Tigris River. It had been a long time since Gaspar had seen him. He didn't want to tell Balthazar, but he wasn't sure Melchior was even still alive. The area where Melchior lived was so unstable some people called it the land of many, the possession of none. So many Mongol, Assyrian, Persian, and Babylonian rulers had reigned over it that a written history was hard to come by.

Even Alexander the Great had tried to rule over the area known as the cradle of civilization. Gaspar only hoped that Melchior had found some way to survive the turmoil and keep the historical parchments, tablets and scrolls safe from harm. Gaspar wasn't sure exactly where to find Melchior, but he knew that someone in Najaf would be able to help them if he was still alive.

With the oasis a distant memory it was becoming harder and harder to understand why they had been in such a hurry to leave it behind. There comes a time when any man, if he is thirsty enough, will trade all that he has for a drink of water.

The time was very near for both men. There might be enough water for one more day and then dehydration would slowly, irreversibly begin to take its toll. They both knew it was bleak when they made camp that night but neither said anything about it. It was bad luck to talk about water in the middle of the desert with no maps and no idea the location of the nearest oasis. All they had were the orbs. Balthazar began to worry the orbs were not guiding them toward anything but were toying with them. With no landmarks it was impossible to tell one dune from another.

Balthazar didn't conceal the orbs any more. Every night he would lay them next to his tent. In the morning, they would re-form themselves on the sand in the shape of an elongated pyramid pointing in the same direction.

As he and Gaspar settled in for the night, Balthazar sat inside his tent staring intently at his clear crystal orbs. He was concerned. For weeks they had been guiding him but what if they weren't really guiding him at all? What if they were just leading him and Gaspar in circles? These depressing thoughts haunted him and made him tired, too tired to think anymore. With his mind full of conflicting thoughts he could only say, "Please help us. We must find water soon."

The orbs reflected the small amount of light filtering into the tent from the torches outside, but they offered no visible sign they had heard his plea. Balthazar opened the front of his tent, laid them on the sand, closed the flap to his tent and said to himself again.

"Please help us."

In the morning, Balthazar smelled the unmistakable scent of coffee. He looked outside his tent and noticed Gaspar had wasted what little water they had left by making a batch of the

Turkish coffee he was so fond of. Balthazar stormed over to Gaspar glaring at him and tapping his foot in the sand.

"I would hate to think that I might have wanted a drink of water today. I hope you choke on that last bit of coffee."

"And good morning to you too, Balthazar. I have some great news this morning. I know we are running low on water, but I'm offended you would think so little of me and accuse me of squandering the last cup of it. Come with me and I will show you where we are going today. Fresh water will soon be in our flasks."

Gaspar led them up the small dune just to the south of their camp and when they topped the crest of the dune it was clearly visible. Najaf. It might be more than a day's travel, but they could make it to Najaf now and they knew it, even with their limited water supply.

"That is a beautiful sight."

Both men said this in unison and it startled them for a minute as they looked at each other and laughed uncomfortably. They both knew how close they had come to dying and becoming one more ghost of the desert.

"This journey is making us more like each other every day," said Gaspar as he turned to make his way back down the dune and into camp.

"The better part of me is rubbing off on you, I would say," teased Balthazar and he followed Gaspar back to camp.

As they packed up their gear that morning the mood had changed dramatically. Gaspar whistled an old Persian song of perseverance, and Balthazar shadowboxed with Jandak as he fed him breakfast. Things were looking up until Balthazar noticed the globes sitting outside his tent. He walked around them gauging the direction they were pointing. Getting down on his hands and knees he looked again. They were pointing away from Najaf!

"No, no," he said, "that just can't be."

He dug a hole in the sand for his belly and lay on the ground as flat as he could eyeing the direction the orbs were pointing. He made a mental note and knew they were not directing him to Najaf.

"What are you doing?" he said sitting on the ground and staring at the orbs.

Balthazar had never thought of it, but this morning he physically picked the orbs up and put them in alignment with Najaf, which was also the same direction as the star. He got up and called Gaspar over.

"Well Gaspar," Balthazar pointed down at the orbs, "it appears we will be traveling to Najaf."

Gaspar cocked his head and stared down at the orbs near his feet. "I don't think so Balthazar. The orbs seem to be pointing more in this direction."

Gaspar looked into the sun and began climbing to the top of the dune in the opposite direction of Najaf.

"What are you talking about?"

The orbs. Sure enough, they had moved and realigned themselves to point up the dune Gaspar was climbing. Balthazar kicked lightly at the globes to turn them back toward Najaf but they did not budge.

"No, no, no." He raised his voice. "We must go this way."

He bent down onto his knees in the sand and facing the globes he moved them again to point toward Najaf. As he held them in that direction, they begin to twist in his hands and move back into their previous position.

"I want to go this way." Now, the gentleness in his voice was gone and anger had made its way to the surface.

"Listen to me. I said this way!" Balthazar yelled.

He pulled and pushed the orbs but no matter what he did they came back together in their familiar arrowhead shape clearly turned away from Najaf.

Gaspar had climbed to the top of the dune and shielding his eyes against the sun he peered into the distance.

"I can't see anything," he yelled down to Balthazar, "but I do hear the strange sound of bells or something…"

"Ringing." Balthazar said under his breath.

He had heard it earlier and chosen to ignore it. He knew what it was—a leper colony. Every town had one and Najaf would be no different. He had seen the devastation caused by it. The lesions and the disfigurement were horrible. His own mother had died from it. He swore he would never enter or go near a leper colony again. Leprosy drove more fear into him than the sand cobra and the dust devil combined.

Everyone in a leper colony had to wear a bell or ring a gong in order to warn others to stay away. It was a terrible existence and he could not face it. The orbs were wrong. They were suddenly trying to divert him away from his goal—Najaf and the star.

"Yes, the orbs are wrong," Balthazar said.

He had made up his mind. He stood in front of the orbs and spit on them. He threw the leather pouch down, turned his back on them and walked away.

"I am going to Najaf," Balthazar said under his breath.

He gathered everything he would need for the one day journey. Then he and Jandak headed in the direction of Najaf, leaving the orbs lying in the sand and Gaspar standing alone at the top of the hill behind him.

"Balthazar, where are you going?" Gaspar's voice echoed across the dunes. "The orbs are pointing this way. We must go this way."

Balthazar sitting on Jandak turned toward Gaspar and yelled, "I cannot go that way, the orbs are wrong. I know they're wrong. They have always pointed me toward the star and that is the direction I am going."

"Well maybe they are leading us to something else we need. Or, maybe there is danger in Najaf and they are trying to protect us."

"Tell me Gaspar. Do you see anything beyond the leper colony? Anything?"

"No. I only see the colony."

"Then that settles it. There is no need to go any closer to the leper colony. Melchior the Magnificent will not be there. It is foolish to even enter a leper colony and we certainly cannot travel with a leper."

"What if Melchior is temporarily at the colony visiting?"

"Gaspar," Balthazar said gritting his teeth. "only a fool would even step foot into a lepers' domain."

Balthazar steered Jandak toward Najaf and yelled over his shoulder.

"No one goes willingly into a world of leprosy. The orbs are wrong and they are not leading anymore. I am."

"But, can't we just see for ourselves."

Balthazar crested the top of the dune. He shook his head and said quietly. "Obviously he has never seen a leper." Balthazar put Jandak into a slow trot. "I can track the star without the orbs. It will be easier since the star has at least slowed its pace. I will gather new tools and instruments in the city and if Melchior the Magnificent is not there…" Balthazar nudged Jandak down the dune and toward Najaf, "then I will continue by myself."

"Come with me Balthazar. What are you afraid of? Don't give up on the orbs now." Gaspar yelled across the expanse of dunes. "I can see water and trees. The lepers might be able to help us."

Balthazar knew what lepers and leprosy were all about and saw no way they could help him. He could not hear the last few muffled words of Gaspar as he descended the dune and headed toward Najaf.

The road to Najaf was well-worn and simple to follow even for Balthazar. He had never been to this part of the world and was already intrigued by what he was witnessing. Balthazar began to see many strange people and sights on his way to the city; he would soon see Najaf was unlike any city he had visited before. It was a transient place, a place full of people from all corners of the world.

At night in Babylon when Balthazar would glance out over his city from the safety of the observatory, there was a quiet calm covering it. In the morning everyone went about their business until the evening when everything would slowly calm down. The only visible people were the sentries manning the ramparts and towers along the stone walls. Najaf was nothing like Balthazar's Babylon. Najaf was a city of perhaps a million people. No one was certain at any one time how many people actually lived inside the city gates. It would be impossible to organize and manage a census in the city that never sleeps and where the gates almost never close.

Balthazar arrived at the city entrance before dusk. Good old Jandak had covered the distance in half the time it would have taken any other camel. As he dismounted from Jandak he realized he was ready for a bath and a good night's sleep. When it came time to pay for a place to sleep and food for Jandak, Balthazar realized he had no gold. He remembered the jewel he had found in the sand, Gaspar's jewel. For a moment as he patted his pockets looking for the jewel, he remembered Gaspar and the predicament he had left him in.

"Well," said Balthazar, "it was his choice to follow the orbs and stay behind, not mine." He pulled the jewel from his pocket and it seemed to satisfy the proprietor. Balthazar wearily walked to his room, ordered a hot bath, and some food and water. Tomorrow would come and things would be better. Perhaps Gaspar would change his mind, follow him to Najaf and leave the leper colony behind.

One last yell of "Wait!" and Gaspar watched as the top of Balthazar's turban dipped below the horizon and disappeared. In the sand, Gaspar tried to run to the bottom of the dune but it was no use. He tripped on the long flowing tail of his tunic and it launched him down the side of the dune. He came sliding to a gritty halt face down in the sand with only his undergarments left on his body. His turban, tunic and trinkets were scattered from one end of the dune to the other. By the time he gathered himself, his camel and started after him,

Balthazar would have a two or three-hour head start. So, Gaspar looked around the campsite, and decided to follow the orbs instead of chasing after Balthazar. Besides, he could always catch up to him if necessary. He was a much more accomplished rider than Balthazar and he had been to Najaf before. Even without any maps, he knew a few shortcuts which would allow him to catch Balthazar near the Tigris River. The shortcuts might not be the safest path to travel, but they were shortcuts nonetheless.

Chapter 7
Najaf

The orbs were still where Balthazar had left them. Gaspar marked the direction they were pointing, then picked them up, put them in the leather pouch and pulled the strap over his neck so the globes hung by his side. He cleaned up the rest of the camp and rather than riding, walked his camel to the top of the dune. Gaspar knew he could reach the leper colony well before nightfall so he decided to walk beside his camel. Every so often he would lay the orbs on the ground and watch them form themselves into their arrow shape.

"Still pointing toward the leper colony are we?" said Gaspar to the orbs. "Then I hope they don't mind visitors."

Well, that was the question. Why was he going toward the lepers? He didn't know if the orbs were trying to guide him to Melchior or lead him into some kind of trap. What if the magic they possessed had gotten twisted and distorted by some stronger evil spell?

"Maybe I should have followed Balthazar. I really knew nothing about you." He said to the orbs.

As he got closer and closer to the leper colony, he could see the back of the colony was protected by a wall of sheer rock. Apparently the desert, after trying for centuries to wear down this formation of stone, had given up and bypassed it altogether. There were several watering holes dotting the landscape and a few groves of palm trees and fig trees here and there. A low stone wall with a gate kept the inhabitants in and strangers out. It didn't seem like such a bad place after all.

Then Gaspar got his first glimpse of a leper. The boils on the skin and the lesions were ghastly and gruesome. Gaspar was turning away from the colony when a leper spying him outside the wall rang his bell fiercely and yelled, "Get away.

Are you a fool? Have you never seen a leper colony before? Get away from here before you get this same curse."

Gaspar looked up at the disfigured man and it made him shudder. He had lived a relatively easy life, sheltered and pampered, never realizing the plight of those much less fortunate than him. Looking away from the man Gaspar mustered up what little courage he had.

"Do you know anything about a man named Melchior?"

"Who did you say?" asked the leper. "It is understood why you do not look me in the eye so say it louder. Who are you looking for?"

"Melchior. Melchior the Magnificent"

"Melchior the Magnificent you say. Hmmm."

Gaspar felt guilty not facing the man so he turned around staring at the ground. He shuffled his feet and decided to grant this leper what dignity he could by at least trying to look him in the eye.

"I beg your forgiveness sir. I am Gaspar. May I ask your name?"

"I am called Laban for the leprosy has made my skin white."

"Do you know of a man named Melchior? I have reason to believe he lives near here."

"Oh, yes. I know of him. I know he is most fortunate to still be alive," said Laban, curious how long this stranger would stay and talk with him. "I also know if you are looking for him you must be no friend of King Mamre."

"And who is King Mamre? If you will pardon my ignorance," begged Gaspar who was gathering more compassion for the leper as they talked. After all, who had made Gaspar the second in command in Persia but chose this man to be a leper? What if Gaspar stood in Laban's shoes and Laban were outside the wall looking in at Gaspar the Leper?

"Are you a stranger in this land?" asked Laban.

"I have not traveled here in many years. When I last saw Melchior he was living in the city of Najaf under the watchful eye of King Lacum." Gaspar looked up now at Laban standing across the stone wall from him. Laban scratched his chin turned his eyes up toward the heavens and counted in his head for a moment.

"That was quite some time ago indeed. You have no idea what has become of Melchior?"

"No. I'm sorry to say that I do not. I only believe he is close by," said Gaspar trying to be patient but realizing he was anxious to find Melchior. "Do you know where he is?"

"Oh, I am very familiar with where he is."

"Can you tell me?"

"I could."

Gaspar waited for the answer. Laban crossed his arms, began humming and looking uninterested. Gaspar's patience was wearing very thin. He wasn't sure if or why Laban was playing games with him. Of course, if Gaspar understood that no one ever came to the leper colony he might have realized Laban's loneliness.

Finally Gaspar broke. He couldn't stand the humming and games Laban appeared to be playing. "I don't mean to be rude but we are on a journey where time is of the essence. Can you please stop dawdling and tell me where he is."

"You said 'We' are on a journey. I don't see anyone else traveling with you."

"Yes... He... went on to Najaf without me to find Melchior."

"Oh, I see," said Laban. Gaspar immediately noticed a change in Laban, an increased sadness.

"Is there something wrong, Laban?" asked Gaspar innocently.

"Your friend, what is his name?"

"Balthazar. He is the most knowledgeable astronomer in the world. He began this journey in Babylon and I joined him in Persia."

"He must be quite the astronomer indeed. Let's just hope he knows not to mention the name Melchior in front of King Mamre."

"Melchior? I don't understand."

"It is a long story. I will not belabor you. Let me just say that Melchior was once the most sought after man in the kingdom. He traveled to far off lands and learned the ways of other races and people. He told any king who would listen that understanding others would only make the kingdom stronger. King Mamre listened initially and Najaf grew from a city of one hundred thousand inhabitants to a city of three hundred thousand. Today, no one is certain how many people live there."

"I don't understand," said a bewildered Gaspar, "That should have made King Mamre very happy."

"It did, but as a king's power grows so do his fears. The King began to see the demons and desires of others in every corner, but what truly sealed Melchior's fate was when he would tell King Mamre of other countries and other kings. In particular King Mamre could not stand hearing the prophecies about future kings. There was one prophecy in particular about a King of Peace."

"The idea of these unknown kings threatened King Mamre?"

"Indeed. King Mamre is no King of Peace. He became particularly obsessed with the prophecy of this unknown King of Peace and demanded Melchior tell him who this king was and when he was to appear; but Melchior did not know. King Mamre presumed Melchior was part of this new king's plan. He thought Melchior was out to kill him and with this new king take his place."

"Listen Laban, I am fascinated by all of this but I really must insist you get to the point and tell me where Melchior is now."

Laban ignored the rudeness and continued with his story. "The king brought in an evil wizard one day and threatened Melchior."

"Tell me who this king is and when he will appear!" King Mamre shrieked at him. He was mad by then and his eyes turned completely white and his face turned livid red with hatred. When Melchior did not reveal this king the wizard struck him with leprosy and Melchior was banished to this colony. That was over ten years ago."

This perked up Gaspar immediately. "So he is here? What of the ancient archives and the old scrolls of the oracles. Are they here too?"

"He is here as are the items you speak of. The old chronicles are all the company Melchior has had since he was banished, cursed with leprosy, and forced to live here with the rest of us."

"Can you take me to him? Can I see him?"

"He is never about during the day. No one is quite sure where he goes inside the colony. I can take you to his cave of magic and history." Laban turned from the stone wall. "Follow me but not too closely." Laban led Gaspar to the front gate of the leper colony and opened it for Gaspar. "Come in."

Gaspar carefully walked through the gate. Laban closed it from behind and led Gaspar through the courtyard that lay between the outer low rock wall and the cliff running along the back of the compound.

At first Gaspar couldn't see anything since dusk was beginning to take its toll on the last vestiges of remaining daylight. But as his eyes began to adjust, he could just make out human shaped forms shuffling around with a stilted gait. Ragged clothes draped over grey and white skin. It was impossible to tell where the rotted clothes ended and the skin began. Color seemed to have been taken away and substituted with a dreary pallet of gray and black. On his walk through the compound a bell or gong would sound. Even the bells and gongs had lost their timbre and sounded monotone. A few lepers lying down along the path were apparently in the last stages of leprosy. They moaned softly, rocking back and forth, too weak to move and find a place of solitude where they could die in peace.

Gaspar turned to look for Laban, but he was gone!

"Balthazar was right. I have walked into a world of death, into a trap." Gaspar panicked but when he looked harder he could see a gap in the sheer rock wall just wide enough for a person to enter. Laban was just disappearing into the rock face.

"Wait here," Laban said.

A moment later he reappeared with a torch and led Gaspar into the cave entrance. The walk across the courtyard had already made Gaspar understand why Balthazar had decided not to follow him. Now he only hoped he had not made the biggest mistake of his life.

The walls of the cave were dry and dusty. Every few steps a little dust would fall from the ceiling to the floor. Laban walked with a shuffling gait and with every step his sandals scraped the floor, but he never stumbled on the roughhewn stone as he led them both down through the dinginess and darkness. The end of the cave came suddenly and Gaspar found himself in a great room. Much of the stone had been carved out to form crude shelves. He had never seen so many parchments and scrolls before. Every wall was lined with them. They were stacked so high even with torchlight he could not see the top most scrolls.

"Laban, you mentioned the archives of Judea, the history of that land. Those interest me and Balthazar a great deal."

"Oh, Melchior has shown them to me many times. They are stored in their own space right over here." On a quiet shelf neatly lined up and stacked were several parchments and stone tablets. Gaspar could tell by how little dust there was on the shelf that these parchments and tablets were looked at often. He was closer to the answer of why the star had appeared, now all he needed was Melchior and... Balthazar! Gaspar's mind panicked like a deer hearing the sound of an arrow whistling in for the kill.

"Laban, I completely forgot about Balthazar! What will happen to him if he mentions Melchior's name in front of King Mamre?"

"He will be killed on the spot."

"What did you say?" Gaspar turned quickly staring at Laban.

"He will most likely be killed. King Mamre lives to kill anyone he considers an enemy. Just looking for Melchior will make Balthazar an enemy."

Gaspar fumbled for the words to say,. "I must not let that happen. The orbs were protecting us. I... I..." Gaspar's mind was spinning. He had to think of a plan to save Balthazar. He had to go into Najaf and get Balthazar out of there before it was too late. Even though Balthazar had abandoned him in the desert, Gaspar could understand his fear of leprosy and his reasoning why the orbs were wrong. Who would think the man they were looking for would be a living prisoner in a leper colony? How could such a man go on any journey with them? It seemed impossible.

Gaspar looked around the room, and quickly spotted what must be Melchior's area for creating magic. He raced over to the shelf where he found a mismatched pile of chemicals and other magical ingredients. He remembered he must be careful what he touched.

"What are you looking for? What orbs are you talking about?" Laban asked.

"Laban, my friend Balthazar is in danger. He has gone to Najaf and most certainly will ask the King about Melchior. Please help me. I have formulated a plan. I will need your help and a few items from this shelf."

"I can't go anywhere with you. Melchior is going to be very upset I even let someone in here."

"Laban, I will not say it again. I need your help."

Laban sensed the fear and panic inside Gaspar.

"Alright, I'll help. What do I need to do?"

Gaspar fumbled with his tunic and pulled three small pouches from inside.

"Put some saltpeter in this pouch and sulfur in that one. Then grab some chalk powder and put it in here."

Gaspar gave the three pouches to Laban, who filled each one with its own ingredient. Gaspar grabbed the pouches, cinched the tops closed and put them back inside his tunic.

"We will need two torches and grab those, too." He pointed to a small pile of tunics lying on the floor. "Does anyone in the colony have transportation?"

"We have one old worn out camel named Jezebel but don't you have your own camel?"

"Yes, I have transportation for me and I suppose Jezebel will have to do. You can ride can't you? And by the way, if you haven't caught on yet, I'm going into Najaf to rescue my friend and you are coming with me. Oh, grab that empty scroll and something to write with."

"Wait, I can't go anywhere. Look at me I'm a leper."

"Do you know where Melchior is?"

"No, I'm not certain."

"Well, we don't have time to find him so it's up to you and me."

"I said I have leprosy. Can't you see? I will be arrested the moment I am discovered."

"I understand," Gaspar said "but I actually need someone with leprosy. It's part of my plan."

Gaspar leaned backwards, put his hands in the air and pointed to an imaginary banner. "Ladies and gentlemen of the court, may I present *Me and My Mummy*." With a flourish Gaspar gestured at the stony opening leading into the hallway. "It is time for us to leave."

Chapter 8
The Imposters

Balthazar was ready for the day. He felt fresh and rejuvenated from his morning breakfast and bath. Even though his accommodations were less than stellar he felt renewed and free of so many burdens. The orbs and Gaspar were gone.

"Good riddance to them both," said Balthazar. The orbs and Gaspar had only succeeded in clouding his mind. Now he could focus on finding Melchior and solving this mystery without any interruptions.

Gaspar was at least a day's journey behind him and was being foolish venturing into the leper colony. No good would come of that. Gaspar was just wasting time...

"Wait, wait, wait." Balthazar said. Maybe Gaspar hadn't even gone to the leper colony. Gaspar had been very eager to join him on this trip, perhaps a bit too eager. He might know something about Melchior and the orbs that he wasn't willing to share. And now Gaspar had the orbs! Gaspar had stayed up every night studying since Balthazar had revealed the orbs to him. He hadn't seemed that surprised by their revelation.

"Gaspar discovered the power of the orbs and now he's using them against me!" Balthazar was fuming and unsettled. "What a fool I was to leave the orbs behind!"

Balthazar paced back and forth in his small room. He had no idea who Melchior the Magnificent was or what he looked like. It may have been a while since Gaspar had seen Melchior, but Gaspar would still recognize him. Unwittingly, Balthazar had handed Gaspar a perfect opportunity to outwit him.

Other thoughts of uncertainty plagued Balthazar. Perhaps Gaspar knew there was gold at the end of the journey. After all, it had been his idea not to bring any with them. And on top of it all, Melchior was Gaspar's friend not Balthazar's.

Gaspar was probably on his way to Najaf right now to find Melchior, steal the gold beneath the star and claim the star as his discovery.

"I should have brought the orbs with me even if they were wrong. Just in case." said Balthazar. "I must meet with the King of Najaf immediately and find Melchior the Magnificent before Gaspar does."

Balthazar was becoming more and more agitated and determined. "I will win this race just like I've won all the others!"

Saying this made Balthazar feel powerful. Knowledge was power and once Balthazar had the answers from Melchior, he would decide who would go and who would stay. "This is my quest," Balthazar said proudly "I'll decide who gets the gold."

Balthazar had one trick up his sleeve he had not shared with Gaspar. He had a royal proclamation from the King of Babylon made just for this purpose. It would grant him an instant audience with any king. Balthazar unrolled the parchment on his bed. It was just the kind of edge Balthazar needed against Gaspar and it was one more reason he always won. He had the edge.

Balthazar left his room with the proclamation and headed straight for the palace. He would introduce himself immediately. The wax seal felt smooth in his hand and the gold band around the proclamation certainly gave it an air of importance. It would be opened immediately.

"This will get me into the king before Gaspar even has time to put on his sandals."

Balthazar promised the steward at the palace gate a gold coin if his scroll made it the king first. Even though Balthazar didn't have any money he wasn't worried. After a few magic tricks he would have the money he needed to pay the steward and the stroll through town would help him gather information about Najaf and its king.

An empty alcove gave Balthazar the perfect place to perform a few magic tricks and in short order he had more than enough gold to pay the steward and purchase any other necessities in town. He was beginning to enjoy Najaf more and more. It was so much more invigorating than boring old Babylon.

That evening there was a knock on Balthazar's door. It was the royal steward returning with the king's answer to Balthazar's proclamation. The steward handed Balthazar a royal scroll. Scouring it gave Balthazar another reason to smile. He had been invited by King Mamre to a grand party in honor of Balthazar.

"Ahh Gaspar, you will be finishing second again."

"I would be most honored to attend," said Balthazar to the steward as he gave him two gold pieces for completing his errand so quickly. The steward bowed deeply and shut the door as he left.

After having seen some of the sights of the city, Balthazar was curious what a party in Najaf would be like. And to his delight, it was incredible. There were influences from Egypt, Persia and even from his far off home of Babylon.

There was a game parlor full of Egyptian men playing senet, a board game of travels through the underworld. The Persians had arranged wrestling matches at an indoor arena. The line was too long to wait for it, but Balthazar loved watching wrestling. There was no room for weakness in that sport. The contingent from Babylon had a wrestling team and a chariot racing team taking on all challengers.

If only there were camel races, thought Balthazar.

Thinking of Babylon and Jandak made him reminisce for a moment. His life was quaint and quiet back home compared to the revelry and liveliness of Najaf. He was beginning to enjoy the difference, and thought Najaf suited him. Perhaps if his star quest did not turn out well he might just return to Najaf and see if King Mamre might be interested in using his talents as an astronomer. The stirring and energy of Najaf was breathing new life into Balthazar.

That night at King Mamre's party the entertainment was creative with elephants, jugglers and knife throwers. There were exotic dancers with gold and jewelry laden costumes, and even a magician. The magician was the last act for the night before Balthazar's presence was to be announced and his proclamation read.

Balthazar had a seat given to him near King Mamre. A royal steward stepped out onto the circular, shiny, black marble surface in the center of the room.

"All court members and guests. We are pleased to announce a late addition to the entertainment tonight; Melitus the Magician and his mummy assistant, also known as Me and My Mummy."

King Mamre laughed so hard he spit a grape out of his mouth hitting Balthazar between the eyes.

Amateurs. I've heard better jokes standing around the fountain in Babylon, thought Balthazar.

The magician came to the center of the circular marble floor and bowed ceremoniously to the king.

"Behold," said the magician as he cleared his throat and pointed to his assistant, a poor soul wrapped in the worst mummy costume Balthazar had ever seen. There was something familiar about the magician but that was true every time Balthazar saw one.

Balthazar scoured the crowd, curious if Melchior was in attendance.

"He would be rolling his eyes at this performance." Balthazar looked back out at the poor magician trying to keep his composure. This magician was performing tricks Balthazar had done since he was a little boy.

"Boring," he said under his breath.

It was nearing the end of the magic act and Balthazar was ready to finally be introduced to King Mamre. As the magician on the floor finished his routine, he came directly to Balthazar and handed him a scroll.

"For me?" Balthazar asked.

The magician only nodded and then made a motion for Balthazar to open the scroll.

"Oh, you want me to open it."

Balthazar took the scroll and unrolled it. On the scroll was written the phrase, 'Don't ask the king about Melchior the Magnificent.'

Now Balthazar realized why the magician seemed so familiar. It was Gaspar in disguise!

So, you've backtracked your way into Najaf and are trying to see the king before me huh, Balthazar thought. You want the orbs and the gold for yourself! I was right about you.

Balthazar sat festering and glowering for a moment but snapped out of it when King Mamre called for order.

"All court guests and members of the council. Tonight we have a very special visitor. From the King's Court of Babylon, welcome the Royal Astronomer, Balthazar."

Balthazar was thrown by this recent turn of events. Rising to the applause of the crowd he said, "I will catch the mouse in his own trap."

He walked to the center of the room surrounded by the royal family and guests sprawled out on lounges, royal purple pillows and blankets woven with gold and silver thread.

"Your Highness King Mamre, and friends of the High Court of Najaf. I bring to you tonight blessings from the King of Babylon. I also bring you something quite unexpected. I will expose tonight an enemy of King Mamre as well."

King Mamre jumped to his feet and the four guards surrounding him came to attention with swords drawn and shields ready.

"Who and what is this danger? Tell me now." Blurted King Mamre.

"Oh King, all in good time. You are in no immediate danger. I have a tiny request and then the enemy shall be revealed."

"I will grant your request. What is it?"

The King settled back into his seat and the guards lowered their swords. The King's eyes darted back and forth nervously looking for the hidden enemy.

"I only ask the great King Mamre grant me a brief audience with his close friend and advisor, Melchior the Magnificent!"

Balthazar had no chance to comprehend what happened next. King Mamre uttered, "Seize him!" Before the king had finished saying "him" Balthazar was thrown to the marble floor. His feet and hands were bound behind him. Two guards appeared and a pole was run beneath the ropes between his hands and feet. He was lifted off the floor suspended between the two guards like a side of beef being taken to a royal meal.

Balthazar thought quickly and screamed, "I am not the threat to you King Mamre. It is this imposter of a magician! He told me to say Melchior the Magnificent. I have no idea who Melchior is. See for yourself! He is not who he says he is. He is a spy from Persia. Seize him not me!"

Without thinking or hesitating, Gaspar pulled a torch from his robe, lit it from a flame burning nearby, and jumped into the center of the floor next to Balthazar and the two guards. Stunned, the two guards stood still not knowing what to do.

"I would stay exactly where you are King Mamre or…"

Gaspar reached into his tunic and threw a handful of saltpeter and sulfur together onto the torch. A flash and flame exploded into the air followed by a cloud of smoke that hid him and Balthazar from view. Unseen by the crowd, Gaspar pulled the pouch of white powder from his tunic and blew it over Balthazar's face and hands. The black and white smoke cleared from the explosion and sank to the floor. The audience stepped back seeing Balthazar's face and hands covered in white.

"…I shall turn you oh King and everyone in this room into a leper." Gaspar repeated the trick of sulfur and salt peter. This time he pointed his torch at Laban.

"Show them what I mean."

Laban moved forward into the room and removed the cloth from his head and hands. The remaining calm in the room quickly turned into pandemonium.

King Mamre began screaming orders no one could hear or obey. Everyone sprang to the sides of the room like the wind parting the wheat as they tried to get as far from the three men in the center as possible. The two guards departed both ends of the pole, and Balthazar fell face first onto the marble floor still tied to the pole. Gaspar hurriedly put one end of the pole on his shoulder and Laban lifted the other as they moved toward the stone archway that led out into the main hall. Balthazar bounced up and down on the pole between them. As the trio of terror entered the hallway leading out of the palace, Gaspar called out.

"Balthazar. Balthazar!"

There was no response. Apparently the drop onto the marble floor had knocked him unconscious.

"We can't wait for him to wake up. We must get to the camel stalls as quickly as possible." Gaspar and Laban hurried out of the great hall and into the open courtyard of King Mamre's palace.

The confusion caused in the great hall had not spread to the stalls near the front gate. Gaspar knew they had to find Jandak and get them all out of Najaf before the Royal Guards arrived. Finding Jandak turned out to be simpler than Gaspar thought. It seems Jandak had beaten every camel in the stalls at one time or another and the camels had all been victims of the gale force winds Jandak could conjure up. There he was in a separate stall, far from the other camels.

Balthazar couldn't ride so they kept him tied to the pole suspended between the two camels. Jandak was tied to the back of Gaspar's camel and Laban rode Jezebel. The camel trainer and the guards at the Gates of Najaf had seen many strange things leave Najaf, but the sight of a man spinning around a pole suspended between two camels was a little unusual even for the City of Najaf.

King Mamre screamed louder and louder but to no avail. The panic of seeing lepers in their midst had driven the crowd out of control. The king finally forced the Royal Steward to blow the brass war horn hanging on the wall. The sound of the horn was brash and loud enough to break the grip of panic in the room.

"Listen to me," said King Mamre. He stepped through the crowd and out onto the floor where Balthazar had been. "Look here."

He knelt down onto the dark marble floor. A light white dust was clearly visible. He took his finger and pointed at the sandal tracks left behind in the chalky dust. He rubbed his hand on the floor and lifted it to show the white residue to everyone.

"Imposters! All of them!" King Mamre stood erect and continued. "Ten-thousand gold coins to anyone who can bring me the head of any of them." Then he froze and a far off look crossed his face. There were three men involved. And somehow he had seen one of them before. He just couldn't place the face. After all, when you have punished and killed as many people as he had, they all looked the same after a while, but the name and the face slowly came to him and King Mamre's face grew cold and stern and hard.

"Melchior," he said under his breath. He remembered now. The face still had the same twisted tormented look frozen into it ten years before. King Mamre's rage and visceral hatred could no longer be contained. "I will give an entire province and any woman in my kingdom as his queen to the man who brings me the head of the leper, Melchior."

A few hours outside Najaf, Gaspar stopped to check on Balthazar. He was still out cold, but Gaspar thought it might be a good time to do a little backtracking and discover if they were being followed. He might even check the orbs just to see if they were off course. Gaspar crept to the top of the nearest hill and gazed back over the dunes behind them. Initially he saw a few faint lights bobbing in the background of the night, but then he saw more, a lot more. More than he could count. It seemed as though the torches outnumbered the stars and the line of them stretched across the horizon of the night. Gaspar ran back down the hill mumbling aloud.

"What is the matter Gaspar?" asked Laban "You seem worried."

"There must be hundreds, no thousands of people following us. It doesn't make any sense. We're just a couple of nobodies, strangers in town. King Mamre has sent his entire kingdom after us."

The fear gripping Gaspar made him uneasy. "We don't have time to check the orbs for direction."

"What do you mean check the orbs for direction?" asked Laban.

Gaspar opened the leather pouch and peeked inside at the orbs. They were all glowing with a soft yellow light. He didn't know if they had ever done that before. Balthazar was the one who had discovered the orbs and might know what the glowing meant.

"I don't have time to explain. We've got to get out of here," said Gaspar.

"Let's go back to the leper colony," said Laban, "It is the one place no one will dare enter, not even King Mamre."

Gaspar didn't like the idea of going back to the leper colony. He knew for certain that Balthazar would never come within ten thousand paces of it. But Laban was right; there was nowhere else to hide safely from the force of fury following them. Gaspar and Laban forced the camels into a trot. Balthazar occasionally moaned suspended from his pole. The strange caravan melted into the dark night, concealing them from the horde hot on their heels.

Chapter 9
The Soul of Man

Balthazar awoke in the morning with a terrible headache. He had dreamed all night of being roasted alive hanging from a pole over a giant fire, but he initially couldn't remember why. Then, it hit him.

"Melchior," he whispered to himself. "I said Melchior the Magnificent."

His mind ran through a strange series of events that were like a foggy morning, some things were crystal clear, others were shrouded. There had been a pole and two guards and sneezing and white powder and Gaspar and a leper? No, that part was a little fuzzy. He remembered trying to pin everything on Gaspar to save his own skin. That part was crystal clear unfortunately, and he wished it wasn't.

It was obvious to him now that the man he had abandoned in the desert, the man he had rejected and suspected of trying to cheat him, was a true friend. Balthazar felt ashamed. Lying there on the cold stone shelf, he cried. He cried so uncontrollably and loudly he did not hear the footsteps running down the tunnel and into his room.

"Balthazar. Are you alright?" asked a concerned Gaspar. "I heard wailing and crying so loud it frightened me."

Balthazar swung his legs over the side of his stone bed. Then he stood up and accidentally banged his head on the low cut ceiling arching over the top of his bed.

"Owww. My head has been leading me down the wrong path. You would think that eventually I would learn to trust my heart a little more, and my head a little less."

He shuffled over to Gaspar and embraced him, hard. New tears formed and each teardrop was a plea for forgiveness as they rolled down the back of Gaspar's tunic and onto the stone floor.

It is said in many languages and places only a few people ever develop a friend closer than a brother. If you could speak to Balthazar today he would tell you it can happen, but it is not the easiest journey to make. He would also tell you the secret to finding a friend is knowing this: no matter how badly you behave nor how many mistakes you make, a true friend never keeps score, always believes in you and will come back for you every time.

"You must be starved," said Gaspar, "Let's see what we can put together for breakfast. But before we eat, I have someone very special I want you to meet."

Gaspar stepped out into the tunnel and grabbed a torch from the wall then lit it inside Balthazar's room. It was a cozy room, as cozy as a cave room can be. There was a modest stone table with a candle and a shelf holding some desert trinkets. A stone stool sat next to the table. Balthazar's tunic and turban were draped over the back of the stool. Balthazar walked over and began putting on his clothes.

"Oh, come on Balthazar, your robe is just fine for now. We're not going to see any kings today. Follow me."

Balthazar followed Gaspar down and around so many turns and openings he felt lost. He had no idea where he was. He guessed he was in a cave of some sort but that was all he knew.

"Gaspar, speaking of not seeing any kings, can you tell me who we are seeing today?"

"Oh, you're just about to find out, and it is quite a surprise. I can't wait to show you our host. He is also the man who helped save your life."

Gaspar and Balthazar finally stepped into an oblong room with six tunnel entrances leading into it. "Balthazar, do you remember anything about last night?"

Balthazar paused. There was the face of King Mamre raging and livid. It was one of the few things he could recall with any clarity.

"Are we in King Mamre's prison?"

Gaspar laughed.

"No, we escaped from Najaf. Don't you remember? I had an assistant with me."

"Vaguely," said Balthazar.

Laban walked out from one of the darkened tunnels just a few feet in front of Gaspar and removed his hood. The torch Gaspar carried only accentuated Laban's scarred features. "Welcome to our…"

"Leper colony," said Balthazar and then he passed out, his head making a hollow thud as it hit the stone floor.

Laban stared at the heap on the floor. "Your friend may be a very wise man, but I hope he has a hard head. I don't think it can take many more falls like that one."

"Oh, he has a hard head alright, but it's good he does. It has gotten us this far. Let's get to work. He'll wake up soon enough."

Gaspar lifted Balthazar onto a shelf just large enough for him to sit on without falling off and tucked his own tunic behind Balthazar's head. Then he and Laban disappeared into the depths of manuscripts and tablets.

Gaspar stared at the unending array of history. He took one of the scrolls and found a nearby table where he could unroll it. He made sure his torch was close enough to clearly read it, but not too close. For a moment he imagined the despair and disaster from catching the place on fire. The excitement he felt as he unfurled the papyrus scroll was squelched almost immediately. Gaspar hadn't seen a word or phrase yet he could read!

He never thought once about the fact Melchior had traveled a great deal and those travels would have taken him to other places and lands with their own languages and cultures.

Gaspar looked up at the mounds and mounds of scrolls, tablets and rolled up parchments. His shoulders sagged. He felt more useless than a three-legged camel. Gaspar was well read and well versed but he was no linguist. Akkadian and Persian were his languages of choice and maybe some Assyrian, but this language in front of him was neither of those.

Gaspar realized they would need Melchior to go with them on their journey. But how could they travel with him if he had leprosy? It would be impossible, and they could not stay here and wait for Melchior to dig through all of this material looking for tidbits of information about the star and the land of Judea.

That was assuming there was any information about the star in this jungle of parchments and scrolls. Somehow, if Melchior could travel, he would have to study and research on the road. They did not have time to sit and sift through all this material especially since Balthazar and Gaspar would be no help.

The star. Gaspar was anxious to find out about its meaning. He grabbed his torch and knew it was time for Laban to take him and Balthazar to see Melchior. Maybe, together they could come up with some kind of feasible plan.

If Melchior had leprosy and couldn't travel, perhaps he would know someone else without leprosy that could interpret the scrolls and go with Gaspar and Balthazar on their journey. There were so many questions and it would take all of them to work together in order to solve this astronomical puzzle.

"Balthazar, Balthazar?" Gaspar flicked his torch back and forth looking for him, but he was gone. In the darkness he could see another torch approaching.

"Oh, Gaspar," said Laban, "I came back to where you had left Balthazar and he was fully awake. I'm not sure if I led him or scared him down the hall, but he has gone into the kitchen. Follow me."

Stepping into the kitchen Gaspar could see a small wooden table with a bench on either side of it. The table was the first thing Gaspar had seen not made of stone. Balthazar barely looked up when they entered. Pacing nervously back and forth, it was obvious he was in denial and refused to admit that he was actually in the middle of the one place he would have never ventured; a leper colony. Gaspar put his arm around Balthazar and led him over to the table to sit down. Laban sat across from them with his back turned away from his guests.

Gaspar placed the pouch containing the orbs on the table. "I know you don't want to hear this Balthazar, but the orbs were right. Melchior is here in the leper colony."

"And so what if he is. We cannot take a leper with us on our journey. We would be banned from entering any city we approach."

"Perhaps Melchior doesn't have leprosy. Maybe he has somehow managed to escape the malady."

There was a pause for a moment. Laban turned to face Gaspar and Balthazar.

"He has been infected," said Laban.

"Is it evident? Could he travel and keep the disease hidden?" asked Gaspar.

"He could not travel. The disease has progressed most severely with him. I suppose it is time you knew the truth."

Laban folded back his hood revealing a pock marked crevasse ridden face.

"I am what once was, Melchior the Magnificent," he said.

The truth, when told, contains real power. Not knowledge. For knowledge can be corrupted by ego and greed and even ignorance. But truth cannot be corrupted by anything. Truth can overcome every evil man has ever concocted to stifle it.

Something deep within the orbs had been waiting for this moment, this place, and these three men to speak and discover the truth about each other. The pouch and the orbs disappeared in a shower of pure light, a light that permeated stone and wood and physical things.

For the rest of their lives when people would ask any of them to describe what pure light was like, they would only shrug and say, "Imagine a light so bright and pure that it blots out every physical thing."

When pestered to elaborate further they would say, "Our souls. We each saw our own soul."

After hearing this answer the person asking the question would typically turn squeamish and awkwardly move away. Men who have seen true, pure light make others who have not experienced it uncomfortable, and that's just the way it is. No one has ever seen a light as pure as the light in that small stone kitchen inside the caves of the leper colony that day, and no one ever will.

Chapter 10
Trapped

When the light dispersed Balthazar, Gaspar and Melchior exchanged glances with each other. The little kitchen was intact and they were alive. The pouch and orbs were still sitting on the table.

Melchior however, had changed. Balthazar and Gaspar both looked at Melchior and could not take their eyes off him.

"Lead us outside to one of the pools Melchior, immediately." said Gaspar. "You are not going to believe what has happened."

Balthazar grabbed the globes and quickly stuffed them back into the pouch and scampered out of the kitchen into the maze of tunnels, trying his best to keep up with Melchior and Gaspar.

As they careened around the last outcropping of rock before stepping outside, they knew something was wrong. The constant drumming had been drowned out by the echoing of their sandals slipping and sliding on the sandy floor of the cave, but now the drumming was distinct and deliberate. When they burst out into the daylight, they were blinded by the sun reflecting from a thousand shields forming a wall in front of the leper colony.

Spreading out as far as they could see was a dark shape of shields and swords, a long snaking line of war. The movements of the troops on the horizon looked like the tail of a giant black scorpion moving slowly back and forth, just waiting for the perfect moment to strike. Yet something was keeping this massive army at bay.

The low lying stone wall which ran along the front of the colony was nothing more than a pebble at the foot of this giant. Melchior knew it was the specter of leprosy saving their lives.

The three of them stood absolutely still, awed by the sheer sight of this massive army.

The drumming stopped. Silence swept across the face of King Mamre's army as he approached the colony keeping a respectful distance. "Ahh, the three imposters," yelled King Mamre. The three men looked around the colony. No one else was in sight. All the colonists had taken to the tunnels. Balthazar and Gaspar did not move, but Melchior, still covered beneath his shroud and tunic, shuffled forward to face the King.

"Yes, oh King! We meet again. Why it only seems like yesterday that…"

"Save the small talk and halfwit remarks for fools with time to listen. I will not tolerate it."

"Well of course, I wouldn't want to irritate the King. Would he like to come in for a visit?"

Melchior removed his shroud and the sun struck his face and features in full force. King Mamre staggered backwards dropping his sword and shield. In an unheard whisper he said, "There is great magic here."

King Mamre ran to his horse and without another word rode directly into the middle of his great army. The only visible sign of him was a thin cloud of dust stirred up by his horse cutting a swath through the solid sea of black clad warriors as he rode toward Najaf. This giant army without its leader soon became a jumbled mess of meandering locusts looking for prey as they scattered into the desert. Never again would King Mamre leave the city of Najaf. From that time on many people would say the decline of his empire began.

"Melchior! Melchior!" Gaspar shouted as he ran toward him.

Melchior stood staring at the site of the bewildered army. "What happened?" He asked as he watched wave after wave of the army move out and away from the leper colony. The ebb and flow of the army's movement stirred the dunes, and when the cloud of sand mixed with the reflection and flashes of the sun it resembled a magic potion being mixed and stirred in a colossal cauldron.

Melchior turned to face the colony. Gaspar was still churning down the path that led to the stone gate at full tilt. A bewildered look crossed Melchior's face.

"I don't understand…"

Gaspar grabbed Melchior in a bear hug so hard Melchior thought he heard a rib crack. Balthazar had finally arrived and together they lifted Melchior up into the air and carried him toward one of the small pools of water. Before Melchior could understand what they were going to do they threw him into the middle of one of the smaller pools.

"What was that for? Are your turbans on too tight? You'll get leprosy now too!"

Balthazar came straggling up behind Gaspar and they both laughed at Melchior. They sat down, crossed their legs and just kept laughing. A flustered Melchior finally stood up in the water. He crossed his arms and glared at the two laughers.

"Calm down Melchior. Just stand there for a moment and let the water settle. Take off that old robe and then glance down," Balthazar said.

The ripples on the water diminished. Melchior took off his old robe and looked down at the shiny surface of the water. He knew something spectacular must have just happened in the caves, but he was unprepared for what he saw in the reflection of the pool. His clothes were white, whiter than he had ever seen them. His tunic appeared to have been dipped in the clouds. His face was smooth and supple, not torn and eaten by the lesions and disfigurement he had lived with for ten years. He rolled up his sleeves and stared at his hands, arms and skin, skin that was vibrant and strong and free of leprosy.

"I, I, I…" he could not continue.

"Oh, let's say it together for him Balthazar," said Gaspar.

"You're healed. You're healed!"

"Yes he is." A low voice said, "I am too."

Houlka, the longest living survivor of the leprosy stepped forward. She was still old and bent over but her skin was clear of the disease. She raised her hands and said, "We all are."

The exuberance and joy of the former lepers gathered at the pool is hard to explain to those who don't believe in miracles. Balthazar, Gaspar and Melchior stood in the pool of water amidst so much shouting and absolute joy no one could hear them speak. But, enough had been said and done. The lepers knew this was a miracle and it had come to pass because two strangers had dared to enter their stone prison. The leper colony was no more.

Chapter 11
Three Wise Men

No one could remember how long the leper colony had been in existence, but Balthazar was still amazed at all of the tunnels and rooms they had built. It was truly incredible what these people had accomplished through the years.

And there was a lot that Balthazar, Gaspar and Melchior now had to do. Balthazar knew there would be at least three men on this journey now. It was beginning to make sense. As he looked around the stone room full of parchments and scrolls he said, "I started this journey by myself, and I actually thought it was one I would finish alone. But, that will not be the case. I don't know how much Gaspar has told you, but I discovered a star, Melchior, and I tracked it for a very long time. I only got so far because my maps were incomplete and I did not have nor know how to make land maps like Gaspar."

"So, you need me for some reason too then. I'm ready to listen. No one enters a leper colony on a whim," said Melchior. "I have seen the power you possess. It is power even King Mamre respects."

Gaspar turned toward Melchior. "I have no power myself," he said, "except for a few magic tricks I have learned here and there."

"I only have the orbs," said Balthazar. "They contain real power. They are no magic trick. You have both witnessed it. The orbs have guided me thus far, but they are not enough. Now I realize they were leading us to you, Melchior. You are one more piece of the puzzle Gaspar and I are missing. We are following a star. It is possibly leading us toward a, uh…"

"A leper colony?" asked Melchior.

"Very funny," said Balthazar.

"Then what?"

"A city of gold? A fountain of eternal youth? To be honest, I don't know. We don't know," said Balthazar nodding at Gaspar.

"Let me guess," said Melchior, "you think the answer to your riddle lies somewhere amongst all of this."

He swept his arm up and over his head. His sleeve fell down around his elbow and he paused staring at his new skin. It was taking time for him to get used to his new body.

"Yes. Yes we do," said Balthazar glancing over at Gaspar. "Gaspar has told me you have been collecting archives and historical works of many nations for a very long time. The star is headed toward Judea, perhaps toward a city called Jerusalem. Gaspar, can you remember enough to draw a simple map?"

Gaspar pulled a large blank scrap of parchment from a nearby shelf and with a piece of black soft stone he drew a rough outline of Judea. He paused and drew another circle inside Judea and marked the city of Jerusalem.

"Balthazar, can you help me remember the names of the cities near Jerusalem?"

Balthazar leaned over the map, took the stone from Gaspar and began writing the names of the other cities.

"Let's see... I remember there was a town north of Jerusalem, it was Hanina. Another city was east of Jerusalem. That was Elzaria. There was Anata and I can't think of the other one. It is just south of Jerusalem."

"Bethlehem." Gaspar said. "I remember it was Bethlehem."

"What city did you say?" asked Melchior.

"Bethlehem," said Balthazar. "Does that mean something?"

Melchior was instantly on his feet straining to see the circle on the map and the city names Balthazar had written.

"Does it mean anything? I have studied these scrolls for years, especially the last ten, and I know exactly which ones I need. Wait right here."

"Well, apparently Bethlehem struck a chord with him," said Gaspar as Melchior whisked out of sight and into the sea of scrolls and tablets.

Balthazar and Gaspar couldn't help looking at each other and smiling. Melchior began rummaging through his stack of Judean scrolls. Occasionally, Balthazar and Gaspar would hear some rustling, and twice they heard crashes and clangs like swords in battle.

"Is everything alright over there?" asked Balthazar.

"Oh, yes quite so, quite so," said Melchior as he rounded the corner and made his way over to the table and the crude map of Jerusalem.

He brushed the map off onto the floor and laid out all the scrolls and parchments on the table rearranging them one at a time.

"Hmmmm. No, that doesn't seem right. I believe this reference should be first."

He rearranged the parchments again like a bird not quite satisfied with its nest. He kept arranging the scrolls and rearranging them. Balthazar and Gaspar were almost at the breaking point when Melchior finally said, "Alright, I think that will do it."

With a flourish and a great sense of pride he turned to face his two guests. "Chronology is important to our story. So, I had to make certain everything was in order here."

Melchior glanced back and forth at Gaspar and Balthazar but neither of the men moved. "Allow me to begin."

And so he did. Melchior pulled the first parchment from the pile and spread it out on the table.

"As you can see here…" Balthazar interrupted Melchior.

"I beg your pardon Melchior, but I may as well be blind. I cannot read a word. What language is this?"

"Hebrew."

Melchior held up the parchment and showed it to Balthazar and Gaspar.

"These scrolls and parchments tell the story of the people of Judea and Judah, the descendants of the patriarch Abraham from the Land of Canaan."

Melchior sat down on a stool he found in the corner and pointed to a stone ledge motioning his friends to sit down.

"This will take some time, but I believe your understanding of Bethlehem and its place in history will be worthwhile. So, make yourselves comfortable and I will be as brief as possible."

Melchior began telling Gaspar and Balthazar the history of Bethlehem as the birthplace of a Hebrew King named David and his father Jesse. He did not tell the stories of great conquest or of David and the giant Goliath or the tales of all the other great kings of Judea. There would be time for that on their long journey ahead.

Melchior knew the history of the descendants of Abraham and thought that would be a good starting point. And so, he began a long story of the Hebrew people. Balthazar and Gaspar were mesmerized, and neither of them realized how long Melchior had been speaking, but Balthazar finally interrupted him.

"Melchior, this is indeed a fascinating history lesson, but how much longer will you be? Can't we just get to the part about why we are following this star?"

"I was just about to tell you why this all excites me so much. It is a very small scroll written by a man, an oracle named Micah, the grandson of a Hebrew named Moses, considered by many to be the first magi. Look right here what he says."

Melchior brought his candle and the two men closer to the parchment. "I will translate this for the two of you."

Melchior grabbed a soft black stone and scribbled a note in his best Akkadian, then slid it across the table in front of the other two men.

"Here. Read this."

'As for you, Bethlehem, seemingly insignificant among the clans of Judea – from you a king will emerge, a child will be born who will rule on my behalf, one whose going out has been purposed from time past, from the eternal days.'

"We are interested in a star Melchior, a star, not some King of Judea," said Balthazar. "What does this have to do with a star?"

He glanced at Gaspar who slowly looked up with a blank stare on his face. Neither wanted to say a word and appear absolutely ignorant, so they sat still waiting and hoping the other would say something intelligent.

"Alright then," said Melchior, "try this, from an earlier manuscript."

Melchior scribbled a few notes on a separate parchment and pushed it toward Balthazar and Gaspar. Both of them read to themselves.

'I see him, but not here and now. I perceive him, but far in the distant future. A star will rise from the east; a scepter will emerge from Judea.'

"So some person is appearing in the future?" asked Gaspar.

"Yes. This scroll was written a long time ago. I believe this writing is referring to the star you are tracking. This future event is happening right now."

Melchior cleared more room on the stony shelf in front of him and laid the crudely drawn map of Jerusalem on it.

"You laid this map out and drew the circle through Bethlehem. These oracles were written hundreds of years apart from each other. What are the odds of that?"

Melchior stood up pacing between his guests and the stone shelf.

"It is apparent to me that Bethlehem is going to be the birthplace of a king. Not just any king but an immortal, eternal king. I don't even have an idea how old this manuscript is but it mentions a star. I believe it is your star."

Melchior stopped pacing and faced both men. "What about this star attracted your attention Balthazar?"

"The orbs initially, but what piqued my curiosity was the fact that this one star traveled in the opposite direction of all the other stars. I began charting its course and I overlaid its path onto my land map. I wanted to know where it was going. Eventually though, my map was inadequate and I knew Gaspar had the best land maps in the world." Balthazar nodded at Gaspar.

"Balthazar came to me and together we discovered the star was slowing down and should stop somewhere near Jerusalem." Gaspar picked his map up off the floor.

"Gaspar is being modest." said Balthazar, "Without him I would not have continued this journey. Gaspar discovered the star was slowing down."

"You say it is only one star?" asked Melchior.

"Yes, only one," answered Balthazar.

"One star which represents one god. Look, the Hebrew people are monotheistic. They only believe in one god, Yahweh. Unlike your people and mine who believe in a god of the sun and a god of the moon and a god of the rain and a hundred other gods. This single star is signaling the birth of a king. That is exactly what I think you have stumbled upon — the star of Judea. The prophesied birth of an immortal king."

Balthazar and Gaspar were beginning to be infected with Melchior's enthusiasm, but they still weren't sure what he was talking about.

"This phrase right here."

Melchior turned back toward the stone shelf and pulled the piece of parchment back in front of him.

"From the eternal days, means Bethlehem will be the birthplace of a king coming to earth whose purpose has been waiting since the beginning of time. And over here," Melchior slid his fingers along a separate tablet, "This is a reference to a star, your star. It's magnificent. We could be witnesses to an historical moment. I have never imagined what it might be like to meet an immortal."

"So," Balthazar began, being very careful with his thoughts, "this would be like Damkina, the Babylonian goddess coming to earth in human form."

"Exactly." said Melchior pleased his students were finally learning. "I believe this star is leading us to the land of Judea — to Bethlehem."

"It's true the star is slowing down," said Gaspar.

"And you did just happen to circle Bethlehem on your map," said Melchior.

Balthazar shrugged his shoulders, "Well, there goes the chance to name the star after my King."

"The earth has been waiting for this person since the beginning of time?" asked Gaspar as confidently as he could.

"Yes. Yes. Yes." said Melchior.

"Then what are we sitting around here for?" added Gaspar. "Let's not keep this king waiting."

Balthazar, Gaspar and Melchior knew they couldn't just leave the colony. The remainder of their journey would require precise planning and patience. Those two things are the hardest to remember when in a hurry: planning and patience. Gaspar found a table and used what instruments were available to begin construction of new maps. These new maps stretched from the land of Mesopotamia to the Mediterranean Sea.

Melchior buried himself in the literature of Judea and the history of that land. He knew he couldn't possibly take all of it with them but he worried that he might leave a critical scroll or parchment behind.

Balthazar found a way to scale the stone wall which formed the back of the colony. At the top of the rock formation he fashioned a small stony observatory and created what instruments he could from Melchior's limited astronomy tools. The high rock wall gave him a great vantage point above the desert floor and allowed him to find the star again.

Over the next few days they all collaborated and cajoled each other into a team of... well, it was tough to say what they were.

"I think we must be able to tell the people we come in contact with who we are and what we are seeking," said Gaspar at dinner one night. "It is dangerous when people ask who you are and what you seek to be unprepared. It breeds suspicion and doubt and together suspicion and doubt create danger."

"I have an idea," said Melchior. "Why don't we tell people we are a trio of traveling troubadours from Troy?

"Why Troy?" asked Gaspar.

"Because, I like the way it sounds," said Melchior.

"Oh, so it's not important if we can sing. Makes perfect sense to me." Balthazar rolled his eyes and glanced at Gaspar struggling to stifle a laugh.

"Can any of us sing?" asked Balthazar. "I know I can't."

"It has been a great while since I heard Gaspar sing," said Melchior, "but the last time I did hear him sing it made the camels cry."

Melchior walked over to Gaspar and patted him on the back. "Somehow, Gaspar's singing sounded more like a camel mating call than singing. The resulting stampede ended the singing contest. But Gaspar was still given a proclamation."

Melchior extended his hands in a mock gesture pretending he was reading a scroll.

"The official decree was for the ability to stampede camels without the use of a horn or physical instrument."

"Ha, ha," said Gaspar.

Balthazar chuckled. "Let's hear your idea Gaspar."

"Well, let me see."

He stretched for a moment and stared up at the torchlight dancing on the ceiling.

"How about this... We aren't kings but what if we pretended to be? What if we came from some place that was so far away no one would know if we were from there or not. What if we said we were from Mongolia? Yes, we will pretend to be from the Far East. We could be the Three Kings of the Orient."

"Oh, I see," said Melchior "We Three Kings of the Orient. The only problem with that is, we're not from the Orient."

"Melchior's right. It doesn't make any sense." said Balthazar, "Who's going to believe that? I have seen people from the orient in Najaf and I bet plenty of people in Jerusalem and Bethlehem have too. Trust me. We definitely don't look oriental. No, there has got to be something else we can call ourselves."

Balthazar scrounged around and managed to find a few pillows. He leaned back into them trying to relax and think. After a few false starts from Melchior and Gaspar, Balthazar finally spoke.

"The Three Wise Men. That's what we will call ourselves. We don't have to pretend or lie about anything. We are three wise men. Melchior has all of this history stored here and in his head; Gaspar has his knowledge of the land; and me, with my curiosity of the stars and the heavens. Together there is no group of men as wise about the world as the three of us sitting in this room. We will name ourselves The Three Wise Men."

"It's royal sounding," said Gaspar.

"It's perfect." Melchior shook his head in agreement. "But what are we seeking? I have seen it written in the manuscripts about a Prince of Peace. Let's tell people we are wise men seeking a Prince of Peace. That should make everyone happy."

"Well spoken," said Balthazar as he stood and stretched, "I think the Three Wise Men would be smart to get a good night's sleep. We need to leave tomorrow. Good night."

Chapter 12
Traveling Troubadours

"You have to hand it to King Mamre. He's persistent," said Gaspar, "Now what do we do? We can't possibly get past all of those men."

Gaspar pointed past the little stone wall where he was standing. Melchior and Balthazar snuck up to the crack in the wall to they could peek out without being seen by any sentries. There they were again, the entire army. There had to be at least twenty-thousand soldiers sitting and waiting. However, King Mamre was apparently not among them. The palatial sized royal tent that had been in the middle of the camp was now missing.

The magic and power King Mamre had seen at the colony scared him off for good. He still had to save face by capturing and killing the three imposters but he wasn't going to waste any of his time on the task. He excused himself by explaining to his army he had more pressing matters to attend to back in Najaf. King Mamre's last advice to Antigone, his commander of the army was, "Starve the colony into submission and make them give up the three imposters."

The soldiers were dealing with a precarious situation. They knew a direct attack was out of the question. One touch from a leper would mean banishment from Najaf. Antigone, King Mamre's Chief of War knew it too, but he was very much a man of action. He called Uzziah, his second-in-command into his headquarters.

"Take a phalanx of my best archers and a squad of spear throwers up close to the colony. Wait for the three men to make a mistake and walk out into the open."

Antigone was, however, not the best strategist. He was more of a bully than a leader and like most bullies, wasn't very smart.

"Look at that," said Melchior as he peeked out of the caves at the troops moving toward the low stone wall in front of the colony. "We would have to be awfully naive to walk out into the courtyard now."

With such a useless show of force Antigone had given up his only advantage: the element of surprise.

Without realizing it, Antigone was giving the Three Wise Men a chance to plan their escape. Balthazar knew the standing army was delaying their plans for leaving but it was also helping them think through their options.

"We are talking about Three Wise Men," he said to himself as he sat in the darkness of the cave with Melchior and Gaspar.

"I know on foot we could easily sneak past the army but that would leave us without transportation. The camels are the problem."

Melchior grabbed a torch from the wall. "Follow me," he said.

Melchior took Gaspar and Balthazar into a small unlit, unkempt room. This room was much smaller than the one filled with the scrolls and maps of Judea and all the other lands Melchior had visited.

"Welcome to the map room." Melchior looked past a few shelves and finally pulled down a non-descript stack of parchments. Each parchment had what appeared to be a maze or tunnel scrawled on it.

"This is the book of tunnels. Remember, I have been here ten years and many of the people have been here much longer. There has been a great deal of time for digging."

Melchior thumbed through the stack of parchments to the last one. He pulled the parchment out of the pile.

"This tunnel," he pointed at the map, "will take us to an oasis behind the stone wall at the back of the colony. It is about a half days journey to the end of this tunnel. Once we get to the end, we will be behind the army and free. The problem is without the camels, we will be free to die in the desert. The tunnel is not big enough for a camel and we won't get far without them."

"Let's think about this over dinner tonight," said Balthazar.

"It is time to eat indeed," said Melchior, "Let me take you to the main dining area. I think you'll be impressed."

The room Melchior walked into with them was large. In the center of it were three tall pillars. Each pillar was engraved with names of people, places and a little history of the colony.

"You certainly were right," said Gaspar, "you have had a lot of time for digging."

"And carving," said Balthazar admiring one of the pillars.

The dinner that night was a feast compared to most of the meals served at the colony. Everyone said so and it made the Three Wise Men proud and humbled to see what the orbs had given to all the former lepers. They were the most gracious and grateful hosts. After dinner, Houlak the old woman stepped up onto a raised platform at the end of the Hall of Feasting.

"May I have your attention everyone? I am Houlak and in honor of our guests, well, I prefer to call them our friends, we have a little entertainment."

Houlak clapped her hands twice and a troupe of performers came up onto the platform. They had silt drums and lyres and flutes and a beautiful young woman, a dancer. Two young men began to sing a Mesopotamian melody and the young woman danced. Gaspar noticed her immediately. Her skin was a deep bronze. Her black hair was darker than the center of her eyes and she was dancing like a...

"Gaspar, Gaspar." Melchior shook him and rudely interrupted his fantasy.

"What is it? Can't it wait?" said Gaspar. "I'm enjoying myself."

"Oh, I can see what you're enjoying. She is astounding isn't she? But yes, this is important. I have a plan for our escape." Melchior waited for the dance to end, and then he walked up onto the platform to speak.

"I hate to interrupt the festivities, but I am afraid I must. My two friends and I would like to thank you for your hospitality. You have been so gracious and kind to us, but now, I must tell you we cannot stay. We are on a journey and time is of the essence. I cannot tell you much about this journey, but I can tell you we will need your help to complete it."

Houlak stood. "We are indebted to you Melchior and, to your two friends. We will do whatever you ask of us." She turned to face the crowd. "Won't we?"

The room erupted in thunderous applause and grateful expressions reverberated from the rock walls.

"I need the two singers and the woman that just performed for us."

Houlak motioned the troupe onto the stage and they introduced themselves.

"I am Joab," said the younger of the two men.

He was about Gaspar's height and build.

"I am Esau," said the older one who was fairly close to Balthazar's height.

"You are Naomi," said Melchior.

"Yes. Yes I am." She said blushing. She stared down at her feet to keep her red cheeks from showing.

Melchior knew who she was. She was one of the few people he did recognize since the leprosy had disappeared. Most of the others living in the colony were so disfigured by the disease it was impossible to know who anyone was by just looking at them. But Naomi was so beautiful that even when she had leprosy it could not totally steal her attractiveness.

Melchior cleared his throat and began speaking. "What I am going to ask you to do is very dangerous; if you are not willing to do it, I understand. Please sit down while I explain." He paced back and forth on stage laying out each step of his plan.

"As you all know there is a tunnel that is a half days journey in length. It leads to a tiny oasis just southeast of the colony. We have used this place for many years to pick up gifts and clothes from the kindness of strangers in Najaf. The entrance to the tunnel is hidden and undiscovered by the army of King Mamre. That is how we will make our escape."

Melchior stopped pacing and looked out into the audience.

"Getting to the oasis is not the problem. The problem is we cannot get far without our camels, and the tunnel is too small to take the camels through. We must have someone bring them to us. It means going outside the walls..."

Melchior paused for a moment. He knew he was asking a lot. No one from the colony had stepped outside the walls until he had done it just a few days earlier.

Houlak stood up. "But we cannot just walk these camels out through the front gate. The army has returned. It would be suicide."

"Yes, I know. That is why these three," Melchior motioned toward Joab, Esau and Naomi, "are going to sneak out tonight far enough away from the colony so that in the morning when they are spotted it will appear they are coming from the west and headed to Najaf."

"But they cannot just pass by without explaining to King Mamre's men who they are and the purpose of their journey," said Houlak.

"I know where this is going." Gaspar stood up from his place in the crowd. "You want them to be the Traveling Tootdoors..."

"Troubadours. Traveling Troubadours," said Melchior.

Gaspar made his way up to the front of the room and onto the stage.

"What are you planning here Melchior? You're not going to send them out to face King Mamre's army alone are you?"

"No. Listen to me," pleaded Melchior. "It will work. When the Traveling Troubadours are stopped by the troops they will offer a small sample of their talents." Melchior walked over to where the troupe was seated. "Naomi will dance and Esau and Joab will entertain them with singing. After that, they will tell the army and its commander they are the featured entertainment for King Mamre's birthday celebration which is just a few days from now."

"Go on," said Balthazar as he stood up and began to make his way to the front of the room and up onto the stage.

"Then the Troubadours will leave; sneak back around to the oasis after they are safely away from the army. We will be waiting inside the tunnel. Once they arrive at the oasis they will set up camp near the tunnel entrance. During the night we will trade places with them inside the tent. They will use the tunnel to come back here."

"Why go through all of that?" asked Balthazar.

"In case some of King Mamre's army follows them or if there are visitors at the oasis. Anyone there will see three people setup the tent and three people take it down the next morning. We will exchange clothes with the Troubadours, and from a distance no one will notice the difference."

Melchior looked down at Naomi, Joab and Esau. "Would you three stand here next to me please?"

Melchior placed Joab next to Gaspar and Esau next to Balthazar and then he stood next to Naomi.

An old man stood up in the crowd and pointed at Esau.

"Esau is going to have to put on some weight if he's going to stand in for him." The old man pointed a gnarled finger at Balthazar. "And I hate to break it to you Melchior, but you are no Naomi!"

The room filled with laughter.

Melchior waved his hands to quiet the room. "I know we'll have to put a little padding on Esau…"

"A little..." said the old man and the room erupted again.

"Alright. A lot of padding but it will work," said Melchior.

"You as Naomi? Now that's something I would pay to see," quipped the old man.

"I will wear Naomi's veil and hide my face."

"Well unless Naomi can grow a beard, you better hide that too."

Melchior lowered his head to hide his grin. "Who are you?"

"Name is Isaac. It's Hebrew for laughter."

"You're from Judea?"

"Yes I am."

"What was your trade in Judea?" asked Balthazar.

"I actually worked in Jerusalem. I was the jester in King Herod's court."

"I believe it," said Balthazar and the room filled with laughter again.

"Well Isaac," said Melchior still smiling, "If you wouldn't mind helping us before we leave, your information about the area in and around Jerusalem and your knowledge of Hebrew could be invaluable to us."

"Be glad to help." Isaac walked up onto the stage with the small group of daring adventurers. He turned to face the room. "Anybody got a better idea than what you just heard?"

The room was quiet. Isaac raised his hands into the air.

"Then what are we waiting for? Let's get started. I believe the Traveling Two by Fours must leave tonight!"

The Hall of Feasting immediately broke into a hive of activity. Like bees buzzing about, a group of women began putting together a costume for Naomi. After measuring Melchior they made him a duplicate of Naomi's outfit. There was more activity around Melchior than any of the other adventurers. Several times during Melchior's fitting, groups of giggles would rise above the verbal banter in the room. Cloth was being cut and sewn. Turbans were twirled into shape and tunics were measured and made. Houlak gathered a group to boil water and create dyes from the chemicals in Melchior's magic room.

When they were done, the costumes looked amazing considering the limited resources the people in the colony had at their disposal. The royal blue sashes made an impressive shape like an upside down pyramid on the chest of Balthazar and Gaspar. The colony had managed to make enough dye to stain Balthazar's tunic a deep red and Gaspar's a bright yellow. The women had done such a good job with Naomi and Melchior's costumes that when they stood side by side it took a good second glance to tell the difference between them. Even though Melchior had to dress like a woman he was glad to be standing next to Naomi.

It was hard to believe how much the colony had changed in the last few days. The leprosy had nearly robbed them of their souls. Now here the colony was helping the Three Wise Men take their next step in a journey filled with uncertainty. The formerly lifeless leper colony and all the people in it were risking their lives for the Three Wise Men. It was amazing to see the difference in people who had been so close to death; they had become like hermits hoarding life. Now they had a chance to make a difference, and they were willing to risk their lives for Melchior and these two foreigners. The colony had become infected with the same driving motivation of the Wise Men; what would they find beneath the star?

Soon the preparations were complete. It was time to send the Traveling Troubadours off on their mission. The Three Wise Men stood in front of the packed Hall of Feasting.

Melchior stepped forward to speak. "Words cannot express how thankful we are for all of you. This journey we are embarking upon has become our mission. It is our destiny, not yours. We could not possibly make this trip without your help. Thank you. However, I must warn you of a few things."

He paused with a concerned look on his face before he continued, "You must still remain a leper colony."

The jubilation and excitement in the room evaporated in an instant.

"Do not be discouraged. Let me explain."

Melchior removed the veil from his face and walked to the very front of the stony stage.

"The only thing protecting you from the wrath of King Mamre and his army is the belief that leprosy is still among us. You must not give them any reason to think otherwise. If there is any clue at all the disease is no longer here, they will rush these tunnels and there will be no mercy shown for any of you."

Houlak stood up at the front of the room to speak.

"He is right. The army cannot stay encamped forever in front of us. They will lose interest eventually, and if King Mamre does not call them back to Najaf, sooner or later they will disband from boredom. It may take a few days or several weeks before they give up. We must remember to ring our bells and cover ourselves as much as possible."

"Plus, by keeping the army occupied in front of the colony you are allowing us a better chance of escaping," said Balthazar. "This is our only chance. If King Mamre catches us you will certainly never see us again."

A small child sitting in her mother's lap was the only soul brave enough to voice the question on everyone's lips.

"Will we see you again?"

Melchior went to the front of the stage and held the girl in his arms.

"It is a long journey and we aren't sure exactly where we are going or what we will encounter. These two men have decided to take me with them and I feel compelled to go. Of course we want to see you all again."

The Traveling Troubadours and the Three Wise Men gathered at the center of the stage and each Troubadour gave his Wise Man twin a hug and a blessing of success. Since Melchior's look-a-like was Naomi he took advantage of the situation and held on to her just a little bit longer than he should have. He wasn't in love, but he was willing to give love a good long look and Naomi a very nice hug. The Troubadours had to leave immediately in order to beat the daylight which would be approaching in just a few hours. The entire colony went to watch them leave just to make certain the Troubadours weren't spotted by the night watchmen. The Troubadours had no problem sneaking away in the dark. The army was encamped a generous distance from the colony and their evening fires were only the tiniest flicker on the horizon.

The Three Wise Men stood at the stone wall until the Troubadours were well out of sight.

"If they are caught and the ruse is uncovered, we shall all be seeing each other in the next life," said Gaspar.

Balthazar turned back toward the tunnels. "Let us not think of such things. This will work," he said as bravely as he could. "It has to."

The gravity and burden of putting other people's lives in jeopardy weighed heavily on all three of them. As they entered the tunnel Melchior could not keep the doubt from his mind. He panicked and ran back outside into the courtyard racing for the gate.

"Naomi…mmmmppphhffff."

Gaspar caught Melchior from behind and stuffed part of a tunic into Melchior's mouth. Balthazar bounded along as best he could and when he arrived Melchior and Gaspar were wrestling in the courtyard. Melchior was desperately twisting and kicking to wriggle out of Gaspar's grasp but Balthazar sat down on top of him just in time to keep him from escaping.

Melchior managed to pull the tail of the tunic out of his mouth and scream, "Let me go! Let me go!" Gaspar deftly stuffed the tunic back into Melchior's mouth and pinned his arms to the rough stone floor of the courtyard.

"Listen to me Melchior. I will pull the stuffing from your mouth if you promise to listen and not scream."

Gaspar stared down at Melchior.

"Shake your head up and down if you promise not to scream."

Melchior shook his head up and down in response and Gaspar removed the tunic from Melchior's mouth.

"I know the feelings you are having," began Gaspar, "I hope you will see her again someday."

"It is not just that."

"What else is it then?"

"I doubt that I shall live to see tomorrow if Balthazar doesn't get off me."

Melchior gulped the night air as Balthazar rolled off him and onto the stone courtyard floor.

"I see your sense of humor has returned," said Balthazar. "You are right Gaspar; I pray we have not sent them off only to find a senseless death."

Gaspar released Melchior's arms and sat down next to him. Balthazar rolled into position on the other side of Melchior and gazed up into the cloudless night sky.

"What am I doing out here?" asked Balthazar.

"Balthazar, you of all people should be the last to doubt," said Gaspar, "Look how far you have come. Look what has happened right here at the leper colony.

Melchior turned to face the two men.

"I do have a feeling about this journey and I must tell you a story about my father which will help you see what I have been trying to understand the last few days."

Melchior shifted his gaze, stared at the ground and lowered his shoulders.

"My father was not feeling well. I was a young boy, but I knew in my heart he was dying. He could barely walk near the end of his life. One day he had a sudden burst of energy and he left the house." The memory of the day stormed into Melchior's mind and he went to another place and time.

"I knew he was sick and I begged him to get back into bed. My father would not listen. He walked to the market and purchased a fig tree. By the time we got home he was leaning heavily on my shoulder. Just outside my bedroom window he began digging a hole."

"Are you digging your own grave?" I screamed, "What are you doing?"

"Do not worry my son; I am not digging my grave," he said, "I am digging a hole for this fig tree."

"Why on earth are you planting a tree?" I cried, "You will never be able to enjoy it. This is no time to plant a tree. You are killing yourself!"

"Ahh, my son you are right. I am dying and I will never live to see this tree grow or enjoy its fruit or shade. But I am not planting the tree for me."

Melchior paused, and looked up at Gaspar and Balthazar. "I do not believe I am making this journey for me. I may not even live to tell about it but I believe my children and my children's children will know I planted a tree."

Balthazar and Gaspar both stared at Melchior as if he were a complete stranger. Neither one of them moved or even blinked.

"You think we're going to die?" asked Gaspar.

"No. But from what I have read about this star so far, I believe this journey is not about us becoming famous or finding a city of gold or being crowned kings in a foreign land."

Melchior struggled as he searched for the words which had deserted him.

"There is no mention in the ancient manuscripts about the people who discover the star. Only the star and the child it represents are mentioned. Even though I believe we were chosen somehow; I'm still not sure what we have been chosen for. But, in order for us to continue on together we must trust each other. Right Balthazar?"

"Yes," said Balthazar, "I almost sabotaged our effort with my mad dash to Najaf."

"And I could have jeopardized us all by trying to stop the Traveling Trapdoors," said Melchior.

"Troubadours. Traveling Troubadours," said Gaspar.

"I'm just glad we stuck them with the name Traveling Troubadours and not us," said Melchior.

They all laughed.

"Wait, wait. Let's all stand up, clasp hands and say it together," said Gaspar. "We are…"

"The Three Wise Men."

The slight echo off the colony walls brought the name back and forth to them as it ricocheted between the stone gate and the sturdy rock wall at the back of the colony. It made them all smile as they looked up into the night sky, curious what tomorrow would bring, and praying the Troubadours would be successful in getting past King Mamre's army with the camels.

In the morning, the Wise Men all agreed that gathering what information they could from Isaac would be the best use of their time. It would be a while before the Troubadours appeared over the horizon and be in sight of King Mamre's army.

"Alright, what would you like to know?" said Isaac, his old but alert eyes darting from face to face.

"Well, for starters," said Balthazar, "how would you describe the city of Jerusalem?"

"It is said by some historians to be like a snowy mountain glittering in the sun. The temples and the hills surrounding Jerusalem are striking. All the marble and gold domes blend and mix into each other making the city visible even during the night."

"Sounds like we won't have any trouble finding it," said Gaspar.

"I would think not. A blind man could feel the sun glinting off the city and find his way to it." Isaac closed his eyes remembering the city and its beauty.

"Can you tell us anything about the king who reigns there?" asked Melchior.

"Should be Herod, unless someone has assassinated him by now." Isaac stared down at the floor and shuffled his feet. "One can only hope."

"That doesn't sound promising," said Balthazar. "Can he be trusted?"

"Does a sand cobra make a good roommate?" asked Isaac.

"I can safely say no to that," said Balthazar as he patted the leather pouch containing the orbs.

"If you make a promise to Herod all I can say is you better keep it. He has a long memory and a short temper," said Isaac.

He got up from his stone stool and grabbed a parchment from a nearby shelf. "Let me see if I can draw up a rough map of Jerusalem, the main roads, where the king's royal palace is located and the interior of the palace."

"That would be most helpful," said Gaspar, "Here. Let's spread the parchment out on this ledge. Why don't you work on the map of the palace and Jerusalem while we prepare for the trip to the oasis."

"I should have this completed in an hour or so." Isaac bent over the table and began scratching a map onto the surface of the papyrus scroll.

Balthazar, Gaspar and Melchior gathered themselves and their belongings in the small kitchen where they had discovered the truth about Melchior.

"That's about it for me. Globes. Check." Balthazar hung the pouch containing the orbs around his neck. The holes from the fangs of the sand cobra still visible.

"Frankincense and Myrrh with me," said Gaspar who just could not stop smiling.

"The colony insisted on giving me something to take on our journey." Melchior held up a small leather pouch. It jingled slightly when he lifted it. "I don't think it's much gold, but it is all they have."

"I would like to go up onto the top of the wall and see if our friends have made their acquaintance with King Mamre's army yet," said Balthazar. "Anyone want to come with me?"

From the top of the wall surrounding the back of the colony the horizon curved in the distance. King Mamre's army was clearly laid out just south of the gate entrance. Balthazar had three different magnifying lenses and he gave one each to Melchior and Gaspar.

"Looking at the terrain, I would think the Troubadours will travel up through that gap between those two large dunes," said Gaspar as he held his magnifying glass close to his right eye. "We should see a slight cloud of dust as they approach."

"Like that?" Melchior pointed just west of where Gaspar was staring.

In the distance and percolating above one of the dunes was a small dust cloud.

"I see one, two, three camels and riders. That must be our group."

Even from this distance and looking through a blurry magnifying lens, Melchior could still make out which rider was Naomi.

Chapter 13
Archery

Naomi, Joab and Esau lurched along at an uneven pace toward the army somewhere to the northeast of them. Just as they were wondering if the army had spotted their small caravan, a pair of sentries appeared at the top of a dune. The sentries stopped for a moment. Their camels partially blocked the sun as Joab spotted them.

"I believe we have been found. We shall have some company from King Mamre's army soon enough," said Joab as he turned to tell the news to Esau and Naomi. "Troubadours forever, right?" For emphasis he pulled three balls from a pouch on his camel and started juggling while riding at the same time. Naomi and Esau stared. "Yes, Joab is full of surprises. Didn't know I could juggle did you?"

For as many soldiers as there were they were surprisingly quick and quiet as they descended down all four sides of the large dune surrounding the Troubadours. It startled Naomi and for a moment she wanted to run but it would have been too late anyway. She sensed the futility of trying to escape and pulled her camel to a halt.

"Who would be so bold and so foolish as to cross King Mamre's desert with no guard or escort?" Uzziah was not quite the bully Antigone was, but he was no smarter either. Uzziah always used his size to intimidate people. His arms were thick and muscular. His body was particularly well defined and sculpted. Sitting behind Jandak on his camel he poked the camel with the tip of his spear. His intention was to make Jandak move out of his way. However, in response Jandak unleashed an infamous cloud of unconsciousness. Uzziah's camel backtracked and quickly dumped Uzziah head first into a dune. It was not a good beginning for the Troubadours.

Joab, Esau, and Naomi stifled their laughter and watched as the stunned soldiers frantically tried to gain the upper hand. Three soldiers hurried over to pull Uzziah and his dignity from the dune. Uzziah was not happy before entering the dune. He was furious coming out of it.

Uzziah glanced at the Troubadours and could see the small smiles they were trying to hide. "Think that's funny do you? Well, I am only going to take two of you back to camp with me." Uzziah fumed and spit sand and grit from his mouth. "Who shall it be?"

Ignoring the threat Esau dismounted and walked over to Uzziah and bowed deeply. "Please accept our most sincere apologies. My name is Esau. And yours?"

"Uzziah. Uzziah from Ur." Uzziah straightened up and shook his head to dispense with as much sand as he could. "So, we have a volunteer willing to die for his friends. How noble."

"Ahhh, who said anything about dying?" said Esau "You surprised my camel and what happened was completely an accident. However, I will give you a chance to regain your honor."

"Regain my what?" asked Uzziah.

"Your honor. I will challenge you in a small game of archery in return for my life and that satchel of gold on your belt." Esau took a bow and arrow from a pack tied to Jandak and fitted an arrow onto the string of the bow. "I see you have a bow also. How about a little game of skill?"

"And what do I get in return?" asked Uzziah.

"Why my beautiful sister Naomi."

Naomi heard her name called, and when she realized the gambit Esau was playing, she fainted and fell face first off her camel. The soldiers laughed and Uzziah walked over to Naomi and rolled her over onto her back.

"Half the gold in my satchel."

"I know how beautiful she is. All of it."

Even with a veil covering half her face Uzziah looked down at her again and realized she was quite attractive.

"Alright," said Uzziah, "What's the game?" He could not back down with all of his men watching and waiting for him to answer such a clear challenge for such a glorious prize. Antigone would be proud.

"Joab, my brother and assistant will take these three balls and toss them into the air one at a time. Whoever can hit the most balls wins. A clean hit counts for two points and a nick counts as one."

"And if we tie?" asked Uzziah.

"We shoot until someone misses. Are you ready?" Esau looked at Joab. "Fifteen paces if you please, Joab."

"His assistant," said Joab under his breath. "I hope he knows what he's doing."

Joab turned and walked the fifteen paces from the group. He stood waiting for Esau to give the signal and toss the first ball.

"Be my guest." Esau motioned Uzziah forward.

Uzziah notched an arrow onto the string of his bow and pulled it back to his eye. "Throw," he said. Joab threw the ball into the air and Uzziah released his arrow immediately. It sliced through the air and the ball, cleaving it neatly in half.

Esau feigned nonchalance by mock clapping. "Oh, that was marvelous." The inside of his mouth went dry. Uzziah pulled an arrow from his quiver, notched it on his bow and said, "Throw." His second arrow flew even quicker this time and it pierced the ball squarely in the center.

Esau's "Uh-oh" was masked by the approval of Uzziah's men. This was an impressive show of skill they had not seen before, neither had Esau. Uzziah was much better than Esau expected.

Joab steadied himself and prepared to throw the third ball into the air. Uzziah was a perfect two for two. How good was Esau? He could not dwell on that and instinctively threw the ball into the air when he heard Uzziah yell, "Throw." The ball arced into the air and Joab watched as the silhouette of the arrow went cleanly through the silhouette of the ball. However, the ball did not travel with the arrow like it had been hit. It fell back down into Joab's hand. Joab searched the ball frantically and finally saw it; a nick on the side of the ball.

"There is a nick on the side of the ball." He raised the ball into the air and walked it over to an impatient Uzziah. Uzziah's men were in a frenzy yelling, "Uzziah, Uzziah!" as they shook their swords and spears in the air.

"Five out of six points. See if you can top that Hee Saw, said Uzziah.

Esau ignored the slight to his name and stepped forward to take his turn. He waited as Joab pulled three more juggling balls from the satchel on his camel. He pulled one arrow from his quiver and clenched it between his teeth. He took another and notched it on the bow string. Esau's mouth was drier than a hundred year drought and his tongue lodged itself at the back of his throat. He could not say anything so he nodded his head to Joab as a signal to let the first ball fly. Esau lined up his bow quickly and sent the first arrow on its way. It whistled through the air and caught the ball dead center.

"Two points," Joab said in a barely audible voice.

Uzziah's men gave a groan. Esau drew another arrow from his quiver, leaving the first arrow still clenched between his teeth. Joab watched for the signal and released the ball, straight up. A drop of sweat fell off Esau's brow and into his eye as he released the shot. The drop of sweat stung his eye, and he could not track the arrow on its way to the target.

"A hit," said Joab as nonchalantly as he could. "That's four points for Esau and five for Uzziah. Esau has one shot remaining."

The men of Uzziah booed and hissed as Esau prepared for his final shot. "What can I do? I have to let them participate, don't I?" said Uzziah as he slapped Esau on the back.

Esau fell to his knees. His heart fluttered and beat in his chest so wildly and loudly he could hear nothing. Hoping to distract him, Uzziah noisily pulled his scimitar from its scabbard making sure the sun reflected off the blade and into

Esau's eyes. Ignoring the threat, Esau stood up and nodded his head again for Joab to release the final ball.

The small ball in Joab's hand weighed more than anything he had ever lifted in his life. He wasn't sure he could even move his arm upward, let alone throw the ball into the air. In a mental fog he tossed it as high as he could. He watched it as it rose into the desert sky and just for a moment it blocked the sun. Joab leaned so far backward he lost his balance and fell onto his back in the sand. The whistling sound of the arrow passed by overhead and the ball began its descent. The ball did not bobble or move as the arrow sped by.

'Esau has missed!' thought Joab as he watched the ball fall toward him. Uzziah's men began to cheer. They did not see Esau pull the second arrow from between his teeth, notch it and let it fly. The ball was just three feet from Joab's face when the second arrow sliced through the air and severed the ball into two perfectly symmetrical halves. Joab watched as one half of the ball fell onto the sand on the left side of his head and the other fell on the right.

"Six points for Esau. Five points for Uzziah," Joab said in a shaky voice from his prone position on the ground.

The groan from Uzziah's men turned into grudging applause and admiration. Even in a losing match sometimes the opponent has to acknowledge the victor. Uzziah knew he had been beaten. He could not lose what respect he had left in front of his men.

"Two shots in one toss… Don't think you can trick me again," said Uzziah as he handed his pouch of gold to Esau. Esau grinned and grabbed Uzziah's hand in hopes it would steady his own.

"Uzziah, allow me to introduce us all. We are the Traveling Troubadours, and we are on our way to Najaf to entertain King Mamre at his birthday party next week. I am Esau. Joab the ball tosser is our juggler and Naomi …" Esau had forgotten she had fainted and was still lying in the sand next to her camel. He ran over and knelt next to her. He quickly grabbed a flask of water from her camel and sat her up to give her a drink. Naomi heard familiar voices, but the person she was listening and looking for the most was just to her left. She let fly a right hook which would have impressed Esau if he had seen it. Her fist connected squarely to Esau's jaw and he collapsed next to her.

Uzziah laughed, "A fiery one she is for sure. I like her already." He pursed his lips in a mock kiss as Naomi prepared a haymaker for him too. Uzziah caught her fist as it came toward him. "Now knocking out the man who saved you from being a slave is no way to treat him."

"I will not go with you and be your slave. I would die here in the desert first."

"I'm talking about your brother. He won the contest. Not me; though I would have been very happy to introduce you to Antigone as my prize." Uzziah paused as he stared at the pouch of gold he had just lost in the archery match. "Speaking of prizes I think I'll just take this back." He pulled the pouch of gold out from under Esau.

Uzziah marched off to his camel. "Stay here with the feisty one and her brothers. If indeed they are her brothers. Bring them all to Antigone's tent." He waved to a group of soldiers, mounted his camel and climbed the dune.

Naomi stood up and poured the remaining water from her flask on Esau. He sputtered, spat, sat up and rubbed his chin. "Wow. Where did that come from?"

"My sister, Naomi. Putting me up as a prize."

Esau motioned for her to be quiet as he whispered to her. "I had to do something. You saw how upset he was. I have no doubt one of us would have gone missing if I hadn't acted. We all have to reach the oasis or the plan won't work." Esau paused and looked at Naomi. He could tell she was still hurt and afraid. "I'm sorry. I really am."

Chapter 14
Entertaining the Troops

"Alright, but I want you to know I am only dancing for Antigone and that's it. No more games or surprises." said Naomi.

"Then let's go entertain the troops." Esau hugged Naomi and they walked over to where Joab was waiting for them.

Joab had already put everything together. They all mounted up and followed the squad of soldiers out of the dunes and into the heart of King Mamre's army.

Joab and Esau set up the tent while Naomi tended to the camels. They were in the middle of camp next to Antigone's palatial sized tent with three spires on top. It looked large enough from the outside to house an entire city. Uzziah walked by and noticed Naomi. He blew her a kiss. Naomi stuck her tongue out at him and he laughed as he entered Antigone's tent.

Esau watched as Naomi stuck her tongue out at Uzziah. "You don't have to antagonize him do you? He may not let you leave with us, and no contest is going to change that. I think he likes you."

"He is disgusting and barbaric. I like men with a little more brain than brawn, a man like Melchior." Naomi realized she had said his name and it made her blush for a moment.

"Melchior? Does he know?" asked Joab.

"Does he know what?"

"That you like him," said Esau.

"I didn't say I liked HIM," said Naomi. "I said I like men like Melchior."

"Well, if you like men like Melchior but you don't like Melchior, what is it about Melchior you don't like?" asked Joab.

"I... well, he... ohhh, you're just being difficult." Naomi turned in a huff and pretended to be tending the camels.

"Women," said Esau.

"Yes," said Joab, "I have often heard it said that no tent is large enough if an angry woman is inside."

"Well, Antigone sure knows how to throw a party," Esau said. The tent was awash in golden candle stands, bejeweled sconces and brass shields. There were so many guards and soldiers it made Esau nervous.

"There must be at least twenty dancers," said Joab "Let me rephrase that, twenty beautiful dancers. Naomi certainly has some competition." Naomi elbowed Joab in the ribs and he grimaced while still trying to walk through the tent and wave at all the party guests. "Of course, Naomi could take on any ten of these girls." Naomi stepped down hard on the arch of Joabs' foot. He tumbled to the tent floor. The merriment ceased immediately and all eyes turned toward Joab. Joab saw what was happening and quickly put one hand under his torso and twisted into a one hand handstand. He turned that into a series of jumps across the tent floor, lifting his body and thrusting himself into the air then landing on one hand and repeating the trick. It was quite a display of strength and was quickly approved of by Antigone with a round of royal applause. The party picked up right where it had left off with dancers, dining and drinking.

"We must get Uzziah to introduce us to Antigone and now would be a nice time since he is in a good mood," Esau said. He stepped forward to lead Joab and Naomi into the group of soldiers and dancers surrounding Antigone.

"Will the most excellent and honorable Uzziah introduce us to Antigone the leader of King Mamre's army?" Esau bent low and tipped his turban to Uzziah. He pulled a flower from behind Uzziah's ear and gave it to the woman sitting next to him. This pleased the woman but not Uzziah.

"You've already beaten me handily today. Would you try and take my woman too?" Uzziah pulled Esau inches from his face and fetched a dagger from behind his back, clinching it tight to Esau's throat. He threw Esau backward forcing him to fall onto his back on the tent floor. This again quieted the tent. Uzziah rose up laughing and walked over to Antigone.

"Antigone," said Uzziah, "Allow me to introduce our entertainment for this evening, The Trolling Troubadours."

"It's the Traveling Troubadours your Excellency." Esau said, as he stood up and bowed in front of Antigone. "I am Esau. This is Joab and Naomi.

Esau motioned for the two of them to step forward. They all bowed in front of Antigone.

"I juggle," said Joab. He threw three balls into the air and began to spin them into a circle in front of him.

Esau walked over to Antigone and whispered into his ear. "Boring isn't it." Antigone nodded.

"Let me borrow a couple of daggers and two torches. This should liven things up a bit."

Without waiting for a response from Antigone, Esau grabbed two daggers from Antigone's belt spun around and threw the daggers and lit torches at Joab one at a time.

Joab grunted and grimaced as the daggers and torches kept coming but he managed not to miss any of the items.

This wasn't in the plan, thought Joab. What is he trying to prove?

Esau whispered again to Antigone. "Still boring isn't it?"

Antigone smiled and nodded. He looked behind where Esau was standing and unlatched a woven basket. Antigone put his hand into the basket and pulled out a writhing snake. He threw it onto the floor at Joab's feet. Joab shrieked then jerked and jumped like a frightened rat in a maze, but he did not drop a single item he was juggling. Somehow he managed to dash and dart his way across the tent floor and jump onto a ledge just high enough to be out of range of the snake. Still juggling he stared at the snake. The tent floor cleared quickly as the snake hissed and spit at Joab. This display really pleased Antigone and he laughed so hard he fell off the pile of pillows beneath him. Still laughing, Antigone walked over to the snake and grabbed its head from behind. He made his way back to his pile of pillows, opened the snake basket and threw it back inside.

"I am amused by these Troubling Troubadours," said Antigone, "but now I want to see her."

He pointed a mangled finger with two golden rings on it directly at Naomi.

"Yes, and you shall," said Esau as he signaled for Naomi to come forward.

Esau watched Antigone place a third ring onto the same finger as the other two rings and then on a piece of papyrus scribble a quick note. Antigone set the papyrus note on top of the pillow he was sitting upon. Esau knew what it said. He had seen Antigone slip the extra gold band onto his finger and he decided to act.

"May I borrow your sash Antigone?" asked Esau.

While helping Antigone remove the sash he slipped the note from the pillow. Esau turned his back and while folding the sash glanced at the note to confirm what it said, then slipped the note into his own tunic and laid the sash beside Antigone.

"During this song, your sash will become a snake," said Esau.

"We will sing and play a Mesopotamian melody as Naomi dances for you." Esau signaled for Joab to stop juggling.

Joab joined Esau and Naomi in the center of the tent. Esau pulled a flute and a small pouch of white powder from his tunic. Joab began to sing. Naomi's movement transcended the dance. She was beautiful and fluid.

Esau poured a small amount of the white powder into his flute and waited for his time to play. He positioned himself above and behind Antigone, and when he began to play a small unnoticeable amount of the powder escaped the flute and floated onto Antigone's face. Antigone froze in mid grin and he sat there still and silent, unblinking and unmoving.

Esau knew the paralyzing powder Melchior had given him was working but didn't know how long its effects would last. Upon finishing his flute solo, he quickly walked around Antigone and laid flat on the floor in front of Naomi and kicked her feet out from under her. She fell onto Esau's feet and he began spinning and juggling her like a human ball. This made the crowd break out in applause except for Antigone. Still affected by the powder, he sat still with a silly half frozen grin on his face.

Joab knew something was not right and he quickly ended the song which raised a respectful amount of applause. Joab bowed and walked on his hands over to Esau and Naomi.

"You will both thank me for this later," said Esau, "Do not argue and do not delay. We must leave without raising any suspicion if we can."

Uzziah was in the vicinity of the powder Esau had blown onto Antigone's face. For a moment it had stunned him too. He still could not move but now his voice rose above the applause of the crowd.

"Get them all. Do not let them escape."

Esau grabbed Naomi and Joab's hands, and ran to the center of the tent. Pulling a dagger from his robe, he cut the master ropes holding the tent up and it began collapsing onto the crowd. A hand grabbed Esau's leg. He stabbed it with the dagger as the tent fell on top of them and the crowd. Esau cut a hole in the top of the collapsed tent just big enough for the three of them to escape. They stepped out onto the outside of the tent and ran for the edge of it, stumbling and tripping over the people still trapped inside.

"What on earth are you doing?" yelled Naomi. "Everything was working perfectly."

The three of them stood just outside the perimeter of the tent. Esau looked at Naomi and Joab.

"I will explain later. You must trust me. We have to leave now. We have very little time."

Esau gave his dagger to Joab.

"Cut all of the camels at that post loose and herd them onto the tent. Naomi and I will get our camels, come back for you and head for the oasis."

Joab stood frozen in place and for a moment Esau thought the powder had affected him too.

"Move! Move! Move!" screamed Esau.

Joab snapped out of his stupor and blindly cut at the ropes holding the camels in place. He herded them onto the top of the collapsed tent and waited for Naomi and Esau. Several soldiers came to see what the commotion was all about.

"Tent malfunction." Joab shrugged his shoulders. "Probably foreign made. You know it's just so hard to get a good tent these days. They just don't make them like they used to."

Naomi and Esau came up to the scene on their camels. Joab noticed one of their camels had been replaced but knew better than to say anything at a time like this. Esau certainly had some explaining to do.

"You can't just leave," said one of the soldiers.

"Oh, but we must. Antigone has directed us to bring these sorry tent makers here so he can give them a message in person," Joab said.

"How do we know you aren't the cause of all this?" asked another soldier standing behind Jandak.

Esau hated to do it but he knew how to silence the soldier. He poked Jandak with the tip of his sword and the unsuspecting soldier was swallowed up in a cloud of gas more powerful than the paralyzing powder of Melchior.

"Is this Antigone's tent?" asked Esau.

One soldier stepped forward. "Yes it is."

"Do you hear him asking to stop us from leaving?"

The soldiers all shook their heads, 'No.'

Of course, half the people inside the tent, including Uzziah, had been knocked senseless by the camel stampede. Antigone however, still sat frozen on his pile of pillows. Esau glancing over at the collapsed tent saw the tips of several spears poking through the top of the tent just about where Antigone's seat would be located. His frozen body draped by the tent created a creepy canvas outline as the sun glinted off the tips of the spears. He knew time was running out.

"Tell Antigone that these evil foreign tent makers will not go unpunished!" yelled Esau, "Tell him the Trampling Troubadours said so."

The three of them turned their camels and quickly rode out of camp. They kept riding until they were a safe distance from the bedlam they had left behind. Naomi pulled her camel to a halt. Joab and Esau stopped and turned to face her.

"Alright Esau," said Naomi, "You have some serious explaining to do and I'm not going anywhere until I hear everything."

"Yes, I do owe you an explanation, but I am afraid it will have to wait." Esau pointed southward.

He said nothing else. He didn't have to. Coming across the horizon was a roiling, boiling wall of sand. It was no dust devil. It was a full-fledged man and beast killing sandstorm.

"We have to try and make it past the leading edge," said Esau. "It is our only hope. We cannot go back to the camp."

Esau knew stealing was wrong but if he had not 'traded' Jezebel for one of Antigone's camels he would have no chance of making it safely past the oncoming sand storm. All three of them wrapped their shemaghs and tunics around their mouths and noses and pushed their camels into a full run. Jandak took a clear lead and Esau could tell by the way he was running even Jandak sensed the coming doom. Jandak widened his lead and the other camels were spurred hard to keep up.

The sand storm was closing in on them but Esau did his best to keep his eyes fixed on Jandak and ignore the shrieking, wailing, wall of sand. Every stride took them one step closer to safety and the oasis.

Joab looked to his left into the heart of the storm. Like an angry child playing in a sandbox the storm picked up everything, looked at it briefly and then threw it back down. He could hear the roar and the swirling sand slashing toward them. He turned away from the storm and focused on his camel and the safety of the horizon just ahead.

The camels were being pushed harder than they had ever run in their lives with each rider lost in their own thoughts. They all gulped for air in deep breaths as they watched the towering wall of sandy death march closer and closer to them.

It was a sudden jolt unlike anything Naomi had ever experienced. At first, she thought her camel had run blindly into a tree, but he had not. The storm had hit her and her camel from the side and she was now in the full grasp of it, lost and tumbling inside the lashing, endless wall of sand.

With all of the tremendous commotion no one could see or hear what was happening to the others. So, Joab and Esau went on with heads down spurring their camels into a frenzied run. Suddenly, they were into and through a small swirling cloud of sand. The noise of the storm began to abate and they knew they had made it past the leading edge of the storm. Joab pulled his camel up next to Esau.

"I have never seen a sand storm such as that," said Joab

"Neither have I," said Esau "Have you, Naomi?"

There was no answer and they both turned around only to see the storm pushing its way across the desert floor.

Esau knew what he had to do and did not hesitate. He pulled a rope from his camel and tossed it to Joab.

"Pull any rope you have from your camel. Tie it to mine. I am going to get Naomi."

"But you cannot go in there," protested Joab.

"Wrong. Both of us cannot go. One of us must stay here and keep the rope taught." Then he turned and spurred Jandak directly into the storm.

Esau and Joab both knew the odds of a person surviving a storm like this were small but they both knew one of them had to go back into the storm. It was the only chance Naomi had. A sandstorm this huge would kill anyone trapped in it within a matter of moments.

Naomi could hear nothing but the storm. She had only a few precious moments before it would fill her mouth and eyes with sand and she would suffocate. She also understood that panic would do her no good so she gathered her garments about her as best she could and prayed.

Esau strained to stay aboard Jandak and keep both of them upright. Each step Jandak took was tricky. Either an unseen sheet of sand was trying to topple them or a blast of hot air was certain to blow them off their feet. Esau had no idea as he squinted into the constant sand pelting him how he would ever see anything in the midst of the maelstrom.

Shimmering and sparkling intermittently in the sand just ahead of him was the tiara they had given Naomi as part of her disguise. He saw a sand drift piling up against a large animal and he knew it was Naomi's camel. He had found her!

Naomi did not see or hear anything but she felt her body being lifted off the ground. The two arms firmly gripping her waist assured her it was not the storm which held her. Esau untied the rope from his waist and tied it around Naomi, then he pulled hard on it.

Joab felt the tug and began reeling in the rope, hoping beyond hope that somehow both of them would be at the end of it.

Esau squinted as Naomi disappeared from sight and now he knew he was the one needing to be rescued. He grabbed the reins of Naomi's camel and he climbed aboard Jandak hoping the world's fastest camel was also the strongest and could weather this storm long enough for them to survive.

Jandak didn't wait for any goading from Esau. His instincts were strong and he knew they had to escape the swirling sand quickly. Jandak bolted ahead. Esau hunkered down, pulled his tunic over his mouth and nose, and then held on tight.

When they finally stumbled out of the storm, it was amazing how quiet and calm the desert appeared. It would have remained so except for the yelp Naomi released when she saw Esau and the two camels stagger out of the storm and collapse onto the sand.

Chapter 15
The Destroyer

Without knowing it, the Traveling Troubadours had just escaped the deadliest storm anyone in the land had ever witnessed. Oh, the people of Najaf would remember this storm for a very long time. Only certain storms get names, special storms, deadly storms. The people of Najaf would call it "The Destroyer". It was one more reason for the decline that befell the once great city.

After the storm passed by Najaf a search party was sent out to see if the army had been spared. It had not. Ten thousand men from the army disappeared. From that day on when the wind blew through Najaf and the surrounding area, it had a sad wailing sound no one remembered hearing before.

Some believed the storm was strong enough that it separated the spirits from the physical bodies of those ten thousand men. The wailing was the sound of those spirits looking for their bodies, which were never found.

Everyone in the colony was safe. The Destroyer passed over the former leper colony just like the thousand other storms before had come and gone.

Finally, all three Troubadours sighed in unison. They were saved by Jandak and the storm. None of the Traveling Troubadours knew how deadly it was, but they hoped it would keep King Mamre and his army at bay. Hopefully, no one would be able to follow them or see them make a turn away from Najaf and toward the oasis.

Joab pulled his camel around next to Esau. "We are not far from the oasis. Given the direction the storm is moving it is likely to have been spared the wrath of it. You still have a great deal of explaining to do." It was the last word spoken between the three travelers that day.

The camp site that night was minimal. No fires were allowed in case someone had managed to escape the storm and was following them, but the real topic of conversation waited in the wings. Naomi and Joab could not think of any possible excuse Esau had for almost getting them all killed.

"Alright," said Joab, "I've waited long enough. What on earth were you thinking back at Antigone's party?"

"I hate to say this," began Esau, "but if I hadn't interrupted the evening we would have been swept up in the sand storm."

"Oh, surely you don't expect us to believe you knew the storm was coming?" asked Joab.

"No, you are right. I did not, but what I did see made me realize we were not going to be allowed to just walk out of there after our performance."

Esau had their attention so he continued. "Did either of you notice Antigone's right hand when we entered the tent?" Neither of them answered. "Antigone had two rings on one finger of his right hand. When he pointed at Naomi and said he wanted to see her, he placed an additional ring on that same finger. There were two women with Antigone at the start of the evening."

"And?" said Joab.

"Antigone was planning on making Naomi number three. It is a custom in Mesopotamia for the king to wear one golden ring for each woman he plans to take with him wherever he goes. I believe Antigone planned on taking Naomi. Do you remember when I threw the two daggers and two torches at you when you were juggling?"

"Is that a trick question?" asked Joab.

Esau ignored the sarcasm.

"Right after that I asked Antigone if I could use his sash for a magic trick. I swiped this note from where Antigone was sitting." Esau threw the note to Naomi. "Read it out loud for Joab."

Naomi unfolded the small parchment and read.

"Kill the two buffoons and bring the girl to me."

She dropped the note onto the ground and began to weep. Joab scooped it up and read the note silently several times.

"Why are you crying, Naomi?" asked Esau.

"I don't understand. Am I so beautiful someone would kill to have me?" She paused for a moment. "I wish I had leprosy again. At the colony people would talk to me because I was Naomi. They had to look past my exterior and see me for who I really am. Even Melchior looks at me differently now the leprosy is gone. We used to just sit and talk and have such a wonderful time. I miss those times. I want him to look at me and talk with me like he did when I had leprosy."

"I cannot think of a better way to say it," said Esau. "And tomorrow you will have the chance to tell him yourself."

Joab and Esau both now understood why Naomi was afraid of seeing Melchior again, Naomi knew she had to tell him the truth. She had finally verbalized it herself and slept better that night than she had in a long time.

Joab and Esau were up early. They scanned the horizon and saw no signs of any significant troop movements or even a small caravan. The brown of the desert on the horizon met the blue of the sky. The sun was just coming up and revealing an unending sea of dunes. The small fire they started left a wisp of smoke, and from Joab's vantage point the smoke appeared to be the only cloud in the sky.

The smell of breakfast startled Naomi and she awoke in a panic. For a few seconds she imagined she was back in Antigone's tent and had not escaped. She quickly dressed and stepped outside into the morning sun.

"Well, well, well. Looks like something finally woke up the sleeping princess," said Esau, "We were about to leave a note for any passing caravan to take you with them." Esau winked at Joab and for the first time since they had begun this ruse and journey they both laughed.

"Ha, ha," said Naomi, "I would be better off with a strange caravan than I would be with the two desert rats I have now."

"Oh, she must have some rats in her tent. She couldn't possibly be referring to us, could she?" teased Joab.

"Perhaps she will change her mind once she sees the nice cache of meats, breads and wine our wonderful friend and host Antigone has shared with us." Joab got up and spread a rug out onto the sand so Naomi could have a place to sit.

"Yes," said Esau, "I didn't want to do it, but if I hadn't traded old Jezebel for Antigone's camel, one of us would not have made it past the sandstorm."

"How do you know it was Antigone's camel?" asked Naomi.

"Oh, the nameplate on the camel was the first clue." Esau got up and walked over to a small stash of miscellaneous satchels, bags and pouches. "And this was a pretty good clue too." He pushed a few things around in the pile and pulled up a scabbard holding a sword.

Even from where she was sitting Naomi could see the lion's golden head at the hilt of the sword. Two silver and gold scorpions sat on the pommel with their tails and stingers curled in towards the blade. Esau pulled the sword out and the sun reflected off the blade, onto the sand, making the sand shimmer like a million tiny diamonds.

This sword was clearly a spectacular weapon of death. In Antigone's hands who knew how many lives it had taken. It was so stunning and magnificent Naomi wanted to touch and feel it. As she got closer she could see it was encrusted with diamonds and rubies. She put her hand on the blade. Up close it was even more astonishing. It made Naomi think of warriors, battles and men. She saw the sword in Melchior's hand. He looked so strong and courageous and powerful. She thoroughly blushed.

"Did you get a little too much sun yesterday?" Esau slipped the sword back into the scabbard and looked at Naomi's face still red from her fantasy.

"I, uhhh, it sure is hot out today isn't it?" She fumbled with her clothing trying to cover her face.

"What did you say? It's hot outside today? It is the desert you know," said Joab.

"I don't think it is the desert which has reddened her cheeks." Esau winked at Joab.

Naomi turned away from them both, mumbled something about how they needed to get going and stepped back into her tent.

"What is wrong with me?" she said to herself.

Everything was suddenly coming up Melchior. The conversation at Antigone's camp, her oversleeping this morning, the sword, the blushing...

She was reeling inside and she wanted it to stop. She was Naomi, not some twelve-year-old school girl with butterflies in her stomach! She had been around Melchior for ten years and never felt this way. She did like him. He was always kind to her and listened to her ranting and non-stop stories about her former life. He had been her friend in the leper colony. Yet, nothing had ever happened between the two of them besides friendship.

The leprosy had always kept Melchior at a comfortable distance. When they both had the disease they knew they could never have a life together. They would never be married or have children. No one could as long as they remained in the leper colony. Now the leprosy was gone, and like a broken dam her heart was crumbling, releasing a river of life and love that had been pent up for so long.

"What if he doesn't want me?" she said quietly. "What if we can't talk like we used to? What if he never returns from the trip to Jerusalem?"

It was a long ride that day for Naomi all the way to the oasis.

Joab stood up on the hump of his camel and peered over the dune. Some scrub brush growing at the top of the dune obscured him from being seen, so he took out his magnifying lens and held it up for a better view. He scanned the horizon for signs of the oasis. Any sign at all. There it was. With his lens he could just make out the top of some Acacia trees and perhaps a Joshua tree as well. That had to be the oasis.

"There it is, just to the east," said Joab, "Couldn't be more than a couple of hours. I can't see the water or the entire oasis but it appears to be empty for now."

"Onward and upward we go, The Trekking Troubadours," said Esau.

All three of them headed their camels toward the oasis and the end of their adventure.

"Another couple of hours," Naomi muttered under her breath.

She knew she had to face Melchior so she began mulling over in her mind how she would start the conversation.

"Hello Melchior, we need to talk." No that sounded too ominous.

"Hi Melchi, you look fabulous." Melchi, a pet name? No. "You look fabulous?" Definitely not.

"Hi Melchior. I want you to look at me and tell me what you see." Naomi thought hard.

She looked horrible after all the things they had been through. Her hair resembled tumbleweed. Her clothing from head to toe was dirty and torn. Everything was filthy and there were several holes in her shawl.

"What will he see?" she said "A mess I'm afraid."

The camels paused at the top of the rise. The oasis was still there. Only a couple of desert gypsies were at the water's edge. Joab looked around and spotted a place to tie up the camels. There was an Acacia tree right by the water's edge. The camels could rest there and have plenty to drink. "There are a couple of gypsies but they should not bother us. They are across the oasis from where we will set up camp. The tunnel entrance should be right behind that row of scrub brush and rocks over there." Joab dismounted and walked his camel over to a tree and tied the camel to it. Esau and Naomi followed suit.

"Well, I hate to admit it," said Esau, "but I am kind of sorry our adventure is over. I thought it was exciting."

"Exciting?" Naomi stormed over to where Esau was standing. "You almost got us all killed at least six times. You call that exciting?"

"Well, yes. Yes I do." Esau looked at her seriously. "After ten years in that stinking leper colony... My life has been given back to me and I am going to live every minute of it." Esau turned toward the scrub brush. "So, in a way, I do wish our adventure could continue. Now, let's set up the tent and find the entrance to the cave."

Joab, Naomi and Esau each took a six foot long bamboo rod and began poking the sand near the rocks and scrub brush. It was taking longer than any of them thought it would. It was Esau who finally hit something besides sand. He pulled back on his bamboo pole slowly and then quickly jammed it as far into the sand as he could. He had definitely hit something.

"Joab, Naomi. I think I found it."

"That's great," said Joab "but I'm afraid it will have to wait. It appears you have gotten your wish. Our adventure is not over yet."

It was true. The couple of desert gypsies they had seen must have been a scouting party. They had been joined by an army of gypsies while the three of them had been distracted, searching for the cave door.

Chapter 16
The Blade of Nineveh

"Well, Naomi," said Esau "The Traveling Touring Doors may have to do some more entertaining. We have guests."

Esau left his pole in the sand and started walking over to the gypsy camp.

"You can't just go into their camp." Naomi pulled on Esau's tunic. "They might not be friendly."

"Well, we can't dig right out here in front of them," said Esau "If they see us digging over here what do you suppose they will think we are digging for? Sand? Hmmm. I doubt it. It looks very suspicious and gypsies don't like suspicion."

Esau stood still for a moment thinking. "Let's put our tent up over the cave entrance. Then we'll cut a hole in the bottom of the tent and dig down to the cave door out of sight."

The tent work was monotonous, but it occupied their time. Esau paced more than he worked. He knew he had to make the first move if he were to keep the suspicion level at a minimum. He walked over to Naomi and Joab.

"I am going over to their camp," Esau said "I don't want them coming here. It's too risky. The best thing to do is to meet them on their side of the oasis."

Naomi and Joab knew it was useless to try and stop him. They watched as he trekked down the dune and around the water toward the gypsy camp.

Esau walked as confidently as he could toward the gypsies. He decided his best tactic would be to maintain the Traveling Troubadours disguise. Even a roving band of gypsies could appreciate some entertainment. The gypsies had several camels tied to a Joshua tree and a few more were already drinking at the edge of the water.

There are too many to fight our way out, thought Esau. Let's hope we have a second act left in us.

Esau headed for the largest tent thinking it would be the leaders. Up close he could tell they had been traveling long and hard; so hopefully they wouldn't be in the mood for a fight of any kind. Esau spotted a burly guard standing at the entrance. Esau ignored the guard and tried entering the tent directly.

"No one walks into Akbar's tent without permission," said the guard drawing his sword.

"Of course not," said Esau, backing up a few steps. "At least not without a gift." Esau pushed the guards' sword away from his neck. "Check your right pocket."

The guard sheathed his sword and stuck his big stubby hand into his pocket. The surprised look on his face told Esau exactly what he wanted to know.

"Pull it out. Come on. Show it to me."

The guard slowly pulled his clenched fist from his pocket. An empty toothless grin crossed his face.

"Well, open your hand. Let me see what you've got there."

The guard opened his hand and a gold coin lay in the middle of his palm.

"Now how did that get there?" Esau winked at the still smiling guard "Well, let's not keep Akbar waiting."

The guard pulled back the flap of the tent and they went inside. From across the oasis Naomi and Joab watched Esau disappear into the tent opening.

"I hate it when he's out of sight. I want to know what's going on inside that tent," said Joab.

"Let's finish setting up our tent. If he's not back by the time we're done... I don't trust him in that tent by himself either."

Naomi stooped down onto the sand as Joab swung the mallet toward the stake she was holding.

Esau was surprised by the interior of the gypsy tent. There was a great deal of activity still going on, but he mentally noted the gypsies had exotic taste. He followed the guard through a gauntlet of gypsy servants, soldiers and even a sword swallower. The floor of the tent was covered in camel hair and all kinds of animal rugs. There were glimmers of gold mugs and silver candle holders. Mugs sitting out in the open were made of bone and tusks set in bases of brass and silver. Pitchers of water and wine were set on a table with four ivory tusks as legs. Several people wearing animal skins and leather sandals put meats, bread and the rarest of sightings in the desert, fruit on wooden trays among the pillows and rugs.

Esau knew it was Akbar before the guard said anything. Much like Antigone, he sat on his throne and was surrounded by at least a dozen women. On the periphery were five or six guards with the largest swords Esau had ever seen. Instinctively he rubbed his neck, said a quick prayer and pushed his way past his escort.

"Ahhh, this must be the desert king I have heard so much about. King Akbar," said Esau while performing a deep bow.

Akbar was no king but he suddenly adopted the demeanor of one. In his own way, maybe he was a king. It was about time someone recognized that fact. Akbar liked this man very much. Here was someone who could spot the potential in people. Akbar took a deep breath and with a dramatic flair motioned for Esau to rise.

"You may kiss my ring," said Akbar.

Esau stood up and leaned into Akbar to kiss his ring. He had won the battle of the mind. It was amazing how just the smallest amount of flattery worked so well, especially on arrogant, insecure men like Akbar. It wasn't hard to see: the over indulgence, the false air of importance while so many in the camp were living in tattered clothes and tents not fit for a desert rat.

Looking around, Esau knew what the gypsies were after. The sandstorm was enormous and it must have been seen for miles in every direction. Akbar was scurrying across the desert and sifting through the aftermath.

Like a vulture of the desert Akbar was following along behind the storm and picking through the debris of the dead and dying. It was evident from the flamboyant but mismatched furnishings that Akbar made a pretty good living being a desert vulture. For now though, Esau would have to call him king.

"Allow me to introduce myself. I am Esau of the Traveling Troubadours."

"Esau, you say," Akbar sat down on his throne "I saw your camp across the way. Only three of you?" Akbar paused baiting the trap.

"Oh yes, there are only three of us. I am here with my sister and my brother. We sing and perform magic."

"Perhaps you can entertain us tonight," said Akbar.

Immediately, Esau realized the mistake he had made. Akbar knew there were only three of them now and if Akbar wanted to he could easily overpower them, take what they had and continue his desert looting spree. Esau had to think of something to give Akbar a reason to leave them alone.

"We can certainly entertain, but I know how we can be of even greater service to you."

"You do?"

"I know why you have traveled so far and fast. You are here to pick up what the great sandstorm has left behind. What used to belong to King Mamre will now belong to King Akbar."

This caught Akbar off guard. Esau was obviously an observant and astute man. Akbar relaxed and leaned back into his throne trying to look nonplussed by this revelation.

"You can help me? How?"

"Let us ride onto Najaf in peace. We will tell King Mamre that a great army is gathering for an attack. He has already suffered one disaster. He will not be in the mood for a battle. He will pull all his troops back to Najaf. This will give you the time you need to pick through what the storm has left behind. By the time King Mamre realizes there is no army, we will be gone and so will you."

"Why are you helping me?" asked Akbar.

"We only want to be your willing servants and treat…" Esau was cut off in mid-sentence.

Naomi rushed inside the tent. She had heard enough.

"We will not be his servants or his slaves or his anything. I knew you were in here selling us out again. Always looking to save your own skin and put mine and Joab's in jeopardy. Well, not this time."

Joab stepped into the tent and stood behind Naomi. He pulled the sword they had taken from Antigone's camel out of the scabbard. The tent went absolutely silent and still. Akbar didn't know what to make of the situation until he fixed his gaze on the sword Joab was wielding.

The legendary Blade of Nineveh! Akbar mentally documented its features: the two scorpions at the pommel, the lion's head on the hilt, the uncompromised and brilliantly shining blade. Through some miracle it had just walked right into his tent.

The stories of the blade were legion. In one battle alone the scorpions on the sword were said to have come to life, and for every person the blade killed, the scorpions killed two more. Akbar knew the stories but he could not believe his eyes. Now the sword was only a few feet from him. The Blade of Nineveh had been rumored to be in the hands of King Mamre, but now here it was. He could not only see it, he could touch it, hold it, possess it.

Akbar's eyes locked onto the sword; nothing else in the room mattered. He walked slowly toward Joab with a wicked and crooked smile on his face. Akbar drew a circle in the air with his right hand and four guards stepped in behind Joab blocking the only exit. Two more forced Esau to the ground and tied his hands behind his back.

No one touched Naomi and she scoured the tent looking for a way out. She was just now realizing the gravity of their situation. Akbar walked past Naomi. For the first time since the disappearance of the leprosy something else was more attractive to a man than her.

Power. The Blade of Nineveh represented it in all its glory. It was the allure of the blade and its legendary power that commanded Akbar's gaze. Power for most men, some would say especially evil men, is more enticing than any woman.

Joab glanced about the room and understood immediately the futility of fighting his way out. Esau was bound and Naomi was trapped inside the tent too. He could see no avenue of escape. So, he did nothing as Akbar came closer and closer to him. Akbar reached out and touched the blade. The Blade of Nineveh. Every fiber of Joab's being screamed inside, *Strike him down. Kill him where he stands,* but he knew that it would only lead to him and Naomi and Esau being taken prisoner or killed. He knew too that it would end any chance the Wise Men would have of completing their journey. He was going to have to wait and see what Akbar would do next.

Akbar gripped the blade tighter and tighter. Joab could see him close his eyes and he watched as Akbar's breathing became trancelike, heavy and deep. A small trickle of blood rolled down the blade and pooled at the feet of the scorpions. Akbar's other hand slipped over Joab's hand as they both gripped the hilt of the sword. Joab's mind became filled with a blackness that took his breath away. The bleak colors of moaning and crying and pain swirled around in his mind. The coldness of death filled him. The room disappeared and Joab sensed something moving through the tent.

He had never even dreamed about the realm of death, but what he saw now must be the spirit of death. It absorbed all color and feeling and space as it passed by him. It moved in the darkness effortlessly closer to Akbar and the blade. Death reached out and touched the trickle of blood on the blade. He laughed and with a wave of his bony hands summoned the three great cohorts of death—Sorrow, Grief and Pain. They all slowly circled Akbar and Joab; then one by one the blade absorbed them. Joab screamed and fell to the ground. He writhed and twisted and shook so hard Naomi thought he might be dying. His skin shriveled and his hair went gray. He lay on the floor twitching and mumbling incoherently.

Naomi knew something terrible and unspeakable had just happened. She had seen nothing but had felt a coldness brush by her. She knelt beside Joab sobbing and begging him to stop shaking. Then she looked up at Akbar. The blade was having the opposite effect on him. It was invigorating him and making him stronger. Akbar turned toward Naomi gazing at her and through her. The air around him became cold and his eyes turned solid black.

The Blade of Nineveh had gone through a metamorphosis, too. It was no longer silver but black as obsidian formed at the base of a volcano. Whenever the sword cut through the air a trail of frozen particles and black smoke followed. Akbar moved the blade in front of his face peering into its black heart of cold and evil. The scorpions surrounding the pommel began to move. Their poisonous tails flicked in and out flexing, ready to do battle. They both struck Akbar's hand at the same time but rather than causing him pain, it made him laugh. He lifted the sword high above his head and blood from the scorpion stings ran down his arm leaving a trail of black dried blood behind.

The Blade of Nineveh had been reborn! For years the whispers of its power and strength had faded into legend and myth, but the blade had merely been waiting for the right heart. A heart deep enough and black enough that it could absorb all the evil and power the blade had to offer. It had finally found that heart in Akbar. Just as there are weapons of good in the world waiting for the right person to grasp and wield them for a righteous cause, there are powers of evil waiting for their own opportunity to spew hatred and bitterness and death. It was the Blade of Nineveh that consumed Akbar, and for the moment the Blade and evil would rule the day.

No one moved. Everyone in the tent knew the world had irrevocably changed. Akbar licked his lips and turned toward Esau.

Akbar spoke but now his voice was different. "You have lied to me."

His tongue had changed; it was thicker and gray. It caused him to speak in low forceful tones.

"You have been to Najaf. You have seen King Mamre or you have killed him." Akbar paced in front of his throne. "It has long been rumored King Mamre had possession of the Blade of Nineveh, but somehow it ends up in your hands? I am most grateful, but tell me why I shouldn't just kill you right now."

Akbar waved the sword in front of Esau; the tails of the scorpions flicking just beyond the reach of Esau's face.

"Yes. I have been to Najaf and seen King Mamre. I am his son. He gave us the sword to take for protection."

"You are lying again," said Akbar.

The blade had taken Akbar's mind and made it wiser in the ways of deceit. He signaled for one of his guards to come forward.

Esau was improvising now. "We are late getting to Najaf and King Mamre will have sent out his army to find us and escort us to Najaf. They will come to this oasis looking for us. They should be here in less than two days."

Akbar sensed it was all a lie but needed time to think and understand the Blade of Nineveh and its abilities. He would give them some time. He could wait two days to kill them.

"Send out scouts in every direction and we will see if he is telling the truth. Tell them to be back here in two days." Akbar went over to his throne and sat down.

"Take them to their tent and put up a guard. We will see if this army appears or not. If it does then we shall use them as hostages. If it does not then we shall use them to test the power of the Blade of Nineveh!"

Akbar thrust the sword above his head and the tent broke out with a roar of approval.

Naomi, Esau and Joab were taken back to their tent on the other side of the oasis and unceremoniously thrown inside. A guard posted outside paced back and forth. His shadow thrown up against the canvas of the tent was the only clue he was there. Joab had returned somewhat to normal but now had a distinct streak of gray hair running right down the center of his head. His skin color had returned to its dark tones and he had stopped shaking.

"Maybe we should have named ourselves the Troubled Troubadours," said Joab. "We have been in trouble from the moment we left the colony."

Joab was racked by another twitching spell.

"Joab, what happened when Akbar grabbed the blade?" asked Esau.

"I saw the spirit of death and three tormentors." For a moment the sadness returned to him and he shuddered. "I do not care to see it again."

Naomi turned her attention to Esau. "What on earth are you doing telling Akbar that an army is coming to rescue us?"

"I said that because we need time. Akbar has given it to us. I may just have a plan that will allow the Wise Men to be on their way and save us too." Esau pulled Naomi and Joab toward the center of the tent. "It's sort of crazy."

"Oh really?" teased Joab. "I was hoping for brilliant."

"Let's get inside the caves and I'll explain everything then." Esau began digging in the sand with his hands. Naomi and Joab plopped down beside him and began digging in earnest.

It only took a couple of hours to reach the wooden door that would open into the cave at the back of the colony. Balthazar, Gaspar, and Melchior were waiting on the other side.

Esau and Joab were excited to finally be back at the colony, but Naomi was more anxious than excited. What was she going to say to Melchior? She stood with her hand inches from the cave door but she could not bring herself to knock. Either heartbreak or love stood on the other side. In a way, the limbo she was in now was worse than the answer she dreaded. She mustered what courage she could and knocked on the thick wooden door.

"Quiet. I heard something from the outside," said Gaspar, "Everyone line up down the wall on both sides."

The entire colony had decided to make the trip to the cave entrance. The Three Wise Men had initially objected but were overruled by the colony's unanimous vote to escort them to the end of the cave and welcome home the heroes from the colony. It had been Houlak's idea to make the tunnel into a welcome home party. She believed the Troubadours would be successful and they would be warmed by the appearance of the entire colony waiting for them. After all, the colony had become more of a home than a prison since the disappearance of the leprosy.

Chapter 17
The Brewing Battle

"Shhh," scolded Gaspar, "Quiet."

A second knock. Gaspar fumbled with the latch. Initially the door was stuck, but with a heave it swung slightly downward into the tunnel. A brief burst of hot desert air blasted Gaspar's face bringing with it a light shower of sand. Gaspar reached up past the door and helped Naomi down into the tunnel. She landed gently onto her feet. In the shifting light it took her a moment to realize the entire colony was lined along the tunnel on both sides of the wall as far as she could see. It made her smile. This was her family and she was finally home. Joab and Esau were quickly lowered into the tunnel and the door was sealed back into place.

"Thank you Gaspar and Balthazar and… Where is Melchior?" Naomi asked as nonchalantly as she could.

Naomi was through fretting and worrying about what Melchior might think of her. Even if he wasn't interested in her, she could at least be rid of the sleepless nights and the worry.

"Has anyone seen Melchior?" Several laughs were heard. Confused, Naomi walked further into the tunnel. "What's so funny?"

A woman walked up behind Naomi and tapped her on the shoulder. Naomi turned to face her. She couldn't tell who it was behind the veil. In fact, since everyone had been healed, it was hard to recognize anyone even if they weren't wearing a veil.

"What interests you about Melchior?" the woman said.

Naomi stared harder at the woman and cocked her head from side to side. There was something odd about this woman but Naomi couldn't quite place what it was.

"I would like to tell him something…" Naomi looked up and down the hall, "in private."

"Well, you can see we have nothing available in private but if you whisper it to me I will carry the message to him in person."

"Why can't I tell him myself?" pleaded Naomi.

"He is back at the colony a half days walk from here. You are needed right here. I will relay the message to him and bring him back myself."

Naomi stepped back and thought for a moment. Even this woman's voice sounded familiar, almost like her own but slightly huskier. Naomi finally gave in. She could wait one more day to hear from Melchior. She leaned into the woman and whispered in her ear. The woman nodded her head turned away from Naomi and stepped out into the hall.

"Has anyone seen Melchior?" the woman asked. Silence. "Anyone?"

"Hey, wait, I thought you said he wasn't here. I don't want the whole colony to know. I thought you knew where he was. I'll find him myself." Naomi turned to continue her search for Melchior but the woman grabbed her arm so firmly it startled her. "Who are you? And why won't you let me find him?"

Melchior smiled broadly beneath his veil and just stared at Naomi. She was beautiful; he could not deny it and he couldn't hide from her any longer. He slowly removed the veil revealing a handsome and clean shaven face.

"Yes," was all he said.

Then he kissed her, brought her close to him, and blocked out the rest of the world. They held each other in the privacy that only love can bring to two people in a dark crowded tunnel.

"Melchior. Melchior."

A faraway voice was calling Melchior out of his private world but he did not want to leave. He and Naomi separated and lingered for a moment.

"Melchior." The voice belonged to Balthazar and it sounded urgent. "So this is what's been wrong with you."

Balthazar shook Melchior just to make sure he didn't slip away again. "Ever since she left you haven't been worth two shekels of lead."

Balthazar grabbed Melchior by the shoulders and led him to the end of the tunnel. The Traveling Troubadours and Gaspar were at the center of a crowd waiting impatiently for Melchior and Balthazar to join them.

"Here we are," announced Balthazar "Melchior had some unfinished business."

"Has he been too close to a torch?" asked Joab, "His face sure is red."

"Oh he's been near a flame alright, just not that kind of flame," said Balthazar "Esau, tell Melchior about this blade. I have never heard of it."

Esau cleared his throat and began.

"I will keep this as short as possible. We ran into a bit of a problem with Antigone, the leader of King Mamre's Army. We traded old Jezebel for Antigone's personal camel. We were in a little bit of a hurry and I couldn't find Jezebel. On the camel we took from Antigone was a sword."

Esau looked at Melchior.

"Neither Joab, Naomi or I had ever heard of it, but it is filled with a great and evil power. You can still see the streak of gray in Joab's hair just from touching it. Akbar, a gypsy who is encamped just across the oasis from us has the sword. He called it the Blade of Nineveh."

Melchior grabbed Esau by the shoulders. "What did you say? The Blade of Nineveh?"

"Yes. Yes. The Blade of Nineveh."

"Well, that's alright. I know a great deal about the Blade of Nineveh. No one has tapped into its power in all the years King Mamre has possessed it. I secured it for King Mamre and mounted it in his throne room. It has hung there well before I was cursed with leprosy only because he could not tap into its power himself." Melchior released his grip on Esau. "I cannot believe King Mamre let it out of his sight. He knows the power it possesses. He must want to kill us very badly."

Melchior stepped back still gazing at Esau. "Everything is fine as long as Akbar has not discovered its power. I doubt he has for it would take a very dark heart to unleash all the evil lurking inside the blade."

Esau could not feel one muscle in his body. He stood as stiff as a stone statue but he somehow muttered, "How would we know if he has unleashed all of its power?"

Well," said Melchior, "You will know if its power has been fully tapped by two things. Here," Melchior pointed toward a stool for Esau, "sit down."

"I don't think I can." Esau was sweating even in the cool dampness of the cave.

"Just to be sure this is the Blade of Nineveh… Did it have two scorpions just above the hilt?

Esau could barely nod, "Yes."

"Were their tails curved in toward the blade?"

Joab looked at Melchior and said, "Their tails were pointed in toward the blade."

"That's the Blade of Nineveh alright," said Melchior "But the power of the blade is minimal unless the scorpions come to life."

Joab felt the tunnel begin to spin and he tried to stop it by spinning in the opposite direction. It didn't help. He ended up on the floor. Melchior looked at Esau but he had become catatonic, his body frozen in place. The only clue he was alive was the sweat which was now streaming off his face. Naomi forced her way to the center of the circle and stood in front of Melchior.

"Yes," she said with surprising confidence, "the scorpions came to life."

Melchior swallowed hard. "That's not the full power of the blade either. I'm certain of what happened next. The scorpions stung Akbar on the hand didn't they?"

"Yes. They stung Akbar on his hand," said Naomi.

"And now Akbar is dead. Right?"

"No. Akbar laughed and raised the sword over his head. The blade turned black and cold and a trail of smoke followed it as it cut a swath through the air. The blood from the cut he sustained turned black on his arm."

Melchior's hands began to shake. He looked nervously at Naomi. "No. No. No. Tell me it is not so."

"It is."

Melchior froze and his eyes became transfixed and unmoving. Balthazar and Gaspar held him. Something that put this much fear into Melchior must be terrible indeed. Balthazar spoke slowly and strongly to him. "Melchior, listen to me. What does this mean?"

"I have heard rumors of its power and I have read the legends and myths, but I never really thought the blade would find a chosen one."

Melchior looked sad and terrified at the same time. He continued, "I thought the blade would be safe with King Mamre. He could not tap into its power and he almost never let it out of his sight for fear a chosen one would find it and wield it someday against him."

Melchior moved away from Balthazar and Gaspar. With his shoulders down and his face staring at the floor he said, "The blade has chosen this Akbar and it means we will not be going anywhere. Once the blade has found a chosen one it will slowly consume that person's soul. Eventually, the wielder of the blade will be able to control the hearts and minds of men and convince them to do its bidding."

A murmur began in the small group and spread from one person to the next like a wild fire. The hall erupted in chaos and fear.

Esau finally escaped from his self-induced coma. "Quiet. Quiet!" He ran down the hall trying to calm the colony.

He finally found a ledge at the side of the cave. He climbed up on it and began to speak. "I have a plan. Please calm down and let me speak."

The hall quieted. The Three Wise Men and the Traveling Troubadours gathered in front of Esau.

"Yes, let him speak," said Balthazar.

Esau continued. "I know why Akbar is at the oasis. He is a vulture of the desert. Did you see the great sandstorm from a few days ago?"

Several people confirmed that it had passed by.

"Well, Akbar saw it too and he knows there will be many dead and dying left in its wake. The dead have no need of weapons or clothes or gold. Akbar is more than happy to relieve them of those things."

There were several gasps as people thought of the gypsies rummaging through and picking over the bodies of the deceased. "It is unfortunate Akbar knew about the Blade and now wields it, but do not give up hope. I told Akbar the army of King Mamre was coming back in two days. So, we have two days to make my plan work. It is good you all have come to welcome us home."

Someone in the hall yelled the question on everyone's mind. "Is King Mamre coming to kill you or all of us?"

Esau sat down on a ledge and motioned for the entire colony to sit as well. "Akbar does not know that King Mamre is not coming. He does not know how much King Mamre would like to see all of us dead. We will be the army of King Mamre."

One of the young men from the colony stood up to speak. "But we are not an army. We have no weapons, no shields, nothing."

"King Mamre will supply us with all our needs." Esau looked into the eyes of those closest to him, but none of them had caught on to his plan. "I told you Akbar has come to pick over the army of King Mamre. We will beat him to it. We must move quickly back to the colony and out into the desert where the army was. Each of us will grab a dead soldier's body, his sword, and shield and any other weapons we can carry. We will bring them back here and during the night two days from now we will station our army of the dead on the hills surrounding the oasis."

"That's crazy," shouted an old man "They'll spot it in a minute."

"We will station enough of us around with the bodies of the dead soldiers so there will be movement. Akbar doesn't have many men and they are not really fighters. They are scavengers. All we need to do is scare them off so the Wise Men can escape and continue their journey."

"It could work." Naomi stepped forward in front of Esau. "I have sensed the heart of Akbar's people. They only serve him out of fear. If we outnumber them they will back down."

Esau stood up next to Naomi. "That is the one weak link in my plan. I am uncertain how to deal with Akbar and the Blade of Nineveh. From what Melchior has said it can control the minds of those around it. Our plan may fail because of the power of the blade."

Melchior, sensing the strength of the others stepped forward to address everyone.

"I am afraid that no matter what happens tomorrow Akbar may choose to fight. He doesn't realize that the blade will begin to control him more and more. The choices he makes will eventually not be his own. This scavenger trip through King Mamre's former army has given me an idea for dealing with Akbar. As I recall, King Mamre had a Royal Guard and those men had shields made of pure silver. We will need those shields if we are to hold back Akbar and the Blade. I think six or so shields would do nicely. Look carefully as you scour the area."

Melchior stood up on a ledge cut in the side of the rock wall.

"Everyone, listen. We have two days to complete this plan. Bring back as many of the dead soldiers and their weapons as you can. Look for the silver shields of the Royal Guard. We have no time to waste. Everyone knows what to do."

"Why do we need these silver shields?" someone asked.

"The sun is our friend and slowly but surely it is becoming Akbar's enemy. The shields are very reflective and might be just the thing we need."

Melchior stepped down off the ledge and walked toward Balthazar.

"That was good leadership Melchior. I knew you would help come up with a plan," said Balthazar "Someone else has noticed, too."

Balthazar pointed over to Naomi, who was beaming at Melchior. Of course, Melchior was thinking the same thing about Naomi, and he was drawing strength and courage from her too.

"Well one part of the plan is in motion," said Gaspar, "Now let's hear how we can defeat Akbar and The Blade of Nineveh." The colonists began making the long trek back to begin scavenging. Left behind were the Three Wise Men and the Troubadours.

"I will need to study the history of the blade to be sure, but I am confident we can be on our way and escape Akbar too," said Melchior.

"Oh that's just grand," said Gaspar, "He's got to read up on how we are all going to die."

"I told you I am confident of my plan but there is one thing of which I must be certain before we proceed. Please be patient and trust me."

The next two days passed in a blur of soldiers, swords, and searching. Everyone was busy looking for the shields of the Royal Guard, combing over the sand for weapons, and dragging dead soldiers back into the tunnel. The colony and all its hopes were placed on the backs of men who could carry no weapon and lead no charge, but if all went well, this army of the dead would only have to make Akbar and his men blink and balk just long enough for the Wise Men to escape and give the colonists time to get back into the protection of the caves.

Melchior paced back and forth, mumbling and mouthing the plan over and over in his head. He knew now how flimsy it was but they had no other chance or choice if they were to defeat Akbar and the Blade. Everything hinged on their faith in each other.

"I have read of the blade, its origin, history and power. The wielder of the blade cannot be defeated."

"What do you mean? Akbar is invincible?" asked Balthazar.

"Well, no but we don't have the Sword of Light. It is the only blade ever mentioned that could possibly defeat the Blade of Nineveh." Melchior paused looking at his army of six. Gaspar, Balthazar, Joab, Esau, Naomi and himself. Melchior had been unable to persuade Naomi to let someone else take her place, and honestly Melchior realized they would need her determination, her sense of purpose and unyielding courage.

"I am afraid Akbar will want to fight and I want to prepare for that chance. The blade has one other physical side effect Akbar will begin to experience. Each day the blade makes the bearer more and more sensitive to light. The darkness at the center of the blade will continue to consume Akbar, making him less and less able to bear the sun. He is destined to living a life in total darkness. Akbar has had the blade with him for two days and he is not yet aware of this. The concentration of sunlight on him from the reflection of the silver shields will expose his inner darkness and..." Melchior knew what he had to say next was the hardest part of the plan.

"And, and what?" pleaded Naomi.

"The dark spirits inhabiting the blade and Akbar will fight back. The Blade of Nineveh will attempt to pierce our unity of purpose. Any doubt we have will fuel Akbar, and he will become stronger than he already is. Should he choose to fight, the reflection of the sun from the shields will keep Akbar at bay long enough for us to escape to the tunnels and the Wise Men to escape. If we are overcome, we will be bound to him and his darkness forever."

The word forever hung in the air and reverberated in the tunnel, washing over each of them again and again. No one said anything but each of them had one word on their minds: Forever.

Melchior continued.

"This will be our last night of sleep before facing Akbar. Remember, the spirits of the blade know your greatest weakness and they will attack it with a fury unlike any other you have ever faced. When the spirits come you must block them out. The faith we have in each other is the only weapon we have in the fight against Akbar without Sword of Light."

"This Sword of Light," said Balthazar. "Would it help? Where is it?"

"Yes, the Sword of light could defeat Akbar, but no one has seen it in centuries. Apparently, the Blade of Nineveh and the Blade of Light were once locked in a great struggle."

Melchior unrolled a scroll. "This scroll tells of a battle between an evil King, King Xon and a man named Horatio. At one point in the battle Horatio was wounded seriously by the Blade of Nineveh. This blow caused Horatio to drop the Sword of Light and fall upon the blade, killing him instantly. Some legends say that killing Horatio broke the swords spirit and it shattered into three pieces."

Melchior rolled up the parchment.

"No one has seen the Sword of Light or those three pieces since that day. Without it, we must avoid direct conflict with Akbar. For as long as he wields the Blade of Nineveh, he cannot be killed by any normal blade – only the Sword of Light.

I believe our army of dead soldiers will be enough to scare Akbar and the gypsies away."

The colony had already moved most of the phantom army out onto the dunes. Houlak reported everything was going according to plan. The torches in the tunnel reflected off the faces of the colonists and the dead soldiers, giving each person just enough light to tell the living from the dead. The few remaining colonists continued to grab dead soldiers, climb up into the tent above ground, and then out onto the dunes to deposit the soldiers around the perimeter of the oasis.

Of course, the sleeping powder Melchior had concocted helped immensely with the guard stationed at the front of their tent. With him out of the way, they had free reign of the desert as long as they kept quiet and low. Everywhere they could, they propped the bodies of the dead soldiers behind trees and on top of dunes and inside the scrub brush surrounding the entire oasis. At first glance it was quite an impressive army indeed.

The process took most of the night and just before daylight the only people left in the tunnel were the Wise Men and the Traveling Troubadours.

Chapter 18
The Sword of Light

"I must say one thing before we go," said Esau. "Today, we shall be the Truthful Troubadours and you three must be the unwavering Wise Men. If all should go as planned..." his voice trailed off as he thought about the Wise Men. "I know we may never see you again. Understand this, we feel a part of you in ways I cannot express. As you leave us, we will continue to travel with you here." He pointed to his heart and turned to prepare for the fight.

Melchior picked up his shield and cinched it tight to his arm. In its reflection, he saw Naomi securing a sword to her side, ready to go with them up into the tent to face the despair and darkness Akbar had undoubtedly prepared for them. Watching her, he knew how the demons and doubts would attack him and he hoped his love for her would help during the coming battle with Akbar.

"The army has arrived Akbar, just as they said it would."

Baal, Akbar's second in command burst into Akbar's chamber. Immediately, he realized his mistake and dropped to his knees.

"Oh mighty Akbar, I ask for your mercy. Do not punish me for arriving unannounced. I only wish to serve you."

Akbar did not even acknowledge Baal's existence. His eyes were rolled up into his skull and only the whites of his eyes were visible. He snapped out of his trance and hurried to the front of his tent. He parted the flap and the early morning sun caused him to blink more than usual. Akbar looked out and around the oasis. He closed the tent flap and returned to his throne. Stewing, he tried to think of a plan. But it was not

Akbar who saw through the false army of the colonists, it was the Blade of Nineveh.

The Blade of Nineveh used all its power to take over Akbar's mind but it wasn't concerned about the colonists and their army of dead soldiers. No. Deep down the Blade could sense the aura of the Sword of Light. It knew the sword was near but there was no one carrying the blade – at least not yet.

The Blade of Nineveh spoke through Akbar. "An army of wind and wishes is all they have. Baal, go and ask of them who their champion will be. I will fight their champion. Tell them if I defeat their champion they will become my slaves. If their champion should win then they may pass freely and go wherever they wish. I will give them one hour to crown a champion."

Baal faced Akbar and bowing low, backed out of the throne room. He walked around the oasis to the Troubadours tent. The guard was yawning and stretching when Baal arrived.

"Have you been sleeping?"

"No, of course not." The guard threw his head back and stared straight ahead.

"Then where did this army come from?"

The guard looked up into the dunes and said nothing.

"It is lucky for you that Akbar has seen through their ruse," Baal pointed toward the tent. "Are they still in there?"

The guard nodded and Baal asked from outside the tent. "Akbar has seen through your ruse and he wishes to know who your champion will be. Who will fight for you today? If Akbar defeats your champion then the matter will be settled. You will become his slaves. If he is defeated he will allow you to pass freely and go wherever you wish. You have one hour to decide."

Baal waited for an answer but was only greeted by the light desert wind whistling through the fabric of the tent.

"One hour," he said again for emphasis and then walked away.

Inside the tent the group sat numb and dumbfounded.

"We are doomed," said Melchior.

This was not how he had envisioned the day at all. None of them could stand against the Blade of Nineveh. Even if they could surround Akbar with the shields, they could not hold him back for long. Now they had totally lost control.

Melchior heard a voice in his head. "You are not in control here. I am." It was a low guttural voice and it took him by surprise. He did not know the voice but nonetheless, it frightened him.

"Akbar." Naomi, Esau, and Joab said in unison.

They had heard the same voice in their minds.

"Why won't he attack us?" asked Naomi.

The voice spoke again but singled out Melchior's mind this time. "Attack? And take a chance of having my future wife die in battle?"

Melchior looked at Naomi and knew she had not heard this latest voice. It was meant only for him. The voice sickened Melchior and he picked up the nearest sword and headed for the tent exit. Esau blocked his way.

"Who designated you as our champion? I didn't."

"You did not hear what he just said to me did you?"

"No, I did not," said Esau. "But I know we have to send a champion to fight for us and you won't be going."

Melchior drew his sword and pulled Esau's throat right up to the blade nicking Esau's neck and drawing blood.

"I go where I please and do what I like," said Melchior.

The Blade of Nineveh looked into Melchior's mind and saw the pure, raw rage mixing with jealousy. This pleased the blade a great deal.

Balthazar shoved his short fat body between them.

"Stop this. Stop it."

Balthazar forced the two men apart.

"Don't you see, Melchior? He is manipulating your mind just as you said he would. If you follow your initial impulses you are playing right into his hands. Remember, he cannot be killed by a normal blade."

Melchior and Esau sat down on opposite sides of the tent from each other. Esau dabbed at his wound and Melchior stared at the tent exit.

"Perhaps his power is growing even faster than we feared," said Gaspar. "He knows he cannot be defeated by any one of us."

Balthazar had reached his limit and he knew they only had one option left. He pulled up the sleeve of Joab's tunic.

"Joab, Esau, Naomi, look at your skin. You have all witnessed the orbs. Have you forgotten so quickly?"

"What good are three glass balls to us Balthazar?" asked Gaspar.

Balthazar pulled the leather satchel from around his neck and opened it to look inside. He gasped and jumped back from the satchel as it fell to the ground and the three orbs rolled out onto the sand.

The orbs were on fire. Multi-colored flames licked the air as the globes formed their familiar triangular pattern. The sand beneath the orbs began to bubble and boil and for a moment the orbs disappeared beneath the surface of the melting sand. Slowly, inexorably from the melting pool of sand an object began to rise. At first it was hard to describe, but as the crystal clear object floated higher and higher it was obvious a sword of some kind was being formed.

The flames from the orbs rose higher and higher but strangely they did not create any heat, just light. Finally, the formation of the sword was complete. Before them was the most magnificent, translucent blade any of them had ever seen. It slowly spun in place floating just above the burning, bubbling pool of sand.

Melchior said, "The Sword of Light. It does exist."

The orbs continued to flare up and the multiple colors of the flames reflected off the blade. It had the appearance of crystal and sometimes would appear invisible but then the flames would flare up briefly and the blade could clearly be seen. There was a bulb on the end of the hilt and inside this bulb was a tiny gold star rotating in the opposite direction of the blade. The star pulsed inside its glass home. The rest of the hilt and even the blade itself had the most intricate designs carved into it. To the casual viewer the sword appeared to be made from water as the intricate designs inside it shifted and changed like a flowing brook. It looked so frail compared to the Blade of Nineveh.

Esau reached out toward the sword, put his hand on the hilt, but could not pull it toward him. Joab and Esau exchanged perplexed glances and then Joab grabbed the blade. But he too, could not pull it from the center of the triangle formed by the burning globes. Balthazar and Gaspar also tried to lift or move the blade from the center of the flames but they could not claim the sword and possess it. Melchior hoped the answer of how to wield the blade was in the manuscripts somewhere.

Most scholars and historians had relegated the Sword of Light to the imagination of the past when men were less enlightened. It was rumored to have been present since time began. Some ancient legends believed the sun was spun from the tip of it in the first great clash of light and darkness at the beginning of the universe.

Melchior ran to his stash of scrolls tucked in the corner of the tent. He had brought the ancient archives concerning the Blade of Nineveh and he remembered the Sword of Light had been mentioned in the same set of scrolls.

"Here, here it is… umm. The Sword of Light is much like the Blade of Nineveh in historical significance, but unlike the Blade of Nineveh, the Sword of Light awaits the touch of someone…"

"It must be you Melchior. You are the only one who has not touched the blade. Go on. Try it," said Balthazar.

Melchior put down the parchment and walked over to the blade. It spun slowly in the air, levitating just above the globes which were still burning, their multi colored flames licking the tip of the crystal blade.

Melchior stared transfixed at the sword. Then he slowly reached for the hilt. Touching it he immediately felt a sense of peace and calm, but when he tried to draw the blade out of the center of the ring of fire, he could not.

"Melchior," said Balthazar "Finish reading what must be done to wield the Sword of Light. Maybe there is something else we have to do."

Melchior walked back to his scrolls and sat down to read some more.

"The wielder of the blade must have great courage and be driven by the purest sense of justice and mercy."

While all of the men had tried to wield The Sword of Light, Naomi had not. The men were all gathered around Melchior listening to the history of the sword and searching for a way to wield it and possibly use it against Akbar. Unseen, Naomi reached for the blade, grasped it and pulled it to her chest.

As fragile as Naomi and the blade both appeared to be, they were strengthened by each other and the courage, justice and mercy the sword craved.

Naomi's world exploded in a flash of light and it took her a moment to understand she was not blinded by the light but merely seeing the spirit of each man as well as their physical body. As she got used to her new sight, she could see the colors of their hurts and fears. The lighter and brighter colors of who their spirit desired to be mixed and mingled with the dark stains caused by fear and doubt and all the things holding each of them captive.

"There must be some spell or potion which will allow one of us to pull this sword from…" Melchior was the only one of the five men looking in the direction of Naomi. He watched as she pulled the sword toward her body and embraced it. He continued to stare with his mouth open as Naomi disappeared into the light of the sword. The rest of the Wise Men and the Troubadours turned just in time to see the light dissipate and

Naomi emerge. Melchior shook his head. This was not the same Naomi. If it were possible for her to be any more beautiful, she was.

Melchior kept staring at her. The sword's power had added something to her aura. At first, it appeared she was encased in glass but the glass moved with her. Armor. That's what it was. Armor so clear and light and fluid it appeared to be an extension of her body. She was completely clothed in white beneath this nearly invisible protective shell.

Balthazar finally stated what everyone knew by now. "Naomi is our champion."

Even though every fiber of his being screamed it could not be so, Melchior knew it was true. Naomi was their champion. All the men circled her staring and stunned, unsure of what to say or do. Naomi finally broke the silence.

"Tell Akbar we have our champion." The voice was Naomi's but the authority behind it came from a different place. Somewhere deep within the blade Naomi had seen the battle that rages between darkness and light. She knew a victory against Akbar was anything but certain, but she also knew she could not shirk from the coming fight.

The Sword of Light had chosen her because the time and place demanded it. She knew there was no other choice. She could not just sit idly by and let darkness rule the day when she had a chance to stop it.

Melchior raced from the tent across the oasis to deliver the message.

"Tell Akbar we have our champion. Tell him to meet us at the west end of the oasis."

Akbar heard Melchior outside his tent and from Melchior's thoughts he knew Naomi had been chosen as their champion.

"Letting a woman do your job." Akbar's thought forced its way into Melchior's mind and it hit him hard. He stumbled to his knees in the sand. Staggering and crawling he made his way back to the tent of the Troubadours and the Wise Men.

"I have told Akbar we will meet him at the west end of the oasis. Since the sun is setting, try and keep him facing the sun. It will be harder for him to fight." Melchior said as he opened the tent flap.

"Remember, Akbar will try and play mind games with us. We must all have absolute faith in Naomi, or it will go badly for her even with the Sword of Light. Do not look at Akbar. The slightest glance at him will offer the spirits of the Blade of Nineveh a chance to enter your mind. Only concentrate on Naomi and believe she can overcome him. Our belief in her will strengthen her armor and the sword. Take a shield of the Royal Guard with you."

Naomi stepped outside the tent; even in bright daylight she shone like a star in the night sky. She led the way down and around the oasis. Akbar stepped out of his tent and the contrast between him and Naomi could not have been greater.

Akbar noticed Naomi's sword glinting in the sunlight. It seemed to appear and disappear as she walked toward the end of the oasis. He was intrigued by the sword but it looked so brittle and frail compared to the Blade of Nineveh. He turned his focus to Naomi.

"She is even more beautiful than before," Akbar said.

The Blade of Nineveh spoke to him and said, "You must destroy her and the sword she carries."

Akbar fought back the thought of killing her. "She is so beautiful."

The Blade of Nineveh tempted him and filled his mind and heart with thoughts of power and kingdoms and all the women he could want. Akbar listened to the Blade of Nineveh. He did not understand anything about the Sword of Light but the Blade of Nineveh, he knew it well. The Blade of Nineveh knew this was its chance to destroy The Sword of Light once and for all. It did not care who carried the Sword of Light into battle. The sword and its bearer must both be destroyed. Akbar marched on toward Naomi ready to defeat her but it was the Blade of Nineveh that was ready to kill.

Akbar sheathed his sword until he was standing in front of Naomi. Then, he pulled it out inches away from her face. He weaved The Blade of Nineveh back and forth hoping its coldness and power would intimidate her. A wisp of cold, black, smoke and ice from the Blade of Nineveh encircled her head. The Blade of Light flashed the colors of the rainbow. Fire shot up and down the full length of its blade. Naomi stared ahead straight into Akbar's eyes and for a second it made him uneasy.

"Draw a circle," said Akbar. "There will be only two rules."

One of Akbar's men took out a sword and drew a circle large enough for the combatants to maneuver.

"Neither Naomi nor I may leave the circle for any reason nor may anyone else enter it. If anyone does enter the circle they will cause their champion to forfeit the fight."

The Wise Men and the Troubadours sat down. Akbar's men chose to stand, and they gathered as close as possible to the edge of the crude arena.

"After you," said Akbar.

He made a sweeping gesture with his sword and Naomi stepped into the circle. With Naomi's back to him, Akbar jumped quickly behind her. He pulled the Blade of Nineveh up high and swiftly brought it down on her left shoulder. Were it not for the protection from the Sword of Light, her arm would have been completely severed from her shoulder, but the sheer, shiny layer of protection provided by the sword blunted the force from the Blade of Nineveh.

Naomi did not escape the blow unharmed. Akbar's sword had crashed into her shoulder causing a deep gash. Sparks of black ice and smoke mixed with colors of the rainbow as Naomi's armor hissed at the Blade of Nineveh and its wielder.

Naomi winced and shuddered as she fell to her knees. She knew now Akbar did not plan to take her as his wife. He planned to kill her. In her heart she thought it would be better to die than live with him. This was not a fight of champions.

It was a battle to the death and if she wanted to live, she had to act, now. She had given Akbar the advantage by turning her back on him. It was a mistake she could not afford to make again.

Naomi could hear Akbar's sword cutting through the air and she spun around pulling up her sword to protect herself. The two blades clashed making sparking and popping noises like a fire loaded with wet wood. Black smoke and rainbows arced outwardly as the blades met again and again. The smell of death and darkness filled Naomi's nostrils and it made her blanch. Akbar came back quickly with a thrust and Naomi ducked away. Her left arm was already feeling the effects of the evil from the Blade of Nineveh. It was turning gray and the muscles in her arm pulled it up tight against her body as she fought the poison that was present. Naomi's mind raced. She dodged and darted inside the circle slipping away from Akbar. She parried another blow from the black blade.

She could not continue to fight a defensive battle. Not only could she not hold out much longer, but she was straining the faith of her friends supporting her. She knew their faith was helping her in the fight. Naomi glanced outside the circle and for a split second saw Melchior sitting and praying for her. Then she saw him open his eyes.

Melchior had closed his eyes before the battle and he did not see the first blow of Akbar. He had only heard the sound of the swords slicing through the air and the clash of the blades as they struck each other. He knew he should not open his eyes but he had to know Naomi was alright.

"Just one quick glance," Melchior said to himself and he opened his eyes. Naomi was looking right at him. He could see she was hurt, and he could see Akbar hurtling toward her from behind.

Melchior screamed and leaped toward the circle. It took Balthazar and Gaspar both to keep him outside the ring. Melchior clawed at the sand and kicked at his friends. Akbar saw his chance and his blade swung down toward Naomi's neck.

She turned her sword toward Akbar but it was not enough. The Blade of Nineveh glanced off the Sword of Light and lodged in Naomi's left thigh. Akbar pushed the blade into her leg and she fell onto her back in the sand dropping the Sword of Light. Her blood mingled with the sand in an eerie mix of red and brown and black. She could no longer stand up, so she crawled away from Akbar and turned to face him again.

Balthazar and Gaspar pulled Melchior back away from the circle. "You must not look at Akbar. You must not enter the circle!" screamed Balthazar. Numb and lost, Melchior closed his eyes and prayed hard.

Strangely, Naomi felt peaceful and calm. Considering her disadvantage, she could not understand why. She had to find a weakness in Akbar. She knew it was there, but before she could form a plan she had to find her sword.

Most evil men portray themselves as confident, but their confidence is cloaked in arrogance and ego. Akbar had his chance to kill Naomi now, but instead of just killing her, he was going to teach her a lesson.

Glancing around the circle, he paused. He wanted everyone to see what happens to those who defy him. That pause. That moment of arrogance gave Naomi the only chance she would have. Her hand sifted through the sand searching for her sword hoping it was nearby. In the sand the sword was almost invisible but finally her outstretched arm felt the hilt of it and she gripped it quickly. Akbar looked back down at her to finish her off, but instead of just plunging the blade into her heart he lifted it higher for a more dramatic and deadly blow. He plunged at Naomi with the Blade of Nineveh as Naomi raised the Sword of Light from the sand toward Akbar. The two swords raced past each other.

The Sword of Light struck first. Naomi twisted the sword upward and into Akbar's body as far as she could. The force of Akbar and the Blade of Nineveh coming at her threw her backwards. The Blade of Nineveh slashed by her head, nicked her right ear then buried itself in the sand.

Akbar staggered backwards then recovered. The Sword of Light protruded from his back, but strangely there was no blood. Akbar, screaming and squealing unintelligible words lunged toward Naomi, intent on killing her.

Hearing the wails of Akbar, Melchior opened his eyes again. Akbar was stumbling toward Naomi with the Blade of Light protruding from his back. It was plain to see Akbar was only interested in killing her.

Melchior had to do something but he understood if he entered the arena Naomi would be gone forever. He remembered the silver shields and he knew they were the last chance he had to save Naomi. He grabbed his shield and focused the sun's rays directly on Akbar.

"Shields!" he yelled.

The Wise Men and the Traveling Troubadours all turned their shields toward the center of the circle focusing the sun's rays onto Akbar.

Chapter 19
City On a Hill

What happened next depends upon the storyteller.

Melchior was temporarily blinded by one of the other shields and following his shout of *'Shields!'* he did not remember seeing or hearing anything else.

Balthazar swore Akbar exploded, and left behind only shards and slivers of black strewn across the desert.

All of Akbar's men said a great and dark spirit left Akbar's body and reentered the Blade of Nineveh.

Joab and Esau saw all the colors of the rainbow erupt from the center of the circle.

Naomi saw the reflections of all the shields and her life flashing in and out of focus. She knew the battle was over and she was still alive. She drew the Sword of Light close to her chest and lay still on the ground.

Melchior sweating uncontrollably and shaking like a reed, raced into the circle. There was nothing left of Akbar except a pall of black smoke that dissipated quickly. Melchior knelt next to Naomi and lifted her head. She was either dead or had passed out. Melchior watched her chest rise and fall with each breath. She was not dead. Gaspar went to her feet. He and Melchior lifted her up.

"Let's take her to our tent," said Gaspar. "She can rest there."

Melchior and Gaspar carried Naomi back to the tent and laid her down on a set of pillows provided by Houlak and some of the other colonists.

Balthazar searched the former arena and spied the hilt of the Blade of Nineveh. He was afraid to touch it but knew he couldn't just leave it out in the open. He certainly didn't want the desert gypsies getting their hands on it again. Fortunately for Balthazar, the gypsies knew what the blade had done to Akbar and they wanted no part of its evil magic. He wrapped his hand in a piece of cloth and pulled the Blade of Nineveh from the sand.

The scorpions on the handle remained frozen with their tails curved inward and the blade had returned to its shining silver state. Joab and Esau picked up the shields and a few other things they had brought with them and followed Balthazar.

The desert gypsies shuffled back to their tents. There was nothing for them to do. They no longer had a champion. They too investigated the circle of sand where the battle had taken place, but nothing remained of Akbar or anything else.

The sand inside the circle had been altered. It was black now, crusty and hard, especially at the spot from where Balthazar had removed the Blade of Nineveh. Most of the gypsies believed when Balthazar pulled the blade from the sand the evil spirits could not stay in the sword and they infused the ground with their poison. It was not long after the battle the entire oasis dried up. To this day it has never filled with water again.

The Troubadours and the Wise Men ignored the gypsies as they took care of Naomi. The rest of that day and all that night Houlak and several of the other women from the colony looked after her. Naomi, barely alive, lay there softly holding the Sword of Light to her chest. No one removed it for fear it was the only thing sustaining her. The wounds caused by the Blade of Nineveh were deep and harsh. The edges of the wounds were puffy and black. Naomi's body was cold and her breathing irregular but she was still with them and for that everyone was grateful.

"Will the poison from the Blade of Nineveh kill her eventually?" asked Gaspar.

No one answered. From one moment to the next her life ebbed and flowed between the world of the living and the underworld of darkness.

Melchior was with Naomi every moment possible, but he could not just sit there and do nothing. He began perusing the scrolls for any information on cures or potions which might help flush the poison from her body. Everyone knew what had happened to Joab. He still had the streak of gray hair to prove it and he had only touched the blade. Naomi was cut deeply and in multiple places. She was fighting for her life and no one could help her.

"I don't know if she will live or not," said Melchior with a delayed answer to Gaspar's question. Then without looking up he returned to reading the scrolls.

Balthazar stepped outside their tent to check and see what the gypsies were doing. "Will the gods be praised," he said. "Gaspar, come take a look."

Gaspar joined him outside the tent and the scene surprised him too. The gypsies were gone. Vanished. But, they had left almost everything behind and the oasis had become a gypsy ghost town. The colonists and guards in charge of King Mamre's dead army said the gypsies disappeared so quickly after the battle it was as if they had melted into the sand itself.

"Perhaps," said Balthazar, "we can finally rest easy for one night."

All the adventures, battles and excitement had taken the star out of his mind. Balthazar went back inside Naomi's tent and stared at the orbs as they sat on the sand and thought about how they had started him on this long journey. The flames were gone and the orbs had returned to their natural crystal clear state. Balthazar put them back into the leather satchel. As he closed the pouch, he knew they would have to be leaving soon. He walked over to Melchior and grabbed his shoulder.

"Melchior, we..."

"I know. We need to be going. I just want to see her wake up and know she is going to be well again."

"Gaspar and I will prepare to leave, and if she is not better by tomorrow morning we must leave."

Melchior looked up at Balthazar. "I hope I am strong enough to go with you."

Balthazar and Gaspar gathered up the camels and necessary supplies, including all of Melchior's scrolls. That night Balthazar even got out his magnifying lens just to see if the star was still there. It was. Inside he knew it would be. This star was more than just a journey now. It was his calling in life. His mission and purpose were intertwined with it, and he could not wait to see what lay beneath the star which always seemed to be just out of reach.

Naomi woke up during the night and when she did the Blade of Light lit up too, filling the tent with a soft glow. The light dimmed as Naomi tried to sit up. She slid back down into her cocoon of pillows breathing heavy and gasping. Melchior jumped up and moved to her head. He stroked her hair and face. He knew now she would be fine; she was a fighter in the truest sense of the word. Naomi and The Sword of Light had defeated Akbar and the poison in her body was no match for her either.

Naomi's recovery would take a while but the colonists would take care of her. Melchior could continue on his mission with Gaspar and Balthazar. Knowing she would be waiting for him after his journey, he hummed a childhood song and sang to her, and then he kissed her on the forehead. Only Naomi noticed the Sword of Light flickering briefly. She smiled, closed her eyes and dreamed of the man she loved.

The three wise men sat on the floor across from Isaac. Isaac pondered over the group sitting across from him. They didn't look much like adventurers, and they didn't appear strong enough to storm a sand castle let alone take on King Herod, but somehow they had made it this far.

"They might make it to Jerusalem," he said in a whisper, "but King Herod will be the end of the road for them."

"Alright," said Isaac, "Any further questions about Jerusalem or King Herod?"

The Wise Men all looked at Isaac waiting for a sarcastic remark or a bad joke but none was forthcoming.

"No," they all said.

They cleared the tent and walked outside into another bright, hot day.

"There is one thing I should warn you about before you go," said Isaac. "I don't know who or what you are looking for beneath this star, but if it is someone or something powerful that could threaten his crown, King Herod will not take kindly to it. News of that nature would best be kept amongst yourselves."

The entire colony was waiting for them to appear. The cheering and admiration for the Three Wise Men was overwhelming and heartfelt. The start of this leg of the journey would be something they would cherish for a long time.

Balthazar was glad to see his trusty steed Jandak again. He patted Jandak on the head and climbed aboard. Gaspar was aboard his camel and ready to go, but Melchior was nowhere in sight. Gaspar spied him hiding beside his camel kissing Naomi. She was still very weak but she had made it to Melchior steadying herself with her sword, using it as a makeshift cane. For a moment Gaspar thought Melchior just might not go. Naomi was a powerful draw for any man, let alone someone newly in love. But Melchior dutifully climbed aboard his camel and signaled he was ready to leave.

The Three Wise Men left the oasis and Melchior resisted looking back for fear he would bolt and abandon their quest. At the last dune before the oasis would pass out of sight, he did glance back. He couldn't see Naomi but he could see the Sword of Light casting a rainbow over the desert.

The three camels and riders traveled quite a distance in silence. Balthazar was continually opening his leather satchel and glancing at the orbs, but there was no change in them.

They remained clear and quiet as the trio traveled along. Gaspar hoped the danger was behind them now, and the journey to Jerusalem would be as dull and boring as possible; he had seen enough excitement for a while. Melchior pondered his feelings for Naomi over and over in his heart. Normally he was focused only on his precious scrolls and learning all he could from them, but now he could only think of one thing.

"Naomi..." he said softly under his breath...

"Watch where you are going," growled Gaspar. "Your camel is drifting in front of mine."

Melchior snapped out of his daydream and rubbed his eyes.

"Why don't you see what else you can find out about this star and what it might reveal to us?" asked Balthazar, knowing Melchior needed something to keep his mind on their journey and its purpose.

"Well, I can't drive my camel and read at the same time, now can I?" huffed Melchior.

He pulled on his camels reins and dropped back into the monotony of plodding along behind Balthazar and Jandak. Unfortunately for Melchior, deep inside Jandak the desert winds were brewing. Melchior passed through an unseen cloud and began a coughing fit.

"What on earth do you feed that thing?" Melchior said pointing at Jandak and pulling alongside Balthazar.

"He's not a thing, and it's just his way," said Balthazar.

"Well, I wish he would have his way, way over there. At least I shouldn't have to ride behind him all the way to Jerusalem."

Melchior pushed his camel into a trot so he could keep ahead of Balthazar and Jandak.

The landscape quickly changed once they left the colony. The desert became more uneven with increasing vegetation and rock formations. That night when the caravan stopped, Balthazar and Gaspar tended the camels and set up the camp site. They were hoping to give Melchior as much study time as possible. Balthazar and Gaspar were anxious to know what Melchior was reading about and learning. But so far, he had said nothing new.

The routine was the same every night. Balthazar and Gaspar would set up the campsite while Melchior searched for some place to spread out his scrolls and study them. He always built a small fire for light while he pored over the parchments and scrolls from right to left. That was one thing Balthazar and Melchior had learned, Hebrew was written from right to left. Balthazar could tell Melchior was making progress but he could not stop the curiosity eating at him.

The next night after watching Melchior study and work his way through the scrolls, Balthazar had to break the silence.

"Melchior, you have been studying and studying. Isn't there anything you can tell us? Anything?"

"There appears to be a great many prophecies and mysteries surrounding this star and its meaning." Melchior looked at the two other men and shook his head. "It is more involved than I knew. I am unsure of all the references to a coming king or prophet or god. I am doing my best."

Melchior got up and stretched his legs. He had been studying for hours.

"It is difficult and I don't want to share with you, unless I can be sure what I am learning relates to the appearance of this star or has some meaning for us and our journey." Melchior stood in front of his two friends. "I just need more time."

Balthazar could see the strain and struggle all the reading and interpretation was putting on Melchior and he knew not to ask again. When the time was right, Melchior would speak.

Melchior was weary from the reading and struggling to understand the scrolls, so for the most part he strapped himself to his camel and slept off and on oblivious to the world around him.

It was faint and faulty, but there it was again. Appearing and disappearing like a vision or a dream just out of reach. Balthazar got out one of his lenses but the light was too far away and the image was not always visible. He spied a sloping path cutting through the rocks in front of them.

"Let's take this path upward. There is something out in front of us. It appears and disappears like a torch or flame, but I cannot make out what it might be." Balthazar strained to see further up the path. "Perhaps, this path will take us to the top of the cliff. The crest of the cliff will offer us a better view of what's out there."

For the next few hours, the three of them wound their way up the loose and rocky path to the top. Sheer drops of several hundred feet greeted them at every turn in the face of the rock and stone cliff. Even though dusk was dropping the sun slowly below the horizon, once on top, they should be able to see further across the valley.

Even without a magnifying glass Balthazar knew they had found it: the city of Jerusalem. The last vestiges of sunlight swept across the valley and on to the city. It shone like a star fallen to earth, glittering and glorious and waiting for their arrival.

The three of them dismounted and began setting up camp. Jandak and the other camels were tied up and fed. Gaspar started a fire which was protected on two sides by a cleft in the rocky top of the plateau. Melchior sat down and rolled out the map of Jerusalem and a few other parchments and scrolls. "I finally have something to tell you both," said Melchior. Surprised, Balthazar and Gaspar sat down with the maps between them and Melchior.

"I have found a prophecy in one of the ancient scrolls. It says, 'For a child shall be born, and a king given. His name will be called wonderful, counselor, and prince of peace. Of his increase and government there shall be no end.'"

"Sounds like an immortal or a god to me," said Balthazar. "His kingdom will have no end? A Prince of Peace born now?"

"Yes. Yes." Melchior pulled out the land map he and Isaac had drawn back at the colony.

"Where did you get that?" asked Gaspar.

"Isaac helped me with this map. He is much smarter than most people think." Melchior straightened out the parchment and began reading. "A king will emerge who will rule over Israel on my behalf, one whose origins are from the beginning of time."

"From the beginning of time?" asked Gaspar. "An immortal being this is indeed."

"I don't know about an immortal," said Melchior, "but a child is being born. I believe that is what we will find beneath the star, a child. A child whose birth is prophesied many times in these old scrolls and tablets. A child who shall be a king, a mighty king whose time has come."

The Three Wise Men sat staring at each other in thoughtful silence. A light wind blew across the top of the plateau stirring the fire and sending a few sparks up into the night. Balthazar followed one of the sparks into the sky and watched it float higher and higher. He fetched a magnifying glass out of his pocket and looked up. The spark continued climbing. Balthazar watched it rise until the ember stopped burning and disappeared. The last faint glow of the floating ember left a tiny trace of smoke that hung in the air for a moment and then evaporated. When the smoke had cleared, there it was—the star! Balthazar reached up with his hand and in his mind he grabbed the star and held it. He had been unsure until now why they had risked so much and come so far. They were so close to a… a… child? A child who would become a king or a god? Maybe this child would be more than he could imagine. The thought made the brisk night breeze seem even colder than it was and Balthazar shivered for a moment. They were so close to solving the mystery. Jerusalem couldn't be more than a half days ride from where they were.

Balthazar, Melchior and Gaspar pulled on the corners of King Herod's palace map until it was stretched out between the three of them. Balthazar lifted his magnifying glass back up to his right eye and stared out at the shimmering city on the hill. "That must be Jerusalem and this is our plan for King Herod." He patted the map and smiled. They were almost there.

Chapter 20
King Herod and Prison

"Oh, it's Jerusalem alright," said an unfamiliar voice.

Balthazar looked at Melchior who shrugged his shoulders. Melchior and Balthazar slowly turned toward Gaspar.

"I didn't say anything."

"Then who did?" asked Balthazar.

"I did," said the voice from behind them. "I am Cornelius, and you are on King Herod's land." Cornelius stepped into the glow of the campfire.

The Three Wise Men turned and were greeted by a Roman soldier who was accompanied by several other soldiers mounted on horses and riding in chariots. Cornelius swung up into the nearest chariot and grabbed the reins from a waiting guard.

"I can tell by your dress and camels you are not from here." Cornelius snapped a whip above the horses' heads and the chariot inched forward, closer to the Wise Men. "King Herod does not take kindly to spies in his land."

"We are not spies," objected Balthazar.

"Oh you're not? Then do you mind explaining to me how and why you have maps and drawings of King Herod's private palace? No one has ever been allowed inside except the king's personal staff." Cornelius shifted his weight and turned to the soldier standing next to him. "I can't wait to hear about your plan for King Herod either. You are assassins sent here to kill the king. I may get a handsome reward for this."

"We have not come to assassinate..." Gaspar was stopped by a sword sliding into place just in front of his neck, the blade just visible in the dark.

"If they don't go peacefully, kill them. I'm certain King Herod would pay something for their heads."

Cornelius turned his chariot and headed back down the rocky path to the bottom of the plateau. The Three Wise Men were ordered onto their camels and taken into Jerusalem as prisoners.

"Well, have you seen anything in the ancient scrolls about three wise men being put in prison?" asked Gaspar sarcastically.

Melchior only glanced up for a moment recognizing the sarcasm and then returned to reading and rummaging through his scrolls.

"Bethlehem is the key. Bethlehem is where we need to be not Jerusalem."

"What are you talking about?" Gaspar said, pacing back and forth in the cell.

"It's right here in the manuscripts. I had only read a portion of it yesterday." Melchior spread the leather bound scroll out onto the floor. "Bethlehem appears to have been the birthplace of two other kings of Judah, King Saul and King David. The evidence is strong that Bethlehem will be the birthplace for this new king too.'"

"Well, that sure would have been nice to know before now. Wouldn't it?" Gaspar said.

"We did know." said Balthazar "That was one of the towns on our original map, Gaspar. Remember?"

"Yes. I remember."

Gaspar continued pacing the cell. He knew every crack in the floor by now and he had counted all the iron bars on the front of their prison cell, a total of thirty. Of course, he had counted all the prisoners, thirty-three, and the steps leading down from the guard's door, twenty-seven. He had even talked to another prisoner, Alexander, who turned out to be King Herod's own son. Alexander was set to be executed the next day.

"Herod is obviously not a king to be trifled with," he muttered under his breath.

Gaspar only stopped pacing when he heard the off key singing of another prisoner, Otisumus. Otisumus was Jerusalem's town crier. He happened to drink a little too much a little too often, and when he did, he would be taken in and paced in a cell until he could sober up. For some reason, King Herod tolerated Otisumus and his shenanigans. Perhaps it was because Otisumus was his nephew. At the moment Otisumus was stuck singing an old Babylonian drinking song, "Camel Girls Won't You Come out Tonight," off-key and loudly.

Gaspar shouted at the top of his lungs, "Can you please stop singing that inane song?"

"What?" said a slurring Otisumus. "I can't remember the last verse."

"It's dance by the light of the moon!"

"Got it," said Otisumus, "and prance in the night by the dune."

"Oh, please tell me you two have a plan for getting us out of here," said Gaspar pleading with Melchior and Balthazar.

"You don't like it here with me?" asked Otisumus "Well why didn't you just say so? Am I talking to myself? Listen. I'll put in a good word for you with King Herod. He's my uncle's cousin on my first mother's side by marriage." Otisumus paused for a moment. "I think that's right." His head bobbed up and down just before he passed out in a corner of his cell singing softly the last refrain of 'Camel Girls'.

"Being in prison might just be the break we have needed," said Melchior looking up from the maps.

"Oh, this I have to hear," said Gaspar. "How is being in prison good?"

"Well," Melchior began, "it will allow us immediate access to King Herod to plead our case." Melchior folded up the papyrus map of the palace and put it away. "Once he hears we are not spies, I'm certain he will let us go and we will be on our way. Maybe even with a king's escort."

"Why don't you talk to Alexander, King Herod's son, about how reasonable his father can be," said Gaspar. "I think Isaac was right. We won't be leaving here anytime soon, if ever."

Balthazar stood up. "I think Melchior is right. Isaac was overplaying his concerns. I think we ought to just tell Herod the truth. We are here looking for a new king. Perhaps Herod will want to come and see for himself. He may even want to offer us a reward."

"Are you insane?" asked Gaspar. "I can't imagine him wanting to do any such thing."

"Well, here we are in prison and I don't think lying is going to get us out of here any sooner than telling the truth," said Balthazar.

Balthazar finished putting away all his maps and scrolls. He stood up and put an arm around Gaspar.

"Isaac hasn't been in Herod's presence in a very long time. I say we just tell Herod the truth. What's wrong with that? Let's just see for ourselves once we are in front of King Herod. Tomorrow we will have to find a way to get a message to him." Looking around, Balthazar realized how late it was and yawned.

He took the remaining blanket in the cell, covered up with it, and fell asleep next to Melchior who had already nodded off.

Gaspar glanced around and noticed most of the other prisoners were already asleep or at least trying to find a dry and comfortable place to lie down in a very dank and dismal dungeon. The few half-burned torches on the walls filled the humid air with a thick, oil laden smoke that didn't help the atmosphere of the place or Gaspar's attitude. He paced back and forth in the cell for most of the night. He could not shake the foreboding he felt inside. Herod was not going to like the fact they were looking for a new king. Gaspar finally and fitfully fell asleep dreaming of being a king himself one day.

"Ohhhhhhhhhh," Otisumus was about to launch into another round of *'Camel Girls'*, but just as he started to sing he realized his head was hurting from his over indulgence. "Ohh, I have a headache."

What little sun could reach the prison was a welcomed sight to everyone. The six slits high up on the wall brought in very little relief from the dampness and humidity, but the light was something to be happy about. The sun was up and they had all survived another day.

Alexander, King Herod's son, was led out early and did not return. Everyone knew what was about to happen, but no one talked about it.

The guards came for Otisumus about the time his headache subsided. He asked the guards to stop for a moment in front of the Wise Men's cell.

"What would you like me to tell King Herod about you?"

"Tell him we are following a star," said Balthazar.

"A star?" asked Otisumus "Who is it? You can tell me. I won't say a word."

"What do you mean, who is it?" said Melchior.

"Oh, let me guess. It's the Queen of Sheba. I have always wanted her to visit. Or it's that Egyptian sword swallower. I can't remember his name though."

"No, no, no, Otisumus," Balthazar interrupted him, "not that kind of star. We're talking about a star, like one in the sky."

"You're following a star in the sky? Which one? Are you sure you want me to tell him that? It sounds a little crazy."

"Then tell him we are looking for a new king."

"You really are cuckoo aren't you."

The guards pushed and jostled Otisumus out of the prison and slammed the door behind them.

"We're dead," said Gaspar "Absolutely dead. Who knows what he's going to tell King Herod."

Seeing Otisumus leave only made the knot in Gaspar's stomach tighter than it already was.

King Herod was lazy. He could see the grapes. They were just barely a knuckles length out of reach but he refused to lean forward. He took a hard wooden cane leaning against his throne and whacked the servant across the chest leaving a rising red welt.

"Bring the tray closer. I cannot reach the grapes."

The servant wincing from the fresh strike moved closer. He closed his eyes assuming another blow would be forthcoming if he had moved too close or not close enough. Herod was not only lazy but also hard to please. Everyone feared him, and that was just the way he liked it. No good king ruled any other way. Fear gets things done.

King Herod had put his own son Alexander to death for being lazy. Alexander had always been enamored with reading and learning or, in King Herod's mind, being lazy. The kingship held no interest for Alexander. So, unfortunately for him, Herod had laid a scheme and accused Alexander of treason. Herod knew it was a lie, but he didn't care if everyone knew it or not. If he were ruthless enough to kill his own son, well, that kind of fear is hard to come by and would go a long way in keeping his court and its officers in line. Besides, he would have other children and other sons; and perhaps one of them would have the courage to be king, a feared king.

"Bring me Otisumus," said King Herod "I could use a little amusement to relieve my mind of my son's unfortunate treason and death."

Two guards departed King Herod's throne room to retrieve Otisumus from the dungeon. Everyone knew that's where he was, even King Herod. Otisumus had been in the prison so many times he had his own private cell.

King Herod liked Otisumus; he could always be counted on to tell the truth. Otisumus was probably the only person in Jerusalem who could tell Herod anything without putting his life in danger. King Herod knew Otisumus was completely harmless and would never be part of a plot to overthrow him or assassinate him. In fact, he could rely on Otisumus to tell him every bit of information he gleaned from the city and the prison. Otisumus was so gullible he would have told Herod about a plot even if he were involved himself.

Otisumus had sobered up a great deal from the night before. His head still hurt a little but he knew the king would want to know what he had learned from the other prisoners, especially the three new ones. He struggled to remember what they had told him. The two guards led him to the front of King Herod's throne.

"So, my dear Otisumus," said King Herod, "what have you learned from the prisoners today? I especially want to know everything about the new prisoners. The three men from foreign lands; what can you tell me about them? Are they assassins?"

"Well, oh king, I do not believe so. They refer to themselves as Three Wise Men."

"Three Wise Men? Hmm, perhaps they have heard of me and have come to consult with me on a matter concerning their own kingdoms." King Herod paused and looked around the room. "After all, I am wise, am I not?"

First one guard answered and then another and another. "Wise you are." "Oh yes, none is wiser." "Long live our wise and noble king." The other noblemen and council men chimed in too. "King Herod, Wise King Herod."

"I see fear has bought you a great deal of false praise today, oh king," said Otisumus bowing deeply with his backside to King Herod.

Herod laughed because he knew Otisumus was telling the truth. All the council and officials of his court always said, *'yes'* to any request from the King.

"But no, these men have not come to consult you." Otisumus stood back up and turned to face King Herod. "They say they have followed a star, and this star possibly foretells of a new king, one that…"

King Herod suddenly threw off the robe gathered at his neck and stood glaring at Otisumus. He reached down and with surprising strength and quickness, put his hand around

Otisumus' neck, and lifted him off the floor. Otisumus' feet flailed and his arms struggled to free himself from Herod's grasp. The hall went silent except for the sharp wheezes and gasps of Otisumus trying to breathe.

"I.... have.... more... news."

Otisumus could feel his life passing before him. Luckily, King Herod released his grip and dropped him onto the marble floor, then sat back down on his throne. Otisumus wheezed and grabbed his neck; it was already bruised from King Herod's grip. He finally caught his breath and continued.

"They are following a star and have been talking about some ancient archives of Judea. They have come to find and worship some child and future king whose time has come."

A small brown mouse scampered across the floor and up onto the arm of Herod's throne. There was a bit of food just too tempting to pass up. Herod was still seething and needed something to quell his insatiable anger. He scooped up the hapless mouse and began squeezing him in his hand. The mouse had no chance and was dead before Herod dropped him onto the marble floor. Herod stood up and puffed out his chest.

"A new king? There will be no new king, and these Wise Men are fools if they think they will leave this palace alive." Herod reached behind his throne and grabbed his sword. "In fact, I will kill them myself." Herod lifted his sword and cut through the air in a sweeping lethal arc. "Bring them to me."

"I'll help bring them," said Otisumus as he ran toward the door leading to the prison below.

Two guards followed him. Otisumus ran ahead and stopped in front of the Wise Men's cell. Gaspar stopped pacing. Melchior and Balthazar looked up from their maps.

"King Herod wishes to see you," said Otisumus, not looking at the Wise Men.

"There," said Melchior, "Otisumus did it. I told you he would get us an audience with the king."

Otisumus turned his back to the cell. "Oh yes, I've done it alright."

The guards unlocked the cell door. Balthazar and Melchior began to pick up their things. Gaspar took up pacing again.

"You probably ought to just leave all your things here," said Otisumus. "You won't need them much longer.

Gaspar turned around abruptly staring at Otisumus. "What do you mean by that?"

Otisumus stared at the wall across the hall from the Wise Men's cell. "Oh, this is a once in a lifetime visit, and we will have someone bring your things to you. I mean, you can come back for your things."

"He won't even look at us," said Gaspar. "Something's up."

"Oh, no, I promise you this meeting will leave you speechless," Otisumus said. "And lifeless," he said under his breath.

"What? What did he say?" Gaspar reached through the bars and spun Otisumus around forcing him to look into the Wise Men's' cell.

"Uhhh, you'll learn a life lesson from this. That's what I said." Otisumus glanced away from Gaspar.

He could say no more. He ran back to the prison door leading up to Herod's chamber and opened it, waiting on the guards and the Wise Men to pass.

"I'm telling you I smell a rat," said Gaspar.

"In this place? It would be impossible not to smell something," said Melchior.

The Wise Men were led out of the prison and into the main hall. Otisumus slammed the door shut behind the doomed men. He wandered back to his cell and locked himself in; he could not bear to follow them to their deaths.

"On your knees," said Seneca, "have you no respect for King Herod?"

Seneca was a complicated man and no one in the court really knew his official title. To King Herod, though, Seneca was indispensable as his Chief Advisor, Court Magician, and Interpreter of Dreams. It was fortunate for Seneca that King Herod needed him as much as he did or Seneca would have been dispatched a long time ago. Seneca was smart, much smarter than Herod. He was dangerous too, but he was also a coward. Only King Herod's ruthlessness kept Seneca cowering and complacent. Seneca would never have the courage to stage a coup against King Herod and Herod knew it.

Balthazar, Melchior, and Gaspar knelt before King Herod, not quite sure what to expect from a man they knew so little about.

"Would you like a blindfold?" asked Herod. He pulled a sword from behind his back as two guards grabbed each of the Wise Men and tied their hands behind their backs.

Gaspar was the first to understand what was happening. "Wait, wait, wait. We are only following a star."

The guards pulled back the head of each Wise Man, exposing their neck. Herod walked down the few steps of his throne to the black and white marble floor. He pulled his blade across the neck of each Wise Man just hard enough to draw a trickle of blood.

"You have drawings of the palace and all its rooms. How did you get them? Who is the spy working with you? They will die beside you."

"Isaac, your former servant, he drew the maps of the palace and Jerusalem for us," said Melchior.

"Isaac? That traitor? You are assassins." The anger in Herod began to swell as he remembered.

Isaac was probably the only other person besides Otisumus who had stood up to Herod and lived to tell about it. When he worked for Herod he was always trying Herod's patience with pleadings for those less fortunate. In the end, when Isaac finally contracted leprosy, Herod was glad to be rid of him for good. The only thing keeping him alive while he worked for King Herod was his sense of humor and the public's admiration for him. Herod had feigned as much sorrow as he could when he said at Isaac's farewell, "Such a man as this is not soon forgotten."

"You have made this even easier. For mentioning him, I will kill you first." Herod walked over to Melchior.

The guard pulled Melchior's head back even further. Melchior looked up into King Herod's eyes and could sense it.

This man has a blacker heart than Akbar. Let us hope he never gets a chance to lift the Blade of Nineveh. He may be the first man I have ever met without a soul, thought Melchior. Then, he closed his eyes and whispered, "I love you Naomi." and prepared to die.

King Herod drew his sword to his left in preparation for a quick kill. Melchior could hear Herod's sword coming for him and as brave as he was, could not help but flinch. The sound of the blade heading for his exposed neck was shattered by two swords crashing into one another. This scared Melchior and the guard holding him so much they both fell backwards onto the cold marble floor.

Melchior flopped on top of the guard holding him like a fresh fish out of water. His hands were tied but he could see no blood and feel no wound. Everything was still intact and he was still alive! Balthazar and Gaspar could not turn their heads to see what had happened and they thought Melchior was dead.

"Wait," echoed a raspy low voice. Stepping from behind the guards was Seneca. It was his blade that had deflected the death blow meant for Melchior. "This is no way to treat such honored guests."

"Seneca," said Herod, "you will be lined up here with them for that. Guards!"

Four men stepped forward and forced Seneca's arms behind him.

"Herod, I believe if you will but have a word with me you will see I am right. This will only take a moment. And if I am wrong then I will take the first blow from your blade."

King Herod could not argue with the logic of that so he lowered his sword.

"You have my ear, and if what I hear is worth it you will have just saved your own head, Seneca. Keep the three fools here until I return."

Seneca and Herod walked across the marble floor out of earshot. Melchior was put back into position in line. Balthazar and Gaspar realized he was still alive.

"King Herod, this was found on their camels: Frankincense and myrrh. They are perfume merchants or magi as they claim, but they are not assassins. Besides, killing these men... What purpose will it serve?" asked Seneca.

"It will prevent them from finding this fictitious new king."

"What if there is a prophecy and it is true? What if there really is a new king?"

"They will be dead that much quicker."

Seneca had been Herod's adviser ever since Herod's father Antipater had been assassinated. Of Antipater's children, Herod was the only one not seen as a threat to succeed his father as king. Yet somehow, Herod as dull as he was, managed to survive every attempt on his life and marry into a local Judean royal family. From King Herod's first day on the throne until now, Seneca had lost count how many times he had saved the king's life or career. Here he was again about to keep Herod from making a mess of the situation.

"Oh wise and kind King Herod," said Seneca with a straight face, "let the wise men go."

Seneca put his arm around Herod and walked further away from the great hall and out into the open courtyard.

"You see all of this?" said Seneca, pointing at the Royal Gardens and fountains, "You are king. Think about it. Let these men lead you to this new king. When they have found him, ask them to bring the child king here so you can worship him also."

Seneca pointed toward the top of King Herod's palace.

"Once inside the palace grounds, you have all the control and advantage. Here in the privacy of your courtyard you can kill them all. Thus, you not only rid yourself of the three foreigners, but any chance of an internal uprising from a new king as well." Seneca stopped and looked at Herod. "With their blood on the floor and each head on the end of a spear, you will show the rulers in Rome how powerful you really are. Think about what that might mean for you. Invitations to visit with Caesar, dine at his table, and you will almost certainly be rewarded for putting down a rebellion."

Herod could see Seneca was right. The three wise men or merchants offered no threat to him. He would let them go and ask them to bring this self-ordained king to him. It would be better to get rid of this king now before he could establish a following. If Seneca's plan worked, then so much the better, thought Herod. In the end, he would still get the credit, and Seneca's plan was so simple it just might do the trick. Of course, it would take the acting job of his life to pull it off, but pretending was one of Herod's shining traits. However, if Seneca's plan failed…

In all of this, one of the reasons Herod had lasted so long as king was he always had a backup plan. And, more often than not it was Herod's second plan which succeeded. No one would even know about Herod's other plan. No one except Abada.

Herod wanted the Wise Men to sweat just a little longer. Plus, he needed information. He sent for all his magicians, stewards and any other currently visiting officers of the court and had them all report anything they knew about this star to him.

"It is true King Herod. There is a prophecy of a star and a coming king mentioned in the old texts of Judea," Seneca looked further at Melchior's manuscripts. "They are telling the truth. However, this prophecy is very old and therefore I think highly unreliable. I doubt any of it is true."

Herod walked over to a long marble table and wrote a message on a piece of papyrus. He poured a patch of hot wax onto the scroll then pressed his ring into the wax giving it his seal. He slipped the secret scroll to a nearby steward.

"See that Abada gets this message," said Herod, "and be quick about it." Herod turned to face Seneca and the palace servants, "Bring me my ceremonial robe and crown."

Several attendants dashed off and returned with the long flowing robe and Herod's golden crown. The robe was a royal purple silk trimmed in lion's mane and zebra and the crown was a simple gold band with encrusted multi colored jewels. Four attendants returned with the robe holding it off the ground, while another stood upon a stool fitting the robe and crown properly onto King Herod.

"Master, King Herod. All the parties are in place and await your return."

The lowly plebe backed out from Herod's presence being careful not to look directly at the king as such an offense was worth a flogging for sure.

Herod felt he was finally ready to make a grand entrance and implement Seneca's plan. Of course, his own plan was already underway, but he would appease Seneca and gauge the Wise Men and their interest in bringing the child and future king to him.

"His royal majesty, King Herod." The palace steward moved aside as King Herod entered the room.

The Wise Men were amazed as the crowd cheered and hailed their king.

"Herod, defender of Jerusalem. Hail King Herod. Hail the great King."

They were about to be executed in front of the entire palace, and the atmosphere was surreal, more like a coronation than an execution.

Two attendants followed along behind Herod. Occasionally, they would pull up and down on the train of his royal robe causing it to ripple. The light in the room reflected off the silk creating a rhythmic, somber, shadow dance on the walls. Herod made his way slowly, regally to his throne and sat down. All the audience bowed deeply waiting for King Herod's blessing.

"Arise my court and staff. Let us welcome our honored guests, these Three Wise Men."

The applause came in waves. The guards cut the Wise Men's bindings and helped them to their feet, then stepped back. Melchior, Gaspar and Balthazar knelt before Herod's throne, their heads bowed. A steward handed Herod his royal scepter and he waved it to quiet the room.

"Oh my guests, I must apologize deeply and sincerely for the ways in which you have been treated since your arrival. I have punished the parties responsible most severely."

Herod sat down. The Wise Men stood up and the room fell quiet.

"Perhaps I should explain my boorish behavior. I have recently been alerted to an assassination attempt upon my life. Three unannounced men have crossed into my kingdom and are looking for a chance to kill me."

Herod shifted his weight and opened his arms wide.

"My overzealous sentries and guards assumed it was you when they found you looking at maps of the city. We have captured the real assassins, so of course I know now you could not possibly be them. I have been told you are on a mission to find a new king. My ministers and astronomers have verified this prophecy of a new king and I wish to meet this King of Peace. After all, who doesn't want peace?"

The room flooded with applause, then settled back down.

"If this child has been prophesied to be the new king then who am I to storm the steps of destiny? I wish to help you in your quest. The finest camels, chariots and horses are at your disposal. Once you have found this new king I would wish you to bring him here to me so all of Jerusalem can celebrate his arrival."

Horns blew. Banners waved. Herod turned in a circle with his arms raised and outstretched, soaking up the adoration and praise of his name.

"Please, introduce yourselves properly to me and my court."

Balthazar was giddy from this turn of events. They were being welcomed as honored guests. This is how he had envisioned it from the moment they had left the colony. He stepped forward.

"We call ourselves Three Wise Men. I am Balthazar and I represent the King of Babylon."

Then he turned to his left and pointed to Melchior.

"I am Melchior and I hail from Mesopotamia." Melchior motioned for Gaspar to step forward.

"I am Gaspar. The King of Persia sends his blessings."

"This is all so wonderful for me to greet you and welcome you to Jerusalem." Herod waited and the room gave him a mild round of applause. "I do have one question for you. Seeing that you have arrived in Jerusalem along with this star, how do you know you have not found the king you seek?"

"I do not understand?" said Gaspar.

"Dullards," Herod said to himself. He straightened up his robe, tightened his sash and held his scepter a little higher. "How do you know the king you seek is not standing before you?"

"Your highness," said Balthazar, "I have been following the star for several months now and I believe it has moved beyond Jerusalem and has settled over the town of Bethlehem." Balthazar turned to Melchior. "Melchior, read to King Herod the prophecy you found in the old manuscripts of Judea."

"But you, Bethlehem, you are little among the towns of Judea, yet out of you shall come forth to me the One to be Ruler in Israel and his star shall rise in the east."

"We believe this star, is fulfilling this ancient prophecy," said Balthazar, "the prophecy also speaks of a small child and you King Herod are certainly no child."

Three attendants came and gave each of the Wise Men a pillow. Balthazar, Melchior and Gaspar all sat down waiting for King Herod to respond.

Herod was livid. He imagined each of the Three Wise Men being decapitated, their heads set on pikes and paraded through the streets. This thought actually made him feel better and he calmed down long enough to maintain a facade of empathy and interest.

King Herod was not about to worship another king. Nonetheless, he was glad to have both plans now in place. These Wise Men and the child had to be stopped. Perhaps Seneca was right and the prophecy was old and unreliable.

It didn't matter if the prophecy was reliable or not, Herod knew Abada was reliable. If there was a child Abada would find him then do whatever it took to get the child back to the palace, dead or alive; especially if the price was right. Herod didn't care which plan worked. He only wanted the child in the palace where he could take care of things away from prying eyes. His fury and scorn were boiling just under the surface. He wanted them all dead. Not in a few days, but right now. However, Herod knew that in order for any of his plans to succeed he would have to keep his poise and not raise any suspicions.

Herod displayed his most sincere smile and descended the steps leading from his throne. The Wise Men knelt again before Herod.

"Arise, you Three Wise Men from afar. I am at your humble service."

Balthazar, Melchior and Gaspar all stood up and looked toward King Herod. Herod clapped his hands three times. A finely dressed palace attendant came forward with a golden box resting on a red velvet pillow. Herod opened the box and pulled out a signet ring, an exact copy of the ring on his right hand.

"Please take this gift, my signet ring. It will open many doors in the city of Bethlehem which might otherwise be closed to you."

He turned Balthazar's palm up and gave him the ring.

"I must remain here in Jerusalem, but once you have found this child and future king be certain no harm comes to him. Bring him and his parents here to me where they shall live all their remaining days in peace and prosperity. If you cannot bring him to me, then at least tell me where I can find him so I may come and crown him as the future king myself."

"It shall be done as you wish," said Balthazar.

Herod was very convincing. Melchior and Balthazar bowed deeply. Gaspar offered a halfhearted bow. No one else had noticed but Gaspar had seen the lifeless mouse fall to the floor. If the steward had not been so quick to clean it up Gaspar might have pointed it out to Balthazar and Melchior. It was frightening. He couldn't quite pin it down. King Herod had gone from almost decapitating them to this sickly sweet caretaker, and all of it had happened after his meeting with Seneca. Gaspar did not trust King Herod or Seneca one bit.

Herod stood before his lavish marble throne and addressed the throng that now filled the room.

"Now may all men in my presence bestow greetings upon these Three Wise Men, Balthazar, Gaspar and Melchior." The throng cheered and then on Herod's command bowed.

"Take whatever you may need from my stables, my palace and armory. May you encounter nothing but peace and safe travels for the remainder of your journey. I especially pray for the child's safety. Let us all worship this child here in Jerusalem together upon your return."

The crowd arose in unison. They banged on drums. They sang. They danced for King Herod and his court. The Three Wise Men bowed before Herod and exited the throne room. They had a great deal to do before they left Jerusalem.

It was amazing. Here they were, reunited and free again! How many times would they be delivered from the brink of death, given new life and a chance to continue this journey?

Balthazar placed King Herod's gold signet ring on his finger. It was a beautiful ring with the kings' crest engraved inside the mouth of a lion. Now they had the power of the king on their side. What could possibly go wrong?

Chapter 21
Abada

Jerusalem was spectacularly beautiful. Color was everywhere. Flowers such as the Anemone and Adonis grew wild and mingled with low lying Jujube trees. The rugged, long-living olive trees grew in gardens and groves and were harvested regularly. People could be seen plucking and storing the olives in clay jars. The jars of olives were then sold, served, or pressed into olive oil, a staple in every Jerusalem home.

There were several especially beautiful gardens. One of them was Gethsemane. In the heart of the garden was the oldest living olive tree in the land. This tree was particularly gnarled and twisted. People would come from miles around to watch its branches and leaves flutter and sway, causing the depth of the tree's shadows to contrast with the trunk, shifting and changing. Every person who looked at the tree and its wavering patterns of light and dark saw something different in its shadows.

The vineyards were tempting since the travelers' supply of wine was completely gone, but they chose not to stop. The draw and the drive of the star was pulling them toward what they hoped was their final destination, Bethlehem.

The Wise Men were enjoying their ride through town. They were glad to be free and back on their quest. But, unbeknownst to them they were being followed.

Abada kept his distance. He couldn't get close enough to see their faces, but occasionally the king's ring which Balthazar wore reflected the sun. Abada could see it glinting as the Wise Men and their camels passed blissfully through Jerusalem unaware of him, King Herod's hired assassin. No one knew what Abada looked like beneath his full cloak and black hood. In fact, no one was sure he even existed. King Herod knew he existed and had given Abada the only other known copy of his signet ring.

Abada was always paid handsomely when King Herod needed to dispose of a troublemaker, but this job was different. Herod offered Abada his own province and enough gold to make him the second richest man in the kingdom. This promised reward was well beyond anything Herod had ever paid before. Abada didn't particularly care why Herod wanted the child and his parents so badly. He only knew that once he had them back at the palace in Herod's hands, he would be rich. Richer than he had ever imagined, and he had a good imagination.

He would need help in order to bring them all back to Herod. Abada had never had to hire anyone before. He would have to find at least two accomplices quickly. He didn't want the Wise Men to get more than a few hours head start. They would be in Bethlehem easily in a day or less even if they decided to spend the night in Jerusalem. He had to find help now. He couldn't just ask people if they would be interested in capturing a few innocent souls. He had to be smarter than that.

It took him the rest of the afternoon to find a couple of perfect stooges, Mirhabad and Sahirabad, twin brothers. He wasn't sure about their abilities or brains but he didn't care. That's what he was hired for, to be the brains of this little operation. After paying them both and explaining the job, Abada decided they would leave within the hour. Even if the three men made it to Bethlehem before him they would easily be found in such a small town, even with a head start.

"Let them have the lead for now," Abada said.

After showing the signet ring around in a few places, someone would remember having seen the other ring on Balthazar. The king's signet ring was hard to forget. One ring would lead to the other.

"Meet me at the city gates in one hour," Abada said to his two new dupes and then he slithered home.

No one ever accused Abada of walking anywhere. His feet never peeked out from beneath his robes and his eerie gait never stirred up any dust. Some believed he had long ago cast a spell on himself and floated everywhere he went.

It was still hard to grasp. Here they were just miles from what they believed would be their final destination: Bethlehem. Balthazar was reminiscing about the start of the whole journey. The orbs, the dreams, the miracles. He would remember this adventure for the rest of his life no matter what happened or what they found beneath the star.

Clouds were rolling through the sky and Balthazar worried he might not be able to see the wandering star. Fumbling through several pockets of his tunic he finally found one of his magnifying lenses. Being this close to Bethlehem, he didn't need to be sitting still in order to find the star. He held the lens up to his right eye and through the patterns of shifting clouds he found it—the Star of Bethlehem. That's what he would call it. Nothing like Okul or Aldhibah, or his king's name. No, he would call this star, The Star of Bethlehem. Balthazar began to wonder what would happen to the star once they found this king. Would it stay as a permanent marker in the heavens? Or once they found the child, would the star disappear leaving him and his friends with only memories of it?

One thing was for certain, he would never forget the smell drifting into his nostrils at that moment.

"What in the world is that smell? It smells like a mixture of wet blankets, mildew and manure. Hold up."

Balthazar stopped Jandak and thought it might be his beloved camel, but even Jandak in his worst day never smelled anything like this.

"Good grief," said Gaspar in a funny voice, as he held his nose closed tightly.

"What died?" asked Melchior in a muffled voice as he slipped part of his tunic over his nose and mouth.

"You are trading in that stink pile you call a camel," said Gaspar. "I'm not breathing this for another minute."

"It's not Jandak." Balthazar dismounted and when his sandal hit the ground he knew he had stepped into a pile of something soft, squishy, and smelly. He wished he had never gotten off his camel. His eyes watered. Maybe he could get back on Jandak and the three of them could make a bold dash out and away from this stench.

"Baaaaa."

It was barely audible. Then it came from behind them.

"Baaaa."

Before any of the Wise Men said it out loud they all knew... They had wandered right into the middle of a substantial herd of sheep. Five, six, a dozen bleats from all around them. The night was filled with the long drawn out monotonous bleats of one sheep after another.

"No wonder Uncle Barabas was written out of our family's will," said Gaspar. "He was a sheep herder."

"We've got to make a run for it, or we'll be goners!" pleaded Melchior. "I don't want someone to find me out here and think I died counting sheep in my sleep."

"So you count sheep in your sleep, huh."

There was someone else nearby. Gaspar could just make out the crook of the shepherd's hook in the moonlit night.

"That's funny 'cause we count camels in ours."

There was more movement in the background and Balthazar could now clearly see the outlines of three shepherds silhouetted against the horizon.

"I am Balthazar. This," motioning behind him, "is Melchior and Gaspar."

"We are three wise men. We represent the kings of Babylon, Persia and Mesopotamia," said Gaspar sliding off his camel and into his own pile of warm, wet, and recent sheep manure.

"I am Boaz. Chief Shepherd of my masters' flock.

Boaz stepped out of the shadows and into the full moonlight. Another shepherd stepped up from behind him with a freshly lit torch.

"I am Mattathias, caretaker of the sheep."

The third shepherd, Timothy, carrying a baby lamb, walked up between Mattathias and Boaz.

"Did he say they were three wise men?"

"Yes. Yes I did." said Balthazar.

"Wise men you say, huh." Timothy pointed in the direction of Melchior, "He must be the smartest."

"Why do you say that?" asked Balthazar.

"He's the only one smart enough to stay on his camel and not get sheep manure all over him," said Timothy.

"Not too wise to be tromping through 'Shepherd's Meadow' in the middle of the night with no torch and no idea where you're headed," said Mattathias.

"We know exactly where we are headed." Balthazar paused wiping manure from his sandal. "We are going to Bethlehem."

"Well then, you've missed it," said Timothy.

Balthazar glanced behind them. A tiny city just barely visible was glowing in the valley. Balthazar realized he had been daydreaming and not paying attention to where they were headed. Trying to save his dignity, he climbed quickly aboard Jandak.

"Hand me my reins," said Balthazar to Boaz.

"I would but they're behind you."

Boaz couldn't help but smile. Beneath his hood and mud ridden tunic, his teeth shone as white as the moon, the only thing visible in the dark.

Balthazar swiveled around in his saddle and grabbed Jandaks reins from Boaz.

"Ewww. What in the world…?" said Balthazar.

"A lowly shepherd once said to a high riding king, leaving your reins on the ground will put on your hands what the reins have found." Boaz threw a tattered partial tunic up to Balthazar. "This will get the manure off but not the smell. That tends to stay with you for a while."

Balthazar turned Jandak around without saying a word and walked him through the herd of sheep toward Bethlehem. He made sure they were going in the right direction this time. "Low life good for nothing shepherds," he mumbled to himself just as he rubbed his sleeve across his face leaving a trail of manure on his cheek. "Ohhh." Balthazar couldn't find anything that didn't have traces of manure on it. It was a slow, smelly ride into Bethlehem.

"This isn't Bethlehem," said Melchior.

"Yes, it is," said Gaspar.

"It can't be," Melchior insisted.

"What's that sign over there say?"

"Bethlehem Stables and Feed Lot." Melchior looked back at Gaspar. "Maybe it's a branch office."

"What about that sign?" Gaspar pointed to their left to an old worn wooden sign. It tilted at a precarious angle making the sign appear to be pointing into the sky.

"Welcome to Bethlehem" was written in four languages - Akkadian, Latin, Hebrew and Aramaic.

"Oh, come on Melchior you know we're in Bethlehem," said Balthazar. "Now, why the argument with Gaspar?"

"I just can't believe anyone important would be born in this dumpy town, let alone a king. The old books of Judea are wrong. Let's go back to Jerusalem and look there."

Balthazar was listening to his friends argue, but he was also earnestly gazing at the night sky.

"We cannot settle this argument here and now. The sky has clouded up. The star is hidden. We shall have to find a place to rest and hope things clear up soon."

"Well, for being such a small town it sure is crowded."

Melchior had moved his camel ahead of Gaspar and Balthazar. He gazed down the street and even on camels it would be difficult to navigate it safely.

"Crowded it is," said an old man standing near the corner. "And you must not be from around here or you would know why."

"Well," said Melchior, "you are right. We are not from this area. So why is it so crowded?"

"It's tax season and the census has been called. Plus, this year King Herod has converted the country to the flat tax system."

"Oh really," said Melchior, he was intrigued with how King Herod taxed his subjects. "What is this flat tax? I am unfamiliar with it."

"Well, with the flat tax the government taxes you until you're flat broke!"

The old man put his scraggly hands into his coat pockets and pulled them inside out. They were empty. He laughed and hobbled across the street cackling the entire way.

"I don't understand how someone so poor can be so happy." Gaspar pulled up next to Melchior.

"Well, why shouldn't he be happy. What money can you take from a man who has none?"

Balthazar finished gazing at the sky. Jandak sauntered over toward Gaspar and Melchior. Everything seemed to finally be going well for the Wise Men except for the cloudy sky. The Wise Men would have to wait it out somewhere.

Jandak stood up stiff and straight on all four legs. Balthazar knew his camel well enough to know something had startled Jandak, but he had no idea what it was. Jandaks head jerked up and down quickly. This sudden motion pulled the reins from Balthazar's hands. Balthazar knew when he dropped the reins he had lost control over Jandak. Not that Balthazar ever had complete control but no control was going to lead to no good.

Jandaks legs became a whirling blur and he darted down the street, cutting a swath through the street vendors, uprooting their tents and booths. One unlucky vendor was tossed into the air and landed squarely on top of a fruit booth and a vendor selling roosters. Bananas, coconuts, grapes, apples, and chickens all flew into the air and onto the street. The roosters were covered in fruit. (Some people believe the term 'fruit cocktail' originated during this incident).

Jandak began slipping on a batch of bananas and each of his four legs went in a different direction. He landed hard on his stomach. His body continued spinning like a top and he cleared the street of vendors and pedestrians from one side to the other.

Jandak regained his feet and was off again down a narrow side street. One poor sentry who was directing the cart and foot traffic at the next intersection never knew what hit him. Jandak lifted him up with his head and threw him backwards. The sentry hit Balthazar full force, knocking Balthazar off his saddle toward Jandak's rear. Balthazar scrambled for something to latch onto. He managed to grab Jandaks tail and held on for dear life. The sentry bounced along Jandaks back and snagged Balthazar's foot. Then, just as quickly as the sentry had dropped in, he lost his grip and fell behind Jandak hitting the street and cartwheeling into a cloud of dust and debris where he disappeared.

Melchior and Gaspar watched the commotion and shrugged their shoulders. Somehow they weren't shocked by the fact that Balthazar was still hanging onto Jandaks tail and flapping like an overstuffed kite sailing in the breeze.

Chapter 22
The Inn

"I guess we better follow him before he lands us all in jail again." Melchior spurred his camel into a light trot.

"Or worse," said Gaspar.

He and his camel fell in line behind Melchior on this dusty, dumpy street, in this dull, dreary town where no king worth his salt would be born. Bethlehem.

Jandak was on some kind of mission and Balthazar was struggling to secure a less precarious position on his camel.

"Whoa! Stop! Slow down!" Balthazar yelled every command he knew trying to slow Jandak down but it was all to no avail.

Balthazar thought he was about to be thrown off and onto the street. Then he spied a couple of carrots bouncing around in one of his many pockets.

"We must have picked these up in our run through the market place," Balthazar said to himself. That's when he knew he had a way to stop Jandak. If there was one thing Jandak loved more than racing it was a juicy carrot.

Clinging to Jandak with one hand Balthazar threw a carrot as far as he could on the street in front of his runaway camel. The carrot landed perfectly in front of them and Jandak stopped instantly. Balthazar had not considered what would happen once Jandak decided to stop. He bounced off Jandaks rump and flew straight up into the air and then back down, somehow managing to land in the saddle. The force of Balthazar landing on his back caused Jandak to collapse onto the street and the reins to fly up and into Balthazar's hands. The result of the stop surprised them both. For a moment they just sat there with Jandaks legs splayed out in every direction, and Balthazar sitting in his saddle, without a scratch on his body.

'The Inn of Bethlehem.' The sign was simple like most things in Bethlehem and it was crooked. Balthazar got Jandak up on his feet again and maneuvered him over to the sign. Looking through his robe and tool bag Balthazar managed to find a hammer and three or four nails. Just enough to nail the sign back up onto the door frame.

Whack. Whack. Ting. Whack. Whack. Ting. Balthazar worked away on the sign until he had it nailed back into position.

The door of the inn opened and a short, thin man with a black beard wearing a smock stepped outside onto the sidewalk.

"What's the racket about out here? Don't you know people are trying to sleep?" The innkeeper now found himself inches from a camels face. "You're making all this noise? A camel?" The innkeeper scratched his head and turned to go inside.

"No, it wasn't my camel, it was me."

Balthazar took one more look at his handiwork and slid off Jandak and onto the sidewalk next to the inn keeper.

"I am Balthazar. I represent the King of Babylon…"

"I don't care who you represent or what you're selling. It's tax season and we're overbooked."

The inn keeper turned away from Balthazar toward the door leading back into the inn. Next to the door Balthazar could now see a sign that said,

One night. One gold piece. Desert Inn Suites.

"The sign says, One night. One gold piece."

"That's when I have rooms available. I told you we're overbooked."

"Perhaps this will change your mind."

Balthazar pulled a coin purse from one of the pockets of his robe and shook it. The gold coins inside the bag jingled.

"Sounds like you have some gold there," said the inn keeper, "and if you have as much as it sounds like you do, I may have just the room you need."

The Inn Keeper stepped aside and motioned for Balthazar to enter the inn.

Balthazar walked past the inn keeper who quickly removed the one gold piece sign and replaced it with one that said *'One night. Four Gold pieces'* in smaller print below it said. *'Blame the government.'*

Melchior and Gaspar stared down another street. Carts were overturned. Storekeepers were fuming and yelling. Pedestrians were shaking their fists.

"Well, we shouldn't have too much trouble finding them," said Melchior.

"Yes," said Gaspar. "All we have to do is keep following the path of destruction."

Abada knew Bethlehem pretty well. There were several places the Wise Men could be but he wasn't worried. He opened a pouch of gold and looking in knew there was enough money to hire plenty of eyes to track and quickly locate the three travelers. Even if he ran out of money the king's ring would get people talking. He would soon know where the Three Wise Men were.

Mirhabad and Sahirabad were having an idiotic conversation about why duck feathers were called down instead of up. Sahirabad's thought was that as you know, ducks can fly which would mean they could go up or down. So, who had decided that duck feathers should be called down? Why not call duck feathers up? Mirhabad's argument was that duck feathers should be called tickly white fluffy things. Period.

The more Abada was with them, the more he realized every conversation ended up in some circular nonsensical world with no beginning, no middle and no end. They would have to do. As long as he was in charge, Abada felt confident he didn't need anyone much more intelligent than a circus monkey. Mirhabad and Sahirabad just barely qualified.

The three assassins set up shop at the marketplace; the center of the city and all its activities. Everything germinated from there. City proclamations were made there. Notices were posted and if anyone was new in town, someone at the marketplace would know about it. Abada didn't enjoy these kinds of social settings; they made him feel uneasy and exposed, so the sooner they dispensed the money and sent their eyes out into the city the better he would like it. Abada was anxious to leave the marketplace and hole up in some dark alley, waiting for their money tree to bear fruit.

"Well, it's no Hanging Gardens of Babylon, but it will do for one night." Balthazar stared at the one wilting flower sitting in a clay vase out on the balcony.

He had insisted on a balcony with an outside view, so he could map the star and Melchior could continue his research of the historical writings of Judea. Balthazar was confident Gaspar and Melchior would manage to follow him and be at the inn before too long. After all, how many inns could there be in Bethlehem? Balthazar was so excited to get to work that he didn't unpack anything except his instruments and maps. There was a table in the room just the right size to lay out his maps and tools. Now he could set up his tools and continue tracking the star. When Gaspar and Melchior arrived, they would quickly compile a few maps of the city, so they could narrow down the birthplace of this new king, or Prince of Peace or whoever he was.

Abada ran up the alley behind a cloaked figure that turned and pointed toward the building across the street from where they stood.

"This is the inn?" asked Abada.

"Yes. Yes. I swear," said the cloaked figure. "Now pay me. Pay me."

"How can I trust you? And how do you know it was them?"

"I saw the ring. I saw the king's ring you mentioned on his hand."

"You saw all three of them?" asked Abada becoming more and more excited.

"No. I only saw the one, but I know I spied the king's ring. It is just like yours."

"I said I would pay for information about all three men. Not just one."

"Pay me or I will warn him you are looking for him." The cloaked man started to run for the inn.

"Alright! Alright!" said Abada. "You will get your reward."

Abada pushed a gold coin hard into the man's hand. The man put the coin into his pocket and ran away from Abada back down the alley. Abada flicked his wrist, and the coin sailed back to him out of the man's pocket. Abada put the coin and the string tied to it into his cloak. He turned to face his accomplices.

"Mirhabad, we must be certain all three of them are together. You take the first watch. Remember, we are looking for three men and one of them is already inside." Abada turned to Sahirabad. "The two of us should sleep while Mirhabad watches the inn. Wake me if you see anything suspicious."

Mirhabad pulled up a stool and slid it against the wall where he still had a good view of the inn. Then he sat down. He knew he was looking for three men and he would not let Abada down. There was that word again, down. Now, how could it mean feathers on a duck and movement and disappointment all at the same time? These sorts of things always gave Mirhabad's very open mind something to think about.

Mirhabad watched as two men on camels pulled up in front of the inn. He was supposed to watch for three men. There were two men in this group, not three but there was something Abada had said about another man. Mirhabad began to toss around some numbers in his head one, two, three, one, two, and three. But, Mirhabad's mind could only toss around one number at a time. So he would think about the number three and then he would think about the number two. Occasionally, the number one would drift into his mind, wait for a moment and leave. For Mirhabad, one was such a lonely number.

Melchior and Gaspar dismounted at the Inn of Bethlehem. Before they could even knock on the door, it flung open wide and the inn keeper motioned them inside welcoming his two special guests.

"Friends of Balthazar are friends of mine," said the inn keeper as he ushered them inside.

He was a greedy but shrewd man. He knew the accommodations in town were limited and if he could milk these men for more money then why shouldn't he; business is business. The inside of the small inn had a bar and it was much more crowded than usual thanks to tax season and the census being called. Balthazar was at the bar. He got up from his stool to introduce his friends to the inn keeper.

"These are my friends Melchior and Gaspar."

Balthazar raised a mug in their honor and handed them both a drink.

"I'm sure they are thirsty and ready for a good night's sleep."

"Certainly, certainly." The inn keeper pushed two customers off nearby stools and slipped them under Melchior and Gaspar.

"You know King Herod has slept in the Desert Inn Suite on more than one occasion. Your friend Balthazar has requested additional bedding and other necessities which will raise the price of the room…"

Melchior rummaged through his pockets and pulled out a small pouch of coins. He dropped a gold coin into the inn keeper's hands.

"Which will mean hiring additional staff and…"

Gaspar looked at Balthazar and silently pleaded for some financial help. Balthazar dropped another gold coin into the inn keeper's palm.

"It is also very late at night and the overtime I will have to pay is outrageous but you know…"

The inn keeper was performing a legal version of robbery. He knew these obviously wealthy men had nowhere else to turn, so he would gladly make a few extra coins for the night. Balthazar deliberately counted out one gold coin at a time into the inn keeper's outstretched hands until he stopped talking and turned his attention to preparing their room for them.

"Welcome my friends to our final destination, Bethlehem." Balthazar lifted his mug and encouraged Melchior and Gaspar to lift theirs also. "Here's to Bethlehem." They all clicked their clay mugs together.

Melchior said under his breath. "Welcome to nowhere I would ever want to live."

He had already forgotten about his ten years in a leper colony. The freedom to go wherever he wanted whenever he wanted was already changing him and making him forgetful and ungrateful.

Mirhabad got up from his stool and stretched for a moment. He looked down the street away from the inn and saw a man leading a slow moving donkey. There was a woman on the donkey and from where he sat Mirhabad thought she looked pregnant.

"Tourists probably," he muttered to himself. If it had been a normal night Mirhabad would have contemplated robbing them, but he was supposed to be looking for a group of three men.

Mirhabad yawned then realized it was time to wake his brother for lookout duty. Mirhabad walked down the alley looking for Sahirabad. He could not find him anywhere and was tempted to wake up Abada. He could see Abada with his cloak pulled over his head lying next to the adobe wall. Abada had pulled a small pile of hay together and was using it for a pillow. Mirhabad decided to make one more sweep of the alley looking for Sahirabad. He stood still listening to the night. He could hear the soft rumbling of sound sleep nearby. He finally found Sahirabad curled up inside a barrel, snoring and fast asleep.

"Get up," Mirhabad whispered into the barrel. "Come on. Get up!"

He picked up Sahibabad's left leg and dropped it, nothing but more snoring. He picked up both legs and dropped them onto the ground, still no response. Mirhabad wiggled his way between the barrel and the wall and pushed the barrel as hard as he could. The barrel rolled across the alley, crashed into the far wall and then splintered into a thousand pieces.

Abada was awake instantly. Sahirabad groggily got up staring and glaring at his brother. Mirhabad could not stop laughing. Sahirabad knew what had happened and charged at his brother, but the steel rungs from the barrel wrapped around his feet making him trip and stumble backwards across the alley. He managed to keep his balance until he got to the back corner of the building. He could see the goat pen but nothing could stop his momentum as he tumbled over the top rung, breaking the gate off its hinges. Three full grown goats and one kid started bleating and blaring warnings as they jumped over Sahirabad making a hasty exit down the alley.

Sahirabad was now fully awake and set on revenge against his brother. He bore at Mirhabad full speed with his head down attempting to ram him. He never quite got there. Abada stuck his leg out tripping him as he ran by. Instead of running into his brother he flew into a wagon breaking it with a shattering crash.

"Why didn't I just hire a barrel of monkeys to help me?" said Abada. "Can you two possibly make more noise?"

Abada turned to Mirhabad.

"Now that the entire neighborhood knows we're here have you seen anything?"

"Yes. Yes I did. I saw two men on camels arrive at the inn," said Mirhabad.

"Two men on camels you say?"

"Yes. They looked like merchants but there were only two of them."

"I see. How many men did I say were already inside the inn?"

Mirhabad knew one man had ridden a camel and was inside the inn. He also knew two more had arrived since. He however, could not make the connection between these two numbers in his mind.

"What," asked Abada, "is one plus two?"

Mirhabad had learned a long time ago when he did not know the answer to a question, it was best to just ask another question.

"One plus two what?"

"One plus two of anything." The veins on Abada's neck were beginning to bulge.

"Well," began Mirhabad, "one gaggle of geese contains at least five geese and a herd of goats might have ten or more."

Abada exploded.

"It's THREE! T-H-R-E-E! One plus two is three!"

Sahirabad sauntered over next to his brother and held up four fingers. He slowly lowered one of them as he counted silently to himself.

"I believe he's right."

Abada glared at Sahirabad.

"Try not to be as dumb as your brother. Stand guard. Since they are all together now, they will most likely stay that way. Wake me if you see them leave, all three of them."

Abada pulled his hood further over his eyes, coiled up against the wall and rebuilt his nest. Mirhabad crawled into the abandoned, broken wagon and fell asleep while Sahirabad took his turn watching the inn.

Chapter 23
Abduction

Gaspar stood up and jubilantly exclaimed.

"I've got it! According to all our calculations and the last position of the star, the child should be born somewhere in this quadrant of the city."

Balthazar ran over to the map table where Gaspar was seated. He stared at a square on the map showing the azimuth and zenith of the star. Compass circles and calculations were scrawled across the entire area except for one open quadrant. Gaspar put an 'X' in the middle of the open area.

"This is where we must search. Now let's go to bed. We can start first thing in the morning."

Balthazar grabbed several magnifying glasses from the table, picked up the map, grabbed the pouch containing the orbs, then put on his tunic and turban and headed for the door. He wasn't about to wait for morning.

"Where are you going?" asked Gaspar.

"I feel a great need and urging to push on and find this child. I cannot explain or describe it. I have been attacked by snakes, almost killed by a sandstorm and thrown into prison. The night will hold no danger greater than what we have already faced. I am going to find this child tonight."

Balthazar was at the door. He turned to face his friends.

"Well, what are you two waiting for? Let's go." Balthazar wiggled out of the room, down the stairs and out the front door of the inn. Melchior and Gaspar packed up the gifts they had brought for this occasion and the other maps and tools. They shut the door, walked down the stairs and followed Balthazar outside. They were uncertain of what to do but curious enough to follow.

Balthazar had ordered the camels and already had them waiting when Melchior and Gaspar came out of the inn.

"It is cloudy. Perhaps the sky will clear. If it does not I…"

The clouds meant they would have to search Bethlehem building by building. He swallowed hard and looking up he knew the clouds were not going away any time soon. Just seeing the star would have lifted his spirits. But, perhaps the stars purpose was finished. It had gotten them this close.

Of all the times the orbs had helped him during this journey, he believed they would help him now. He opened the well-worn leather pouch. All three of the orbs were inside sitting quietly beside each other. He closed the pouch and moved Jandak out into the street.

"If the sky doesn't clear then what?" asked Melchior. "You didn't finish your thought."

"If the sky doesn't clear then I hope the orbs have something left in them to help us one more time."

Balthazar stared at the map and began navigating the streets in the direction of Gaspar's "X" and the last known position of the star.

Sahirabad felt like he was being controlled by a string running right through the top of his head. Every couple of minutes his head would flop over onto his chest. He would slap his face fighting the sleep determined to bring him down. However, sleep finally won and Sahirabad tumbled forward into the middle of the alley kicking his stool over into a brass pot. The thud and resounding clanging of the brass pot woke Abada again.

He stormed over to Sahirabad and kicked him in the stomach. "You fool. You fell asleep didn't you? How are we supposed to know if they…"

Across the street the front door of the inn opened and Balthazar stepped out onto the walkway. Abada threw himself against the building and pinned Sahirabad to the ground with his foot. The only sound was Mirhabad's snoring drifting across the street. Abada picked up a rock and threw it at Mirhabad. The stone made a hollow sound like it had hit an empty wooden bowl. Mirhabad woke up with a start and fell out of the wagon.

"Shhhh," said Abada.

He turned his attention to the inn. Abada watched Balthazar bring three camels around to the front of the inn.

"He must be waiting for his two friends," said Abada.

This was the chance he had been looking for. Abada released his foot from Sahirabad's head and motioned for Mirhabad to come over to the wall.

"Mirhabad, when the Wise Men came in earlier were any of them carrying a baby or was anyone else with them?" asked Abada.

"No. No one was carrying a baby and they were alone."

"Good. It means they haven't found the child yet. The only reason they would be leaving now must mean they are still searching for it."

Abada walked back to the corner and looked out across the street at the Wise Men. He pulled a magnifying glass from his pocket and watched as Balthazar studied a map. Abada could see an "X" on the map from the available moonlight. He watched as the three men headed down the street.

"They have a map with them but it looks incomplete. I think we should wait until they have completed more of their search. Let them do as much of the work as possible. Then we'll take the map, find the child and finish the job."

"What is so important about this child?" asked Sahirabad as he dusted off his clothes.

"I don't know and I don't care," said Abada as he glanced once more at the Wise Men. "Now take me to this child."

Abada rushed to the back of the alley and untied their camels. "Stay close. Stay silent. Stay in the shadows."

He nudged his camel out into the street as the Wise Men turned the corner. He looked back at his two accomplices.

"Come on you two, we don't have all night." The assassins snuck out into the street, staying in the shadows.

Abada began thinking of names for his new province. Mirhabad and Sahirabad thought as little as possible. Following the Wise Men was easy for Abada. He had tracked hundreds of people in the darkness. Abada was about to announce his plan for capturing the Wise Men when they inexplicably stopped at an intersection. The three assassins stopped too, ducking into an alley. Abada strained to see what had brought the Wise Men to a halt.

Abada heard the bleating before he saw them. The Wise Men had stumbled upon a herd of sheep and were now surrounded. Abada's mind worked quickly. This was the perfect opportunity to take the Wise Men out of the picture, steal the map and find the child.

"We will charge into the intersection and create a stampede. During the chaos I'll grab the map."

Abada pulled his magnifying glass out and scoured the situation. Still looking down the street he worked out his plan.

"Mirhabad, you will take the man on the left. Sahirabad, you will take the man on the right. I shall take the man holding the map. If either of you needs help I will be next to you. Do you understand?"

Mirhabad and Sahirabad nodded. Abada hoped they did. He turned his camel around and prepared to stampede the sheep, steal the map and take out the Wise Men.

"We must do this as fast as possible."

He pulled a club from the folds of his robe, spurred his camel, turned the corner and raced down the street.

"I smell something don't you?" asked Balthazar.

"Yes. I believe I smell a pool of sewage. No. No that's not quite it. Oh, I know, it's a shepherd," said Gaspar,

"Same thing," said Melchior. "Shepherd. Sewage."

"Well perhaps this is the first time you have ever met a man who actually works for a living. That smell would be the sweat of a working man and to some it is a sweet aroma," said Boaz.

"Listen, we are in a bit of a hurry so if you and your animals would kindly clear the intersection we will continue our search," said Balthazar.

"What are you searching for?" asked Boaz.

"For a child," said Gaspar.

"What kind of child?" asked Boaz.

"A future king," said Balthazar, "one whose coming has been prophesied since the beginning of time."

"We are looking for a child too. He is to be born in a manger." Mattathias stepped forward into the moonlight.

Balthazar turned Jandak in Boaz's direction.

"Well, we most certainly must not be looking for the same child. We are looking for a king. What would a king want with a group of sloppy, smelly, uncivilized shepherds? And why would he be born in a stable full of animals?"

"I wouldn't be so sure. What if we're both looking for..."

Boaz was unable to finish his sentence.

Abada stormed into the intersection scattering the sheep and striking Balthazar across the back of the head with a thick wooden club. Balthazar's turban lessened the blow, but he nonetheless shuddered, slid off Jandak, and fell onto the street.

Balthazar landed directly in front of Boaz and for a moment there was a brief glimpse of recognition and curiosity. What were the odds they could both possibly be searching for the same child? There was no time to ponder the question. In the next instant, there was an explosion of sheep, camels, clubs, and men. The screams and groans of the wise men, shepherds and assassins mingled with camels baying and sheep bleating.

Sahirabad had practiced using a rope his entire life and was good with it in his hands. He tossed a lasso from the back of his camel in full stride. The loop of rope settled so gently over Gaspar's arms he didn't even realize what had happened until it was too late. Sahirabad and his camel sped by pulling

Gaspar off his camel and onto the ground. However, Sahirabad left his rope tied to the saddle of his camel and now his camel bolted pulling Gaspar, Sahirabad and several sheep in circles.

Mirhabad crashed into the back of Melchior's camel, and hit Melchior squarely in the back. They both tumbled down onto the street and into the stampeding herd of sheep.

The intersection disappeared in a thick cloud of dust and debris. Occasionally a head, hand or foot would poke out of the cloud only to be sucked back into the vortex of man and beast. Boaz was the only one unaffected by this sudden attack. He knew they had to separate from the chaos. The shepherds could not afford to become involved in whatever was going on in the intersection.

"Mattathias, Timothy?"

Boaz raised his voice to be heard above the bedlam.

"We have got to get out of here!"

"What's going on?" asked Mattathias.

"Assassins or mercenaries would be my guess," said Boaz.

"Mercenaries? Assassins? Who sent them and why?" asked Timothy.

Boaz knew. He had seen the signet ring on Abada's hand. King Herod had sent them and that could only mean bad things. Confused but knowing this was neither the time nor the place to discuss anything, Boaz skirted around the melee and maneuvered several sheep with him into a corner out of harm's way.

"Follow me. Take what sheep you can but follow me now. Hurry!"

Mattathias and Timothy appeared from the midst of the dust cloud and followed Boaz down a side street and into an alley until they came to a dead end.

"We will build a pen here for what sheep we can find. Then after the coast is clear we will go back and pick up any stragglers."

It only took a few minutes and the street fight had calmed down. Boaz crept back toward the intersection keeping next to the buildings and running from one dark shadow to the next. The three assassins and the Three Wise Men were nowhere in sight. Boaz gave a quick pluck of two notes on his shepherds harp. The notes were the signal to Mattathias and Timothy the danger had passed.

"Come on," said Boaz pushing a few more stragglers into their makeshift pen. "There are only a few mangers in this area. Let's see how quickly we can find this child. We're taking the sheep with us. There will be food for them at the manger."

A few lilting bleats from the sheep were the only sounds heard as the shepherds mingled and meandered along the street, looking for a manger.

Balthazar tried to straighten up.

"Who are you? We are here on behalf of King Herod."

"Shut up," said Abada in a hushed, menacing tone. "King Herod means nothing to me."

Balthazar sensed danger was coming but had no time to react. Abada's blow across the front of his face hurt badly and threw him backwards. Abada slipped the ring from Balthazar's finger as he fell. Balthazar could not break his fall and landed hard on the leather pouch slung over his back. He heard the orbs shatter and it made his heart sink as he passed out from the blow.

The three assassins rummaged over their victims. They tugged at the Wise Men's turbans and cloaks looking for anything worth stealing or bartering with at the market.

"What's this?"

Mirhabad slipped a leather pouch off Balthazar. He untied the leather thong and peered inside. He could see nothing as he inserted his hand feeling along the sides of the pouch.

"Ouch!" He yanked his hand from the pouch and licked the drop of blood from the end of his finger.

"Well whatever it was it's broken now."

He threw the pouch on the ground and picked up Gaspar's turban.

"Very nice." He said and the rummaging continued.

Sahirabad discovered two long ornate glass vases plugged with corks. "Wine." he thought.

He lifted it toward his mouth, biting into the cork plug. Sputtering he immediately spit the piece of cork out. "It's some kind of perfume."

He dropped the vase onto the street and looked at a second one lying on its side. This one he picked up and sniffed the cork first.

"More perfume. What kind of men are they, carrying perfume with them?"

He dropped the second vase on the street next to the first one.

"Must be perfume merchants," Mirhabad said.

"The vases are irrelevant. We must find the map. Tie them up and leave them here." Abada went back out into the intersection looking for the map. A chilly wind was blowing. Abada's hood caught a stiff breeze, and the hood blew off his head and over onto his back. He pulled his hood back up cursing the wind while it pelted him with sand. An empty wine skin flew past him. An awning tore loose from a wall and flapped against a window waking up a weary store owner. A piece of parchment picked up by the breeze caught him squarely across the face. Abada sputtered, spit and cursed even more as he peeled the parchment away from his face. Just before he threw it down the markings on it caught his eye.

"The gods are truly smiling on me now," he said.

It was the map made by the Wise Men! Several blocks of buildings had been crossed out. There were only a few spaces not filled in on the map. He knew he could find this child now. His spirits lifted and so did his price tag to King Herod. He didn't want just a province anymore. He wanted a palace to go with it. If he gave the three fools to King Herod, along with the child, he might just get his province and a palace.

Chapter 24
Isaac and Naomi

Naomi had been unable to sleep through the night ever since Melchior, Gaspar and Balthazar had left the colony. Her dreams were filled with fire and smoke and faces she did not know. Images of a town and a child haunted her even during the daylight hours. She woke up one night and her neck was bleeding from a small cut. She got up to bandage herself and realized her bedroom had turned darker than usual.

The Sword of Light always filled her room with just enough light to see, but not tonight. The hilt of the sword had turned dark and in the night, almost invisible. Naomi pulled the Sword of Light from its scabbard. It felt cold and lifeless in her hands. She stared at the sword. Moving across the flat surface of the blade was the distorted face of a man wearing a crown? She laid the sword on her bed and ran to get Isaac. He was the closest thing the colony had to a magi now that Melchior was gone. Maybe he would know the face in the sword and understand the changes in her blade.

Isaac lifted the sword gently from Naomi's bed. He wasn't quite sure he should even be allowed to touch it. He could feel the coldness and the heaviness of it but he could see no faces or images. Naomi laid her hand on the hilt and immediately the sword felt even colder and heavier. Isaac saw a face flowing across the width of the blade. Images of blood and death mixed with each other. He shrieked so loudly they both released the sword and it fell back onto Naomi's bed. Isaac backed across the room into a corner sobbing.

"Isaac."

Naomi shook him and looked into his eyes. They were empty of the light and joy she was used to seeing. Naomi thought someone had taken over his soul and it frightened her.

"Isaac!" She shook him harder.

He hung his head and mumbled. "Herod. King Herod."

Isaac looked up at Naomi with so much sadness in his eyes.

"He intends to kill them. All of them."

He stumbled forward into Naomi's arms. Naomi moved the sword from her bed and laid Isaac down. His mouth was moving, but he made no sound. His eyes rolled back into his head, and Naomi was afraid letting him touch the sword had been a bad idea. She had allowed no one else to touch it since she had pulled it from the grasp of the orbs. But, Isaac had touched it, and seen things not meant to be seen. The sword had obviously shown him King Herod but what did Isaac mean Herod would kill them all? Kill who? The whole town of Jerusalem? His own family? The baby? The Three Wise Men and the baby? Without even asking she knew that was it. King Herod for some reason was going to kill the baby and the Wise Men.

Instantly she was shaking Isaac.

"Has he killed them already? Answer me!"

Naomi shook Isaac harder than she should have, but she wanted an answer. The pit in her stomach was growing by the second. Her desperation was getting the best of her. Isaac was unresponsive. Naomi dropped him back onto her bed and began to pack for a trip to Jerusalem or Bethlehem or wherever she had to go. After all they had been through; Melchior had to still be alive. She paused for a moment. Then she brushed the thought from her mind, the thought of what she would do to the poor soul who would dare take Melchior's life. It was gruesome, too gruesome for words and she knew the Sword of Light would be against her if she thought of it again.

Naomi gently picked up the sword thinking it would show her some sign of hope, some sign of life, but it did not. It sat in her hand lifeless and filled with an impenetrable blackness only the mind of the most evil can embrace.

"What has happened to my blade?" Naomi turned it over and over in her hand. Was it only showing her the depths of how evil some men could be to spur her into action?

She had already made up her mind. She was leaving. Now. And, like it or not, Isaac was coming with her. His knowledge of Jerusalem and the surrounding area would be invaluable. Plus, she was hoping he could tell her more of what he had seen in the sword. And maybe, just maybe, if they prepared themselves, together they would hold the sword again and take another gaze into the blade. Naomi couldn't help herself. Her blade, her body, her heart, her mind were all screaming for her to find the Wise Men and this baby. She would find them and save them somehow. It didn't seem like much of a plan, but she knew the Wise Men would do no less for her; they would come for her no matter what, and she could do no less for Melchior and the other Wise Men.

Chapter 25
No Trouble

Balthazar snapped out of his stupor. He was awakened by a searing pain at the base of his head. He knew he had been knocked out. He knew he was tied up and lying on the ground somewhere in Bethlehem. And unfortunately, he knew something terrible had happened to the orbs he had been carrying. He strained to move his back off the ground. The broken orbs grated and cracked beneath him. They were shattered along with his hopes of somehow pulling one last miracle out of them. After being robbed and losing the map, their chances of finding the child with the orbs was slim. Without them... well he didn't want to think about failure but it was hard to see anything positive about their current situation.

The robbers had taken almost everything. The only reason they had left the orbs was because they were broken. The robbers hadn't even done that! Balthazar had broken them by falling on them. Balthazar struggled against the ropes but they were expertly tied by the assassins.

"Gaspar."

No answer.

"Melchior."

A foggy, feeble voice replied.

"Yes. I am here but I cannot escape these bindings."

Melchior, too, was struggling to remove the ropes from his hands but was having no success. Gaspar, leaning against the wall, was unmoving and unresponsive. Balthazar was afraid he might not even be alive until he saw Gaspar's breaths warming the chilly air.

"One more miracle," Balthazar said out loud.

He tried sitting up but only managed to cut his hand on a piece of the broken orbs.

"Ouch."

"What's the matter?" asked Melchior.

"Oh, I was hoping the orbs might have one last miracle in them but I have fallen on them and broken them. Now they have abandoned me too by cutting my hand."

"Did you say cutting your hand?"

"Yes I did."

"What about using a broken piece of orb to cut the ropes?"

Balthazar was a very smart man but his despair from breaking the orbs had blinded him to the fact that maybe by breaking them they were giving him the miracle he needed. He would have never voluntarily broken them no matter how desperate the situation might have been. It was an unintended miracle, but a miracle nonetheless.

Balthazar, still on his back, sifted through the dirt of the street until he felt the cold hard shard of a sliver from the shattered orbs in his hand. He turned the sliver over and cut through the ropes so easily it surprised him. The ropes fell away from his wrists. He sat up and used the shard to cut the ropes from his feet.

"You did it Balthazar. You are free! Now come and cut my bindings."

Melchior sat up in the middle of the alley and held his bound hands out behind his back. Balthazar sliced through the ropes, and crept over to Gaspar. Gaspar's stuttered breaths came and went like a fire running low on fuel. Balthazar freed Gaspar's hands and feet and gently shook him.

"Gaspar. Gaspar. Wake up. We must get out of here."

Gaspar mumbled something, but Balthazar could not understand him. It didn't matter what Gaspar was saying they had to get up and get going.

"Melchior. Come here. I am afraid we may have to help Gaspar to his feet."

Melchior came over and together they lifted Gaspar up.

"I, uhhh, fell off my camel. That's all I remember," muttered Gaspar as he feebly took a few steps.

"Gaspar. Are you alright? Can you ride?" asked Balthazar.

"I think so. Just give me some time to clear my head. I'll be fine."

He craned his neck from side to side and felt his jaw. He was going to be sore tomorrow but thought he could ride.

"We have no map. We have searched all the quadrants in the area except for a few. Whoever robbed us has taken our camels and left theirs behind."

Balthazar turned toward a still woozy Gaspar.

"Gaspar we need your help. Can you remember from the map which area we have yet to search?"

Gaspar did his best to ease his throbbing head and quickly drew a map in the dirt from memory. He sketched in the buildings and streets they had not inspected yet.

"You see. There is only a very small area where the child must be."

Balthazar looked up into the sky and sure enough the clouds were still there in full force. The orbs were gone now and the star was nowhere in sight. It was up to them. They would have to search block by block. But what kind of building or home were they looking for? Where would such a child king be born? He wished he knew, but it certainly wouldn't be in some nasty barn full of animals and smelly shepherds. Balthazar surveyed the alley one more time and saw the pouch lying on the street. He thought about leaving it, but changed his mind. He picked up what pieces of the broken orbs he could find and placed them inside the pouch.

The colony had gone through the belongings left behind by Akbar and the desert gypsies and now there were two things in particular Naomi and Isaac would need, the Arabian horses. Naomi went to Houlak and inquired about them.

"Oh my dear," said Houlak, "They are fine horses indeed, king quality. Highly bred for speed and endurance. Why do you ask?"

"I am going to find Melchior, Gaspar and Balthazar. I am taking Isaac with me."

"You can't take Isaac back there. Herod will kill him."

"I must have Isaac with me. I cannot find Jerusalem and the Wise Men without him. He knows the area so well."

Houlak knew Naomi was serious. Naomi was a different woman since the Sword of Light had arrived. It had definitely made her more confident and purposeful. Houlak could sense Naomi would not be swayed.

"Prepare for your journey. The horses and provisions will be made ready for you immediately."

Naomi dashed off to prepare herself and deliver the news to Isaac. She did not have time to bring the colony together and make a formal announcement; Houlak would have to inform the others. Naomi went back to her room. The Sword of Light was softly glowing again. It had not returned fully to its former self but seeing it glow gave Naomi the confidence she was doing the right thing. She only packed a few absolutely necessary things and then went to get Isaac.

Isaac looked at Naomi like she had three heads.

"You want me to go back to Jerusalem?"

He paused and stared incredulously at her.

"Listen to me Naomi. Have you heard the old saying about King Herod? He only says goodbye once."

Isaac shook his head.

"It means if you manage to escape from his grasp once you won't do it again. No one ever has. If he even thinks I am back in the area, I'm dead. Do you understand that?"

Naomi gave Isaac a desperate look. He knew he was going whether he wanted to or not.

"You must go with me. You are my only hope in getting to Jerusalem and Bethlehem. Once there I will release you to return on your own if you so choose, but you will go with me, and you will do so now."

Isaac turned and began to roll up his bed.

"Let me grab these few maps I have put together."

"The colony is providing everything we will need. Meet me in front of the stone wall outside the gate."

Naomi turned to go but glanced back at Isaac.

"I will protect you with my life and the Sword of Light. I will see to it that you arrive back here safely; even if I do not. I swear it."

She was gone before Isaac could even reply. He was not comforted by what she had said. The sword was no match for Herod. Isaac knew about Herod and his spies. He knew about Abada and knew if Herod were still king, Abada would be close at hand. Isaac was one of only a handful of people who could say they had met Abada, or seen Abada and lived to tell about it.

Isaac knew Abada well and if they should meet him, Isaac would be prepared. He made a special trip to pick up the one item which might save their lives. No one could see him or discover it until they were gone. He could not even tell Naomi. She would forbid it and not understand.

Naomi and Isaac mounted their horses. Houlak stood still, holding the horses' reins. She could not raise her head to look at them. She thought she would never see either of them again. Naomi understood but it could not be helped. She and Isaac may already be too late.

"Naomi," Houlak began, "these are fine horses but they cannot make it to Jerusalem without stopping. I am afraid even these horses will be driven beyond their limits."

"We will do what we must. The Arabian horses are almost like camels. They can manage a great distance quickly and without water."

Naomi knew the horses might not make it, but if she was willing to sacrifice her own life, she was willing to sacrifice the horses if necessary. They had been left by the gypsies and she could think of no more noble purpose than to save Melchior, Balthazar and Gaspar. She had learned enough about their pilgrimage to know they would give their own lives in order to complete their journey to this child. She could now do no less.

"Hiyaaah."

Naomi and Isaac turned their steeds into the night leaving the colony behind. Houlak had a sick and sad feeling about them not returning. She hoped she was wrong, but the uneasiness she felt stayed with her.

"All clear," said Balthazar.

They moved out into the street. He let Gaspar take the lead since Gaspar knew the area they had yet to search better than he or Melchior. Balthazar kept a close eye on Gaspar, hoping the wooziness would not get the better of him. It was funny in a way, for the first time ever Gaspar was on a camel and ahead of him. It made Balthazar smile and he didn't even know why.

They crept slowly down the street and stopped occasionally, listening for a baby's cry and watching for a late night flickering torch. Most of Bethlehem was fast asleep and the buildings were dark. Balthazar guessed if a baby was being born there would have to be some kind of light nearby, either a fireplace which they could smell or a torch or two they could see through a window or a crack in a door. Babies were known to cry so the Wise Men were being as quiet as possible.

'The Three Wise Men'. Melchior liked the thought of it. At first he hadn't, but the more he dwelt on the name the more he realized he was growing fond of it. He knew why too. He, Gaspar and Balthazar were truly becoming friends. He was looking forward to remembering this time together and remaining friends for life. It was a pleasant thought but it left his mind as he spotted a small crack of light at the end of the street. There was no mistaking it. Through a partially opened door he caught the quick flicker of a torch.

"Look." Melchior said loudly enough for Gaspar and Balthazar to hear.

"Torchlight, in the building at the end of the street."

Melchior strained to see through the darkness and he shook his head. It was a stable.

"Never mind," he said. "It's just a stable for feeding animals. The king child we are searching for won't be born there."

"Oh, and who says so?"

Boaz, Timothy and Mattathias stepped out from the shadows of a nearby building. Several sheep smelled the feed in the stable, and like a beacon, they followed the aroma of food down the street. Boaz stepped forward standing in front of Gaspar and his camel.

"Listen. We don't want any trouble OK?" Boaz looked up at Gaspar.

"And neither do we," said Gaspar.

Balthazar dismounted, hoping that being on the same level as the shepherds would ease some of the tension.

"We are looking for a child," said Balthazar.

"My two friends and I have been following a star. It has led us here to Bethlehem. We believe it is a sign of great importance, possibly the sign of an immortal or a king's birth."

"Well, before the bandits attacked us I was trying to tell you we have seen heavenly hosts," said Boaz. "Some might call them seraphim or angels."

"Yes," said Timothy, "their shouts were so loud we were thrown to the ground. And when they blew their trumpets, the earth shook."

Mattathias shuffled his feet and said, "I thought we were about to die. There were thousands of these shimmering creatures filled with light and fire. They sang and spoke to us. One of them had a glass sword and read from a scroll."

Melchior, still sitting on his camel felt smug and he could not help himself. "Ridiculous," he said.

"A glass sword?" asked Balthazar.

"Yes," said Boaz. "It was so beautiful and it filled the sky with rainbows and fire."

"We know of another glass sword. Maybe their story isn't so ridiculous Melchior."

"We were told the baby would be found in a manger," Boaz said as he turned and pointed to the end of the street.

"And in case you didn't know it, that is a stable, and inside every stable is a manger."

"Our guidance has been a star. We call it the Star of Bethlehem," said Balthazar.

"Oh, I see. And just where is this star of yours?"

Boaz stepped back away from the Wise Men and gazed into the sky.

"So, we have heard angels and you are following a star. Which one sounds crazier to you? Which star are you chasing? I see one through the clouds right over there."

Mattathias pointed at a shooting star gliding in and out of the clouds.

"There goes a shooting star. Looks like it made a rainbow. There must be a pot of gold over there."

Mattathias walked up next to Balthazar. He was ready for a little trouble no matter what Boaz had said. "Sounds to me like someone has had their head in the clouds a little too long."

"There will be a manger inside that stable." Boaz said it again and he headed in the direction of the stable door.

"Are you certain the angels said a manger?" asked Balthazar. "Maybe you misunderstood. It does seem like an odd place for a king to be born, doesn't it?"

"Perhaps he is being born in the lowliest place of all on purpose," Mattathias said. "If he were born in a palace he would represent royalty. Being born in a manger, anyone, even shepherds and animals, could claim him as their own."

Boaz and Balthazar were stunned. Neither of them had ever thought of this. Mattathias had uncovered the reason for shepherds and kings both being invited to this special birth in such an unlikely place.

"You may be right," Balthazar said. "You may just be right. Let's all go together."

Chapter 26
The Manger

The three assassins sauntered onto the street. Abada had a firm grip on the map fluttering in the breeze. Looking around, he saw movement just ahead of him. Spilling onto the street from some type of low lying building was a shaft of light. Abada stared harder and now could see the shifting shadows of shepherd hooks and camels between him and the light.

"Dismount," he said. "Tie up the camels and block the street with them. Do it now and be quiet."

Sahirabad and Mirhabad pulled their camels to a halt. Mirhabad tied his camel to a post on one side of the street and Sahirabad tied his to a post on the opposite side. Jandak was tied to the front of one camel and the back of the other so he completed the blockade.

Abada pulled Mirhabad and Sahirabad off to the side next to one of the buildings to lay out his plan of attack.

"Our three friends have managed to escape, and have arrived before us. For some reason they appear to be preparing to enter a stable at the far end of the street."

Abada turned to confirm the group was still heading for the stable. "It doesn't seem like anyone has made it there yet. There are some shepherds with them as well. Could be the group we ran into earlier. I don't know."

Abada took a dagger from his cloak and drew an outline of the scene on the back of the Wise Men's map.

"Mirhabad, you will go behind this row of buildings to the next street over. Run ahead of us to the end of the street then cut over one block and wait here in the shadows just outside the stable doors. Sahirabad, you will do the same thing, but you will go behind the buildings on the opposite side of the street behind us. I will track them down the street in front of us. When I give the signal, one clap, you two will block the entrance to the stable and I will keep them from coming this way back down the street. Got it?"

"What do we do if they fight back?" asked Mirhabad.

"We have already taken what weapons the Wise Men had. The other three appear to be shepherds armed only with shepherd hooks."

Abada stared past his two assassins and shrugged his shoulders.

"They will back down once they see our blades."

He patted the sword hanging by his side.

"Now go. Run quickly to get ahead of them."

Sahirabad and Mirhabad ran down the alley. Abada waited, giving them time to reach their positions.

The faint cries of a woman in the midst of childbirth filled the air and Balthazar knew the shepherds were right. This was the place. All the doubt about a stable and all the struggles melted away as he stepped toward the stable door.

Balthazar heard a faint clap but it meant nothing to him until Mirhabad and Sahirabad stepped out of the shadows and blocked his way.

Balthazar thought perhaps others had come to celebrate with the Wise Men and the shepherds.

"Oh, have you come to see the new king?" he said.

It suddenly dawned upon him they had not when they shoved him back from the door and drew their swords. The shepherds and Wise Men turned away from the assassins only to be confronted by Abada.

"No. No. I'm afraid we haven't come to see the new king," said Abada. "And I'm quite certain you won't be seeing him tonight either, and none of you will live to see tomorrow if you make so much as a whisper."

Abada walked backwards down the street motioning Mirhabad and Sahirabad to move the group away from the stable door.

After walking everyone away from the door and backing them into an alley, Abada spoke.

"Line them up here." He drew a line in the sand with his sword. "Get them on their knees and tie their hands and feet behind their backs."

Mirhabad and Sahirabad shoved their blades into the backs of each Wise Man and forced them to their knees. Sahirabad, the expert knot tier, checked the ropes and pulled them even tighter.

The Wise Men and the shepherds faced Abada whose back was against the wall at the end of the alley. Abada paced back and forth in front of them becoming more and more pleased with this turn of events. It had been so easy.

"I must congratulate all of you on making it this far. But you are in Abada's territory now and only what I say happens in Bethlehem."

Abada stopped pacing and stared hard at his captives. Melchior could just make out Abada's eyes flitting back and forth, nervously, excitedly.

"You have all run out of options, I'm afraid," said Abada pacing once again.

"Oh, I think they have at least one more."

Even though the voice came from behind him, Melchior instantly recognized it. Naomi!

Melchior forgetting about Abada for the moment spun around on the street until he was facing her.

"Naomi," he said in a whisper.

The moonlight outlined her with a soft white glow. A light breeze blew across her body and the wind brushed her face with her hair. If it hadn't been Naomi, Melchior might have thought he was seeing an angel.

"Melchior," Naomi replied.

Abada grabbed Melchior's shoulders and forced him face first onto the ground.

"So, we have someone coming to the rescue for, what did you say his name was again, Melchior?"

Naomi pulled the Blade of Light from its scabbard. It spun off a shower of colorful sparks that fell to the ground and slowly died out. The Blade itself was crawling with light and more colors than a rainbow. Abada was no fool. Even though he could have attacked, he thought better of it. He knew this woman Naomi had acquired some sort of magical blade and without understanding what powers it might possess, he was in no mood to challenge her. Plus, he could see there was someone else with her, and until he knew how many people there were, he was in a bad spot with nowhere to run or hide.

Abada forced Melchior onto his feet.

"Since you seem to have some feelings for this one, I will take him with me as a hostage, and you my dear lady are going to back out into the street to let me and my cohorts pass."

Abada cut the ropes binding Melchior's feet, and with a sword at his throat, Melchior and Abada walked out into the nearby safety of the street. Now, if he needed it Abada at least had some running room.

Mirhabad and Sahirabad followed forcing their way down the alley leaving the prisoners tied up and still on their knees.

"It's alright," Melchior said. "I'll be with you all soon enough. He will have to release me eventually."

"Oh yes," said Abada, "I will release you as soon as I have the baby and am on my way."

Isaac knew Abada had never released anyone. Death was the only thing Abada understood; and as Herod's chief executioner, any human feelings he had once upon a time were long forgotten.

Unheard and unseen, Isaac pulled a garment bag from his camel. He unfurled the bag and peered inside. Naomi would have never let him bring it, but Isaac knew Abada could be bribed and turned against whoever he was working for. Greed can always be turned, and Isaac was about to offer Abada something worth more than Herod's entire kingdom.

Isaac pulled the drawstring tight, tucked the garment bag beneath an arm and rushed past Naomi toward Abada.

"Abada," Isaac said. "Remember me?"

Isaac pulled the hood from his head to reveal his face in the moonlight.

Abada, holding Melchior looked into the dimly lit face of Isaac. "Why, it cannot be. You had leprosy and were banished. Your name... Isaac, that's it!"

"Ah, it is true Abada. I had leprosy." Isaac tightened his grip on the garment bag and moved closer to Abada. "Now, I have a trade for you."

Isaac stretched out his arm holding the bag loosely in his hand. "What I have in this bag is worth more than all the gold in Herod's kingdom."

"You couldn't possibly offer me more. You're lying."

"Here in this bag is more power and riches than you could ever hope to possess. I promise."

"Oh, and you expect me to look into this bag and find myself staring face to face with a sand cobra."

Isaac moved closer. "Here, I will look first."

Isaac loosened the drawstring and stuck his arm into the bag all the way up to his shoulder. "You see? Nothing dangerous."

Abada wasn't in general a very curious person, but for some reason he was intrigued enough to take a look inside the bag. He handed Melchior over to Mirhabad then stared into the sack Isaac was still holding open for him.

It was not possible. Abada thought it might be a trick, but then, the impact of what it was hit him. Even in the darkness of the bag he could see just enough of its size and shape to recognize it. Without hesitating he reached his hand inside the bag, secured what was inside and thrust it above his head. The Blade of Nineveh!

No one could tell if the blade had found a completely willing host or not, but evil often grows on people in stages. The Blade of Nineveh was wasting no time making itself at home. The evil, hatred and death it contained coursed through Abada. His tongue hung loosely from his mouth, and drool formed at the corners of his lips. His eyes turned red and the blade, only knowing death, looked for its closest victim. Before Naomi or anyone else realized what was happening, Abada thrust the blade into Isaac, lifting him off the ground. For a moment, he dangled silently in the air, before sliding off the sword and onto the ground in a heap.

Naomi could not help herself. Anger, hatred and despair welled up inside her and she charged toward Abada. She carried the Sword of Light in front of her, but it was turning curiously dark again. With every step she took, it became heavier and darker. By the time she got close enough to Abada to strike him, she could barely keep it in the air. Abada saw her coming and the Blade of Nineveh was ready for her.

"What is wrong with you?" Naomi screamed at the Sword of Light. She had little time to dwell upon what was happening. The Blade of Nineveh crashed into the Sword of Light and for the first time her beautiful sword showed signs of damage. Part of the blade shattered and dark, black shards of crystal fell to the street.

Naomi staggered backwards into Melchior and Mirhabad. Melchior knew what was wrong and he whispered into her ear as she fell against him.

"The blade is useless if you attack in anger and hatred. It is the Sword of Light. You must wield it only with thoughts of justice and mercy. Use it to protect yourself and those you love. It understands those things."

Melchior saw Abada charging toward Naomi from behind. He thrust the weight of his body against her throwing her out of the path of danger. The Blade of Nineveh whistled by Naomi's head narrowly missing her but it nonetheless found a victim. Melchior instantly knew he would not survive the mortal wound as he crumpled to the ground.

The world stopped for Naomi. Every breath was agony and every fiber of her being was in denial. Isaac and Melchior, the two men she cared the most about in the entire world lay either dead or dying. One she loved with all her heart and the other she had sworn to protect with her own life.

The battle had been quick and quiet, and now the street was absolutely still. No one moved, and nothing could be heard except for the cries of a woman wafting from the nearby stable.

Gaspar began weeping openly and his cries mingled with the woman's. He closed his eyes, but even with them closed, he could still see his friend Melchior lifeless and blood covered, lying on the ground.

Naomi, standing in the middle of the street, struggled with all her might to remember what Melchior had just said. Here she stood trying to kill someone with no thought of the life she wanted to take. Now she willed within herself the mercy and justice Melchior said would feed and fuel the Sword of Light. The sword began to glow and at its very tip a small globe of orange and yellow light began to form.

Naomi kept her head down concentrating on the sword and the good it had inside just waiting to be released. The entire blade began to burn brightly with streaks of color never seen before or since. The sword became lighter in Naomi's hand and she raised it above her head. A single streak of light tore from the tip of the sword shooting into the night sky. This flash of light disappeared into the clouds sweeping them aside in its wake. Balthazar watched as this ball of light and the Star of Bethlehem collided.

Melchior, mortally wounded, blinked and then closed his eyes. The burst of light created by the collision was so bright it pushed through his tightly closed eyelids and permeated his entire body.

"The Light of all light has come," he said to himself.

And then, just as quickly as it had appeared, the light was gone and the street was dark and quiet again. But something was different, very different. Balthazar looked to the spot where Melchior had been lying in the street. He was no longer prone but was sitting up and patting his body with his hands. The blood stain on the front of his tunic had vanished. And the ropes! All the Wise Men's bindings were cut and coiled at their feet.

"I, I, don't... What happened?" Melchior got to his feet checking his body for the mortal wound that surely was still there.

Mirhabad and Sahirabad had seen enough. Without even looking at Abada, or waiting for him, they mounted their camels and rode them down the street away from the stable and the powerful magic they had just witnessed. Abada too decided the time to leave had come. He had the Blade of Nineveh. He didn't need the child or King Herod or anyone else. Isaac was right; he could have whatever kingdom he wanted. Now was a good time to prove the worth of the blade and form his own kingdom.

Isaac, however, was still and unmoving. Naomi rushed to him and rolled him over. His wound was serious and blood continued to seep onto the street.

"Isaac." Naomi slid her arms beneath his head and lifted him toward her face. "You are..."

"Dying. Yes I know." Isaac sputtered and the trickle of blood increased as it flowed from the corners of his mouth.

"I have finished my journey. I am part of the old order of things. I do not belong here anymore."

"I don't understand. What do you mean the old order?"

"The light you have just seen and felt has opened the door to a new city. I have arrived at the gate, but I cannot enter."

Isaac used what remaining strength he had to lift himself up and rest against Naomi's shoulder.

"This day you have been changed. The world has been changed. Things will no longer be as they were and I will not be a part of what they are to become. Look through the historical archives Melchior has gathered, the manuscripts of Judea and the old kings. Then perhaps you will understand. May you be given eyes to see and ears to hear."

Isaac slumped forward. Naomi knew he was gone. Melchior walked over to them and gently touched Naomi on the shoulder. He moved Isaac from her arms and laid him on the ground. The shepherds and the Wise Men surrounded them both in a somber circle of friends. They picked Isaac up and carried him over to the side of the street and placed him on the walkway.

Naomi stood over Isaac and addressed the Wise Men and the shepherds.

"I do not yet understand the things Isaac has spoken of tonight. I only know we each have a different path to travel." A single tear fell from her face. "I cannot allow Abada and the Blade of Nineveh to continue their rampage and kill at will. I must stop him before he and the Blade become one and he realizes its true power. That is my path, my destiny."

Naomi paused and in the stillness another cry could be heard wafting from the stable.

"Your path lies at the end of this street. Go, meet your king. I will take care of Abada."

Naomi knelt down next to Isaac and gave him one last kiss on the cheek. Then she walked over to her Arabian horse and untied it from its post.

Melchior handed her the reins as she settled into the saddle. "Will I ever see you again?"

"I don't know," Naomi said. "But I do know I love you."

She turned away from him and urged the horse into a full trot. Her eyes were stinging but it was not from the dust stirred up by her horse. She dared not look back.

The shepherds and the Wise Men knew there was nothing they could do for Isaac. They moved him off the sidewalk and into an alley. Gaspar covered him with his own royal tunic.

"He gave his life in order for us to finish our journey," said Balthazar.

No one else uttered a word. It was the crying of a baby that turned their attention once more to the stable door.

The Wise Men gathered their camels and what few belongings they still had. Somehow, the vials of frankincense and myrrh had made it through everything. Balthazar panicked realizing he had lost every gold piece he had brought with him. Despondent, he didn't even have the orbs any more. All he had was the old leather pouch containing the few remaining pieces of the broken globes. Opening the pouch Balthazar looked inside and somehow a single gold piece had managed to find its way inside the pouch. He pulled the coin out hoping it would be enough for a king. It was now all he had left.

Melchior, Gaspar and Balthazar mounted their camels and headed toward the stable door.

"Hey wait a minute." Balthazar stopped Jandak and looked back at the shepherds. "Aren't you coming with us? The child, the king is waiting."

"Yes. We will come with you," said Boaz.

"I have an idea," said Balthazar. "You shepherds should lead the way."

Mattathias was happy to be leading the group. He hesitated as he reached the stable door. He gingerly pushed it open and immediately took two steps backward sprinting as fast as he could back to Boaz.

"We cannot go in there." Mattathias shook as he said it.

"What are you talking about?" said Boaz

"There is a lion in there."

"A lion?"

"Oh that's impossible. Move over and let me take a look."

Boaz crept up to the stable door and through the crack he peered inside. It was a wondrous sight to behold. Animals of every kind were gathered in the stable. And yes, right in front of the door was a grand, majestic lion. Next to the lion were three sheep, quiet and resting. There were donkeys and cows and more animals than Boaz could count or name. And there, beneath his parent's gaze, in the center of the stable, was a baby wrapped in swaddling clothes, lying in a manger.

"Peace on earth. That's what the angel said," Boaz told the group. And for a moment, there was peace on earth. Boaz stepped back from the stable door, opened it wide and led them all inside.

Balthazar hung back for a moment. They were finally here. He looked up into the sky searching for the star, his star, the Star of Bethlehem. He couldn't seem to locate it. Scouring the night, he pulled out one of his magnifying glasses. The star was definitely gone. He had wondered if it would remain once he had found the child. He knew it was gone for good, its purpose completed. Then he smiled, entered the stable and closed the door behind him.

Chapter 27
Night Visitor

"I am going to tell King Herod about the child," said Balthazar.

"That would be suicide," said Gaspar.

"I don't see why we should," said Melchior.

Balthazar looked down at the ground and picked up a stray piece of wood and threw it onto the fire.

"I made a promise. I cannot go back on my word."

Balthazar walked around to the far side of the fire to keep the smoke from his eyes. The wind outside the city of Jerusalem had shifted. He gazed up into the night sky. Even though the heavens were filled with stars, it seemed empty to him now.

"What does it all mean? Maybe Herod knows," Balthazar said to no one in particular. "I surely don't understand."

He rolled up his star map, and put it away for the last time. "I must go see King Herod. If you choose not to go with me, that's fine, but I made a vow," said Balthazar.

"I understand vows, but this vow is one you must break."

Balthazar turned and looked through the flames of the fire at his friends, but it was not Gaspar or Melchior speaking.

"You cannot go to King Herod with the news of this child and his location."

Balthazar, Melchior and Gaspar all began circling the fire trying to discern where the voice was coming from. Slowly, as they continued walking around the fire, they could see the outline of a ghost or an angel; something in the fire was speaking to them.

"The voice is coming from the fire," said Balthazar.

"Yes. It is," replied Melchior.

Gaspar reached out toward the figure in the fire and the flames shot higher and outward, burning the hair on his hands and arms.

"Ouch." Gaspar jumped back from the fiery figure and blew on his arm.

"You cannot touch me so do not try again. No harm will come to you. I promise. I am only here to warn you not to return to King Herod."

"Why should we trust you? My arms! You have singed the hair on my arms," cried Gaspar.

"Look again," said the fiery visitor.

The hair on Gaspar's arms was completely restored and he couldn't even smell the scent of burnt hair.

"Come out of the fire and let us see you more clearly," said Balthazar. "We will keep our distance."

The fire billowed upward like a furnace being stoked and the flames turned from a burnt orange and yellow to a thousand shades of blue and white. A creature much taller and larger than any human emerged from the fire. It was filled with the shifting shades of blue and white flames just like the fire. His hair was so long it mingled with the flowing garment covering his body, and somewhere the hair, the garment and the fire all merged and became one just above the ground.

All three of the Wise Men stared at this marvelous being in awe, but Balthazar was undeterred in his decision to see King Herod.

"Balthazar, you don't mind if I call you by your name do you? I know you made a vow to return to King Herod," said the figure.

"How do you know my name?"

"I only know what has been given to me by the one who sees and knows all things. You have a great deal to learn about the mysteries of Him who has sent me my magi friend."

Balthazar swallowed hard. There were a great many things he did not understand and he decided against testing the fiery visitor's knowledge. He would just let this creature say whatever it felt was necessary, and then he would go see King Herod anyway.

"You are a stubborn man, Balthazar of Babylon."

Balthazar stepped behind Gaspar to avoid any further eye contact. This creature was obviously probing his mind.

"I will show you why you must not entertain any thoughts of returning to King Herod."

The fiery guest did an abrupt about face, waved his arms at the now blue and white campfire. He whispered a few unintelligible words and the flames widened out and leaped upwards flickering at the edges. Inside this broadened wall of flame a palace appeared. The Wise Men recognized it as Herod's palace.

"This is Herod's plan," said the visitor. "Listen."

The flames shifted and in the blue and white fire King Herod's face appeared. It was even more twisted and demonic than it had been when he was initially threatening the Wise Men. Herod's eyes were darker and his face was sunken and hollow.

"The Wise Men. The Foolish Men... I don't care what they call themselves. I will kill them and the child once they arrive here. There will be no king in Judea other than King Herod!"

The wall of flame dissipated leaving behind a veil of smoke hanging in the air displaying the disfigured, frozen face of King Herod. Then, as if it had never happened, the campfire returned to normal and the smoky face of King Herod disappeared.

"Alright." Balthazar hung his head, "I will not go to the palace and tell King Herod. None of us will."

Balthazar looked up at their visitor. He had so many questions. He didn't even know where to begin.

"I understand you have many things puzzling you, but tonight is neither the time nor the place for solving all the riddles from your journey. I will answer the most pressing question for you."

The visitor pulled three logs out of the fire and when he did, they were made whole again, like they had never been put into the blaze.

"Please, sit down for a moment and I will tell you what you need to know and why."

The flaming guest sat down on the sand across from the Wise Men.

"None of you can ever tell your kings about this child. They would have no more love for him than Herod. They have their earthly kingdoms, and they will spare nothing to keep those kingdoms in their grasp. You three have each experienced this before and during your journey. Every king is threatened by a new king, especially one who is proclaimed to be the King of Kings, and the Great I Am. This child you have seen will someday reveal himself to the world, but that time is not yet to be."

The visitor peered into each of the Wise Men and asked them all if they understood, but his lips did not move, and he did not speak. Gaspar, Melchior and Balthazar all nodded affirmatively.

"Good. Allow me to continue. Each of you will not be able to remember the child's name nor his parents' names. That too is for the baby's protection, and yours. Should anyone ask you information about him you will not be able to recall his name or location."

Balthazar drummed his fingers on the ground. Gaspar raised his hands to his head and Melchior merely scratched his chin.

"He's right," said Melchior. "I can't remember his name, but his mother's name was…"

Gaspar put his head in his hands. "Ummmm. I, I." He looked up into the burning blue eyes of their visitor. "I can't remember."

Balthazar didn't seem overly concerned. His other memories were so vivid; he would never forget the rest of what he had endured: the sand cobra, the dust storm, the leper colony… giving the gifts of gold, frankincense and myrrh. All of those things and so many more would stay with him forever.

"The Alpha and the Omega," said Balthazar.

"One of many titles written in the ancient scrolls which will someday be ascribed to him," said their fiery visitor.

The visitor arose and walked over to the three men. He laid a hand upon each of them.

"You will each be blessed in many ways, but fame and fortune will not be yours for what you have done. In return for your service and sacrifice, a tradition will be started in your honor, and it begins now. Balthazar let me see your trusty leather pouch which has been through so much."

Balthazar took the pouch from around his neck and handed it to the visitor. The pouch appeared so small in the fiery creatures enormous hands.

"I have something for you Balthazar." The visitor motioned for Balthazar to come forward. He lowered the small leather bag and Balthazar reached inside pulling out a crystal globe. It was just like the ones Balthazar had smashed into pieces but there was something inside this orb; a single, gold, spinning star.

"Inside this orb is a star. Your star. The Star of Bethlehem. It has been taken from the heavens and given to you because of your faith to begin this journey."

Then the blue fiery visitor turned to Gaspar. "Reach your hand inside. Pull out what you find."

Gaspar put his hand inside the pouch and pulled out an orb similar to Balthazar's. Inside his orb was a golden sand dune and a star resting just above it.

"You Gaspar did not give up when Balthazar walked away at Najaf. This dune is the place where you picked up the dream Balthazar left behind. You had hope when there was none."

Lastly, the figure turned to Melchior. The creature leaned the bag toward Melchior and rocked it gently back and forth. "There is something inside for you as well, Melchior."

Melchior was hesitant but finally reached into the pouch and pulled out an orb, an empty crystal orb. Melchior rolled it around in his hands, but there was nothing inside it.

'I am an empty fool I guess,' he thought.

"Oh no, you are no fool Melchior."

The fact this creature knew all their thoughts still startled each of them. Melchior looked up into the visitor's eyes and waited for him to explain.

"Put the orb inside your coat, next to your heart, and then remove it."

Melchior did so and when he removed the orb from inside his coat, he saw a portrait of Naomi's face cut out of gold.

"The globe has filled itself with love. You have loved Naomi since you first saw her. When she had leprosy, you loved her even though you could not be with her. You have been given this orb as a token of your love for each other."

The Wise Men stood up, each one admiring their own crystal globe. The visitor stood in the center of the small group.

"You will not see this child or each other again. You were given an opportunity to honor him and you have done that."

For a moment the visitor was silent.

"What of our children?" asked Melchior "Will they know him?"

"Perhaps. I cannot say for certain. I do not have all knowledge of the future. These globes will be the only reminder of what you have done for the child by worshiping and honoring him. Generations from now will honor this night and your sacrifices by exchanging gifts and globes very similar to these."

Each of the Wise Men stared at their own globe, and they forgot about the fiery visitor. When they looked back up, they realized he was gone. They didn't even know his name.

Gaspar knew he would return to Persia. He had nowhere else to go and could not stay near Jerusalem. If King Herod ever found him, he would be killed.

Melchior realized he had forgotten to ask the visitor about Naomi. What had become of her? Perhaps Abada had somehow killed her? In the distance, behind Melchior a ray of light appeared followed by a glowing rainbow in the night sky. Balthazar saw the rainbow and knew what was on Melchior's mind. He didn't need the mysterious night guest to understand what Melchior was thinking.

"My friend, don't worry. Naomi is fine, and you will see her again. I feel certain of it."

Balthazar smiled. Babylon was where he belonged. He knew his days of adventure were over. He looked inside his orb at the golden star—the Star of Bethlehem—taken from the sky and put inside a crystal globe just for him.

Epilogue

The Three Wise Men never saw each other again. Balthazar returned to Babylon and continued his duties as Royal Astronomer. The king failed to ever ask him what he had found or why he had left. Balthazar knew the fiery visitor outside Jerusalem had probably paid a visit to the king.

The globe with the spinning star inside was the only thing Balthazar kept for himself when he was no longer able to perform his duties as Royal Astronomer. It is rumored that after a time, shortly before he died, he gave his precious orb to the next incoming Royal Astronomer, along with these words of wisdom. "Allow your dreams to spur you into action, for no dream ever came true without a little faith and doing."

He never did marry. Everyone in the kingdom nicknamed him 'Old Bachelor Balthazar.' However, he did have a soft spot for children and every time he had the chance, he would give children gifts and copies of his magical orb. It always made him and the children smile.

Balthazar and Jandak never raced again. Jandak was retired upon his return to Babylon and became content giving guided tours. Other riders and camels won the Desert 100 Race, but no camel before or since Jandak has ever won as many races as the camel with the magical, mystical winds. Of course, after Jandak retired, the palm leaf fans installed alongside the track were no longer necessary. They were promptly removed in order to make room for more trackside seating and royal suites. The strangest thing happened when Jandak stopped racing. His stomach settled down and his gastro intestinal time bomb stopped ticking.

Gaspar returned to Persia and resumed his role as second in command. He eventually became king, and his first decree was to create a festival of giving. He used his globe as an example for his kingdom. Everyone loved the idea. It seemed so simple. Create a globe out of anything, and put a gift inside; something important to you. Then, give it to someone you loved or someone less fortunate. Some of the ornaments created at this festival are still in existence today.

About Melchior. Yes, he did finally find and marry Naomi. The wedding was splendid and the only thing missing were his two magi friends. He sent couriers out telling them about the wedding and they both replied back saying Melchior was the luckiest man in the world and Naomi's luck would eventually turn around some day. Naomi and Melchior lived for each other and loved each other until the end of their lives.

The former little leper colony became a thriving city. One of the gift shops there sold the most beautiful crystal ornaments anyone had ever seen. Inspired by Melchior's small crystal globe, a skilled artisan would create an orb and put a keepsake or small gift inside. When Melchior later died, Naomi placed his original precious orb in the tomb with him.

There was only one thing Naomi refused to talk about with Melchior, the battle with Abada. She would only say Ababa had been defeated, and the Blade of Nineveh had been hidden somewhere, never to be found.

The Sword of Light? It was buried with Naomi upon her death. Sometimes at night in the desert, Naomi can still be seen carrying the sword and dancing through the desert sky. Legend has it that to this day travelers continue to occasionally see a rainbow of unknown origin in the desert night sky.

Joab and Esau created the 'Greatest Show on Dirt' a traveling circus. One of their major attractions was a group of three men called the 'Flying Assassins.' Two of the men in the act were not too bright. The third man walked with a limp and could not speak. His vocal cords had been severed in a fierce sword battle, but that was all anyone knew about him. Occasionally, he would pull out a disfigured gold ring and stare at it for hours, daydreaming. No one really ever knew why.

Fewer and fewer people in today's world believe this adventurous tale of three magi. But on a certain day each year set aside for gifts and giving, it is hard to ignore all those ornaments and a simple tradition begun with a single star.

THE END

Made in the USA
Middletown, DE
11 October 2022